Praise for the novels of

MaryJanice Davidson

"A hilarious romp full of goofy twists and turns, great fun for fans of humorous vampire romance." —*Locus*

"Delightful, wicked fun!"
—Christine Feehan, #1 *New York Times* bestselling author of *Dark Predator*

"Move over, Buffy. Betsy's in town, and she rocks! . . . I don't care what mood you are in; if you open this book, you are practically guaranteed to laugh . . . top-notch humor and a fascinating perspective of the vampire world."
—ParaNormal Romance.org

"One of the funniest, most satisfying series to come along lately. If you're [a fan] of Sookie Stackhouse and Anita Blake, don't miss Betsy Taylor. She rocks."
—*The Best Reviews*

"*Undead and Unwed* is an irreverently hilarious, superbly entertaining novel of love, lust, and designer shoes. Betsy Taylor is an unrepentant fiend—about shoes. She is shallow, vain, and immensely entertaining. Her journey from life to death, or the undead, is so amusing I found myself laughing out loud while reading. Between her human friends, vampire allies, and her undead enemies, her first week as the newly undead is never boring . . . a reading experience that will leave you laughing and 'dying' for more from the talented pen of MaryJanice Davi

"Creative, sophisticated
—Catherine

Titles by MaryJanice Davidson and Anthony Alongi

Jennifer Scales and the Ancient Furnace
Jennifer Scales and the Messenger of Light
The Silver Moon Elm: A Jennifer Scales Novel
Seraph of Sorrow: A Jennifer Scales Novel
Rise of the Poison Moon: A Jennifer Scales Novel
Evangelina: A Jennifer Scales Novel

***

Titles by MaryJanice Davidson

Undead and Unwed
Undead and Unemployed
Undead and Unappreciated
Undead and Unreturnable
Undead and Unpopular
Undead and Uneasy
Undead and Unworthy
Undead and Unwelcome
Undead and Unfinished
Undead and Undermined

Derik's Bane

Sleeping with the Fishes
Swimming Without a Net
Fish out of Water

Anthologies

Cravings
(with Laurell K. Hamilton, Rebecca York, Eileen Wilks)

Bite
(with Laurell K. Hamilton, Charlaine Harris, Angela Knight, Vickie Taylor)

Kick Ass
(with Maggie Shayne, Angela Knight, Jacey Ford)

Men at Work
(with Janelle Denison, Nina Bangs)

Dead and Loving It

Surf's Up
(with Janelle Denison, Nina Bangs)

Mysteria
(with P. C. Cast, Gena Showalter, Susan Grant)

Over the Moon
(with Angela Knight, Virginia Kantra, Sunny)

Demon's Delight
(with Emma Holly, Vickie Taylor, Catherine Spangler)

Dead Over Heels

Mysteria Lane
(with P. C. Cast, Gena Showalter, Susan Grant)

Mysteria Nights
(with P. C. Cast, Susan Grant, Gena Showalter)

Evangelina

A JENNIFER SCALES NOVEL

MaryJanice Davidson
and
Anthony Alongi

ACE BOOKS, NEW YORK

THE BERKLEY PUBLISHING GROUP
Published by the Penguin Group
Penguin Group (USA) Inc.
375 Hudson Street, New York, New York 10014, USA
Penguin Group (Canada), 90 Eglinton Avenue East, Suite 700, Toronto, Ontario M4P 2Y3, Canada
(a division of Pearson Penguin Canada Inc.)
Penguin Books Ltd., 80 Strand, London WC2R 0RL, England
Penguin Group Ireland, 25 St. Stephen's Green, Dublin 2, Ireland (a division of Penguin Books Ltd.)
Penguin Group (Australia), 250 Camberwell Road, Camberwell, Victoria 3124, Australia
(a division of Pearson Australia Group Pty. Ltd.)
Penguin Books India Pvt. Ltd., 11 Community Centre, Panchsheel Park, New Delhi—110 017, India
Penguin Group (NZ), 67 Apollo Drive, Rosedale, Auckland 0632, New Zealand
(a division of Pearson New Zealand Ltd.)
Penguin Books (South Africa) (Pty.) Ltd., 24 Sturdee Avenue, Rosebank, Johannesburg 2196,
South Africa

Penguin Books Ltd., Registered Offices: 80 Strand, London WC2R 0RL, England

EVANGELINA

An Ace Book / published by arrangement with the authors

PRINTING HISTORY
Ace mass-market edition / September 2011

Cover art by Danny O'Leary.
Cover design by Lesley Worrell.

For information, address: The Berkley Publishing Group,
a division of Penguin Group (USA) Inc.,
375 Hudson Street, New York, New York 10014.

ISBN: 978-0-441-02079-9

ACE
Ace Books are published by The Berkley Publishing Group,
a division of Penguin Group (USA) Inc.,
375 Hudson Street, New York, New York 10014.
ACE and the "A" design are trademarks of Penguin Group (USA) Inc.

PRINTED IN THE UNITED STATES OF AMERICA

10 9 8 7 6 5 4 3 2 1

For our children,
who tolerate our deadlines with good humor.
They are better people than we were at their age.

For aught that I could ever read,
Could ever hear by tale or history,
The course of true love never did run smooth.

—WILLIAM SHAKESPEARE,
A MIDSUMMER NIGHT'S DREAM

Well, possible motives for murder are profit, revenge, jealousy, to conceal a crime, to avoid humiliation and disgrace, or plain old homicidal mania.

—*THE GENERAL'S DAUGHTER*

Hey, gang! Guess which author wanted the lame Shakespeare quote? Now guess which one wanted the line uttered with perfect coolness by John Travolta? A game the whole family can play!

—A & MJ

AUTHORS' NOTE

This is the sixth book in the Jennifer Scales series. The first five formed a long story arc, which finished in *Rise of the Poison Moon*. If you haven't read any of those five books, don't worry: you'll have no trouble figuring things out. Welcome to the race.

Our thanks to Leis Pederson at The Berkley Publishing Group for her patience and assistance.

PROLOGUE

The following is a transcript of a recording recovered from the Saint George's Secure Medical Facility in Moorston, Minnesota.

According to staff at the facility, the conversation took place in a secured room in what would have been the facility's psychiatric emergency care center.

Authorities have blacked out some offensive language and certain names of people under investigation regarding the death of Dr. Collin Loxos, severe injuries to several staff, the disappearance of at least one other patient at the facility, and the fire that consumed two wings of the main building.

[Recording begins.]

LOXOS: September 18, 5:12 P.M. Dr. Collin Loxos, conducting our second interview with a female patient, age approximately twenty, height five feet eleven inches, weight one hundred fifty-five pounds, hair black, eyes gray, refers to herself as ████████, no given surname. ████████ has been with us at Saint George's for just under twenty-four hours; she was a voluntary self-admit. She has barely spoken to anyone since her arrival. Her first interview an hour after entry was, in the words of my colleague Dr. Eisenstadt, "an hour-long staring match with the table." Since then patient has become increasingly agitated. Under Dr. Eisenstadt's direction, staff have attempted sedation with a progressive schedule of benzodiazepines. None have had any discernable effect. Patient has submitted to restraints, which I have recommended due to the increasing danger she presents to staff and herself. ████████ has made multiple vague references to deaths, and to the town of Winoka. This has caught our attention, for obvious reasons. I have notified authorities, but would like to see if I can learn more prior to their arrival. ████████, I am Dr. Loxos. You can call me Collin.

[Long silence.]

LOXOS: ████████? Are we going to have another staring match with the table?

████████: ████ you, Collin.

LOXOS: ████████, I wonder if you can tell me why you came here.

████████: *I* wonder if you can tell me what you think these restraints and all the drugs are for.

LOXOS: We're taking measures for your safety, and the community's.

████████: I've heard that line before.

LOXOS: Where? In Winoka?

████████: I didn't come here to talk about Winoka.

LOXOS: But you're from there, right?

████████: You don't know ███ about Winoka.

LOXOS: I know there was a natural disaster there—

████████: The Regiment is *not* a natural disaster.

LOXOS: What is the Regiment?

██████: You know what the Regiment is. They run this place, or run those who do. That's why I'm here. Well, it's the first reason I'm here. You're taping this interview, which means they'll get a transcript. Right?

LOXOS: Let's suppose for now that this "Regiment" exists. What message would you like to send?

██████: I would like to tell them, they are wasting their time.

LOXOS: How so?

██████: The people they're hunting don't have the information they want.

LOXOS: This Regiment is hunting people?

██████: Doing a good job of it, too. I'm sure you've seen the occasional headline.

LOXOS: I have. Some of the details in these cases are gruesome.

██████: Nothing worse than what I've seen for years. It's easy to treat people like that, when you consider them "not human."

LOXOS: What do you mean, "not human"?

██████: Don't insult my intelligence, Collin. Everyone listening to this tape or reading this transcript is going to know who's dying and why.

LOXOS: Because this "Regiment" of yours is killing them, is that right?

██████: It's not my Regiment, Collin. It's yours. You're a member.

LOXOS: Who else is a member?

██████: What, you want a directory? Pay your membership fee. I don't know. I just know you—

LOXOS: ██████ . . . have you considered that *you* may be a member of this Regiment? Or more precisely, that the Regiment is nothing more than a psychic construct you use to distance yourself from your own awful actions? That all of the hunting you are talking about . . . that it's *you* doing it?

████████: That's not true. That's not who I am.

LOXOS: You're so sure of that?

████████: I'm sure. You're not going to confuse me with psychiatric games, Collin.

LOXOS: You think these are games. Yet you checked yourself in here. Nobody came in with you to St. George's. How long have you been alone, ████████?

████████: Months. Maybe years.

LOXOS: What about before that? Did you live in—

████████: Let's stop talking about Winoka. You're trying to pump me for information. You're stalling until the authorities show. It's not going to work. I'm here because I want to be here, Dr. Loxos. Like I said, I wanted to get a message to your friends in the Regiment.

LOXOS: Yes, you said that was the "first" reason you were here. Was there another reason?

████████: Yes. I wonder if you know a ██████ ██████?

LOXOS: Of course I do. She's a patient here.

████████: Why?

LOXOS: I don't see why that's relevant—

████████: Let's get to the point. You preach the fiction that ████████████ suffers from severe, chronic psychosis.

LOXOS: She's been experiencing secondary delusions since she got here. Possibly since childhood.

████████: Her "delusions" are reality. The facts are documented and disseminated worldwide, on unedited video—

LOXOS: Please, ████████. We both know the Internet is a storage house for manufactured fantasy. Those special effect films she crafted to impress the world were nothing more than a clever stunt to get attention, after the death of her mother and subsequent emotional abandonment of her father—

████████: Who believed her, after the rise of the poison moon.

LOXOS: You are referring, I presume, to the unusual but completely explicable phenomenon of the "green moon," which happened most notably in Winoka. Astronomers have noted that certain phases of the moon, when viewed through an aurora borealis, can give the impression—

██████: You and I can interrupt each other all day long, Collin, but we know ██████████ has never suffered a psychotic episode. Neither did her father.

LOXOS: Well, he's no longer alive to tell us what he has seen, is he?

██████: Yes, that's very convenient for the Regiment.

LOXOS: Convenience has nothing to do with it. He died in a military training exercise at the air base he commanded. He was highly decorated and received a hero's funeral. I suspect he would be very sad, as are we all, to see the depths to which his daughter sank after his demise.

██████: The Regiment is all over the military. All over law enforcement. And it's growing . . .

LOXOS: You're suggesting that the Regiment killed ██████████'s highly trained and decorated father, during a military exercise. That doing so somehow supported their false case that she should be committed. That she never suffered any delusions about dragons, and enormous spiders, and interdimensional travel, and pixie dust. That these things actually exist. That there is a conspiracy to hide this truth.

██████: Not hide it, Collin. Destroy it. Murder it.

LOXOS: Murder it, like you've murdered innocent people?

██████: I've never murdered anyone. Not in this lifetime. Not yet. You might be the first, Collin.

LOXOS: You believe that will scare me? I don't know *who* you think you are, but let me tell you *where* you are. First, you're strapped down in a bed with steel and leather restraints.

████████: I noticed.

LOXOS: That bed is in a locked room, here with me, inside the most secure wing of the most secure psychiatric facility known to North America, and likely the world.

████████: I'm feeling more repressed by the minute.

LOXOS: We use highly trained private security forces, at an unprecedented guard-to-guest ratio, to ensure the safety of everyone inside and the surrounding community. You walked in here, ████████, but you are not walking out. You're a woman with deep emotional problems, who likes to hurt people to avoid the awful truth.

████████: What truth is that, Collin?

LOXOS: You're a monster. And you belong here. You cannot be cured of your need to kill.

████████: Why don't you turn off that recorder so we can have an honest conversation about your intentions, Collin?

LOXOS: What are my intentions?

████████: You do the Regiment's bidding. You're not going to hold me here—at least, not for any longer than it takes for the Regiment's assassins to arrive.

LOXOS: If this is a place where we assassinate people, why wouldn't we have killed your friend ██████ by now?

████████: She's not a problem to the Regiment, now that she's in here. The Regiment only murders those it fears.

LOXOS: The Regiment being . . . you.

████████: Are the authorities here yet?

LOXOS: Probably. Why?

████████: Because I want to interrogate them after I'm done.

LOXOS: What do you—*what do you think you're doing?!* [Snapping sounds.]

████████: I think I'm getting up off this table.

LOXOS: There's no—

████████: No, no, it's my turn to talk. Then I'm taking

out your guards, disarming any Regiment assassins, and beating on them until I learn something useful. Then I think I'm rescuing my friend from a lobotomy factory. How much of this institution remains standing, will depend on how well she is when I find her.

[Crackling noises.]

LOXOS: Oh, ████. Nurse!

[Struggling noises.]

LOXOS: Shit. Officers! *Officers!*

[Shrieking, followed by gurgling, followed by crashing.]

[Recording ends.]

PART ONE

Lue

CHAPTER 1

Lue was the first officer to David Webber's house. It was, as it seemed so often with him, serendipity.

In this case he immediately felt both regret and a thrill. Regret, because this was definitely a crime scene that could have used a friendly "you'd better brace yourself, Detective" from a junior, sweat-soaked, pale officer who'd already have been there. Thrill, because getting here so quickly meant he almost caught . . . *it*.

What was it? His first thought was a bear, partly due to its size and partly due to the amount of blood and wreckage it left behind. Bear sightings were not unheard of in northern Minnesota, even on the fringes of small cities like Moorston.

But bear *attacks* were rare . . . and this "bear" was upright and moving through the backyard of the small house with furtive intelligence. Plus, a half-second glance at the corpse and blood patch visible on the twilit porch revealed a slit throat—*not exactly ursine M.O.,* he realized.

"Police!" He drew his gun. "Hold it!"

It did not "hold it"—in fact, it spread two massive, bat-like wings, hissed, and lurched toward him.

Not human.

He squeezed off three rounds, aiming for its leg. The thing shrieked, turned, and vaulted over the eight-foot cedar fence that lined the backyard.

Adrenaline simultaneously quickened and slowed his senses, giving him time for three thoughts: first, he was sure he had hit the animal.

Then: I have fired my weapon; they are going to take it when I get back to the station. Even if that was an animal. He thought glumly of his backup piece, the .40 cal Glock. Smaller and lighter than the Browning Hi-Power. And wimpier!

And then: *I should probably focus now and report this.*

Taking one hand off his soon-to-be-surrendered piece, he tapped the radio on his shoulder. "Requesting ambulance and backup at 2605 Snapdragon Avenue. Ten fifty-four *D*. Suspect has fled and is on . . . foot, heading south. He or she is large, over six feet tall, and dressed in . . . black." He winced at his own description. "Likely armed with a blade. May be injured. Officer in pursuit."

That sounded fine. Not weird at all. Everything Under Control.

As he slid behind the cedar fence and gave chase, he thought back to the blonde who had waved down his car half a block away with a report of commotion behind the modest ranch home with cheap tan siding. She had been wearing long-sleeved athletic gear suitable for autumn, her color-treated hair pulled back in a ponytail—*office job, got home by six, changed clothes, routine jog,* he had guessed as he instructed her to remain with his vehicle. That had not been all he had noticed. *Late twenties. No ring. Light makeup. Expensive headphones and leather-lined water bottle. Name-brand jogging shoes from an upscale depart-*

ment store . . . Macy's or Nordstrom. Heading out from the new riverfront condos.

A recent transplant from the Twin Cities, in all likelihood. She would stay safely by the car and give a statement to the other officers when they arrived. *Hurrah for solid citizens.*

The light brush behind the fence hindered Lue as he navigated the property line. He picked up the trail quickly—bent and broken branches pointed down a straight path into the adjoining property. His mother had told him there was a Sioux somewhere back in the family woodpile, but he didn't need any special ancestry to follow this trail. The thing was the size of a small car. With wings!

He pounded after it, reminding himself that this, *this* was why he forced himself into a four-mile jog three times a week. Sure, there were freezing dark mornings when his alarm went off and his first instinct was to burst into tears, but then there were times like this, when winded was a long way away, when he remembered he was a fellow in his prime, well armed and well shod (*thank you, Kenneth Cole*), when he could run down a killer on foot, have the cuffs on (*it*) him, and read Miranda without even being out of . . .

Damn.

He'd bolted around a corner and was startled and crushed to see nothing ahead of him but an orderly procession of cars filled with commuters headed home. There was no sign of any suspect, human or animal or otherwise. Just cars and traffic lights and street signs. No one had so much as hit their brakes. Peaceful commuters as far as the eye could see.

Gone.

He holstered his weapon, and one thought cheered him, like a shaft of sunshine through storm clouds: *At least I can go back and interview that jogger.*

CHAPTER 2

"His name was David Webber. He worked at Saint George's."

"Was he a security guard?" Lue looked over David Webber's living room.

The patrol officer cocked his head. "You knew him?"

"No. But he had an athletic build, and the only furniture he kept in this room was the couch, the television, a coffee table, an end table, and that gun cabinet." He pointed to the pine structure with glass doors, which held an array of rifles, shotguns, and pistols. It was securely locked. "We will need to check all those, by the way."

"You bet. I don't know that I'd jump to conclusions on this guy, though, Lue. Lots of guys in Moorston have full gun cabinets. Irregardless, it doesn't mean they're, you know, dangerous terrorists or anything. We hunt out here, y'know." The patrol officer's smile was a mixture of friendly and patronizing.

Lue tried to swallow his irritation, and kept his words crisp and separate. "There is no such word as 'irregardless,' *Mark.* That word didn't even belong there. And I know about hunting in Minnesota; I have done it all my life."

"Okay, but—"

"If he was a hunter, where are the trophies? Where are the photos? Where is the room full of dead stuffed heads with shiny marble eyes?" *Which, I swear, follow you as you walk across the room.* He walked down the hallway, almost tracing the bare walls with his fingertips. "Maybe we can find a top-loading freezer full of venison in the garage, and a reloading bench, but I doubt it. This guy was *not* a hunter."

The officer swallowed. "Didn't mean to offend you, Lieutenant. I just figured you're new around here."

Lue didn't acknowledge the nonapology; it wasn't the first time he'd run across this prejudice since he came to this town. His head was already poking into the spare bedroom, which had nothing in it, and the master bedroom, which had very little beyond a bed. *Nothing to leave behind. Did not expect to stay long . . . or needed to be ready to move instantly.*

"No signs of struggle anywhere inside," Mark offered. "Looks like everything happened out on the porch. Victim had this." He held out a plastic evidence bag, and his arm sunk a bit with the extended weight.

Lue whistled. "That is a Grizzly Mark V."

Mark nodded. He looked surprised Lue knew what it was, but didn't remark on it. "Hell of a thing to keep at your side while sipping lemonade and watching the sunset on the back porch. He discharged four rounds. That's probably what got the attention of our jogger." He gave Lue an expectant look: *how about that woman, eh?*

"Did any of those shots hit anything?"

"Nothing that bleeds. The only fresh blood that's not his, is a splatter by the fence, but we figure that's one of your shots. We'll get samples into the lab and see if it gets any hits."

"Thanks. Please bring the results to me back at the station."

Mark nodded again, though his look seemed sour. Lue tried to care, but found he could not. He left without another word.

All he cared about was finding that thing that had flown over the wall and disappeared.

Sixteen Years Ago

They cannot find me!

So thought Evangelina Scales, age four, a precocious child who was still at an age where if she hid her eyes, she knew they couldn't see her.

Not ever!

Sometimes it took her "Niffer," Jennifer, and her aunt Susan a long time to find her. Hours and days (though they told her it was only twenty minutes, but she knew that wasn't so . . . she had to wait for them and wait for them).

But today, Evangelina was determined never to be found. They would look and look and look and then they would give up and then they would make supper and she would come strolling in because she would be hungry by then anyway and they would be soooo surprised!

It would be a wonderful surprise.

The wolves were far back, they were still running for the farm. She got there first! That was good because of the plan. She could hear the wolves crying their pretty howls; for some reason when wolves cried it sounded like music. She could always hear the music, no matter how far away the wolves were, so good! Good, she was the only one at the farm.

She cast about for the perfect hiding place, the perfect . . . what was the word she learned? Yes! Lair. She would find the perfect lair, and lair there. She would be such a good lairer they would never find her lair.

So she dove into the silo and instantly regretted it.

Evangelina had been warned. The old farm on the edge of town had a working barn, and cats, too. And electricity and running water and bales of sweet-smelling hay. And a chicken coop and a place where sheep used to be. And a silo. It was all Not-a-Playground.

She knew. She did so know! She did: the farm, this silo, was Not-a-Playground. But that didn't mean it wasn't a good lair—a lair so good, it made sense they wouldn't want her to go in there! Besides, the silo had a ladder on the outside, just like a playground. And some playgrounds had hatches and chutes. Anyway, the warnings were silly. Choking? Drowning? There was corn in there! She loved corn!

And here had been an aluminum-encased pond of loose, scratchy kernels. No water at all! Just corn and corn dust—so much dust that she could see it now in the air, like stripes. This wasn't anything like a lake you could jump in and realize too late that it was deep . . .

She clawed for the surface; she fought for air. And it seemed like every warning she'd been given was now being shouted through her poor thirsty brain.

You can drown just like in a lake . . .

. . . I know it sounds silly, but you could suffocate . . .

. . . You have to stay out of there; if you fall in you could drown . . .

. . . Where is that kid? She's such a crazy kid . . .

. . . Aw, c'mon, Vange, let's get this done, show yourself, Mom wants me to pick up pasta for supper . . .

And okay, that was proof she was lost, lost and drowning in the silo because she was thinking thoughts that weren't her thoughts. She was thinking thoughts that tasted like Aunt Susan and Niffer.

So she tore and scrabbled and fought for the surface and now there was air now there was room and she could get all the corn out of her throat and the best way the best way the best way to do that was . . .

Evangelina puked.

She puked black.

I'm scared this isn't right

Was that Vange?

Is that her? She sounds hurt. Where is she?

She felt their panic and added her own.

Here here HERE I'm in HERE

Something flailed about her—legs like stalks, and at first she thought she was about to be devoured by an enormous spider, which was a shame because she loved spiders and the way they worked so hard on their webs and gobbled up bugs, and then she brought her hand to her mouth to wipe the puke away and the leg moved with her

(oh . . . OOOHHH . . . !)

and she was wriggling her legs and puking and climbing and

(are those wings too?!)

and she was so big and everywhere was corn, there were heaps of it and she'd thrown up black and had wings and lots of legs.

The next thing she knew, there was someone next to her in the corn, helping her stay afloat.

That was Evangelina's first memory—Aunt Susan diving directly next to her, uncaring of the mess or the monster in the corn.

That, and looking up at her own sister's face against the sky beyond the hatch, seeing the shock in the young woman's face, and hearing her unfiltered thoughts.

CHAPTER 3

A man is what he thinks about all day long, it occurred to Lue. *Thoreau. Wait, no. Emerson.* Whoever it was, they would think Detective Lue Vue was insane.

The Saint George's Secure Medical Facility, where the victim David Webber had worked, had been on his mind since he left the crime scene. Lue was learning from a late-night Internet search that Saint George's was a two hundred bed "purely forensic facility" that opened over a decade ago in Moorston. It did evaluations of competency to stand trial and mental state opinions, and also admitted criminal suspects judged not guilty for reasons of insanity.

Here, they would be admitted for long-term treatment and, the website assured the reader, "eventual return to the community if possible . . . we are a Hospital, not a Prison."

Perhaps capitalizing all those unnecessary words makes them feel more important. He smirked as he read on.

Saint George's had won awards from something called

NAMI for being "Best Hospital in Terms of Reducing Seclusions and Restraints." *No doubt,* Lue thought, *their acceptance speech was a landmark event. If nothing else, they probably took ninety minutes to say "thanks."*

"Looking for a new wife already, Lue? Feels soon."

He smiled as he turned. "When I want to marry another problem personality, Chief, I will start by looking around here."

"Tsk-tsk. We frown on fraternization within the ranks, Lue. Best to stick to the asylums." Chief Linda Smiling Bear rubbed her nose with a stout thumb, leaned against his desk, and nodded toward the screen. "Related to earlier today?"

He nodded. "David Webber worked at Saint George's for nearly eight years as a security guard. He had a Spartan lifestyle, and I doubt the crime scene will tell us much. I plan to go to Saint George's tomorrow and scan his personnel file."

The chief hooked a nearby office chair with her toe, pulled it toward her, then sank into it. She wasn't what Lue would call beautiful, more cheerfully attractive. Her shining tan eyes were trained on him with almost unnerving intensity.

"You see any possible connection between this guy and what happened at Saint George's a few months ago?"

"You sure you want my opinion, Chief? I hear that Saint George's incident is a political hot potato."

She laughed. "My favorite meal."

Out of curiosity, he'd done some research when he first came to work for her, and found she was independently wealthy. She wasn't shy about that, either. "God bless gambling, Native Americans, and white guilt," she often said good-naturedly. Her financial independence and lack of family ties made her not only an incredibly eligible bachelorette, but also as close to politically invulnerable as a police chief could be. Her fellow officers, the elected leaders of the community, and everyone else knew why she came to work—to get things done, and only to get things done.

"Okay, if you want to handle it, here it comes. I figure coincidence is not possible. This guy had a loaded Grizzly Mark V on him when he was off duty. He could have been upset by the idea that so many of his coworkers were killed. He could have been generally fearful, or the kind of guy who likes whipping out his pistol to show the ladies. He could have known more about what happened that day than most of us."

"Knew more? You talking about that Regiment rumor?" She leaned back in her chair and chuckled. She was short, with the generous figure often referred to as zaftig. "That's awfully conspiratorial of you, Detective."

"With all due respect, I think you mean 'paranoid,' Chief. Conspiratorial would suggest that I—"

"Lue, it's me. I hired you, remember? You don't have to prove your superior grasp of English."

"—would suggest that I am part of the Regiment, an entity that may or may not exist."

"I should never have given you that Grammar Gecko book for Christmas. That was an ironic statement, you realize. Not a criticism."

He blinked in genuine surprise. "I loved that book, Chief. The Grammar Gecko fine-tuned my usage."

"You never needed to fine-tune your usage, Lue. You grew up in Brainerd. You taught your parents English while you were in fourth grade. They probably owe their jobs to that. School's over, dude. You scored great. We, the good people of Moorston, are in awe. Ease up."

"There can always be a higher score. And since when are you society's spokesperson?"

She watched him return his attention to the computer screen and sighed. "I suppose this means you won't be taking your vacation days next week, as planned."

"It depends on how quickly I can close this case."

"Jeez, Lue." Chief Smiling Bear stifled a chuckle. "I almost feel sorry for the suspect."

"That reminds me—if he is injured, he will be looking for medical attention."

"Sure he's injured. You hit him."

He finished his thought. "We should get an APB put out on him, and an advisory to the area hospitals and clinics."

"We did that. You're not the only high performer here, you know."

Her brusque tone recaptured his attention. "Sorry, Chief. Yeah, I will probably skip vacation. I had nowhere to go anyway, and no money to get there."

"Oh, is that my cue to offer you a raise?"

"That would be splendid, but I still plan to work next week."

"I'd be more sympathetic if I thought you knew what to do with your hard-earned doubloons."

"Doubloons?" he said, delighted. *Great word.* And even greater to hear it in a sentence in the middle of the Cop Shop.

"Perhaps you shouldn't keep giving all of your pieces of eight to the former Ms. Vue."

"It was always Sato, Chief. She was proud of her heritage, and so was I."

"Again: being ironic. You're evading my point."

"Nancy needs to go to community college. It's the only way she won't still be cleaning toilets ten years from now."

"Nancy Sato is not your project. This was true even when you were married. She doesn't need improvement. Well, maybe she does. But that's up to her, not you."

"Thanks, Doctor. Am I fit for duty now?"

"Don't forget to turn in your gun."

"I already did. Per department policy, I'm currently down to a Taser and a wad of spit."

"More than enough for someone of your skills and instincts. We'll have your piece back quick."

"Quick*ly*. And thank you for those words of reassurance. I remain undaunted as I know the department shall *quickly* process all paperwork and give my weapon back in a *quick* seventy-two months."

"Get a life. Take it from me: it's possible to be single and not be such a dork." She grinned, patted him on the neck, and left him alone to work.

CHAPTER 4

"Hey, new kid."

Lue found a smile from somewhere as he passed the desk sergeant, a grizzled veteran of the streets who looked all of twenty-four.

He supposed the "new kid" moniker would stick for at least a year. *Should have come in through Booking. Also should have gone through the academy earlier . . . or grown a full beard to look older.*

He dodged and weaved, carrying a cup of steaming green tea and holding a bag of trail mix in his teeth, nodding to the cops he knew and the administrative assistants he didn't—anyone with half a brain made nice with the men and women who could, with a phone call or an inconvenient sick day, delay paychecks, benefits paperwork, processing of expense reports, and meal vouchers.

It was almost like a dance . . . dip, weave, open door for the intern du jour. Glide, wave, nod, dip. *I should have been a ballet dancer . . . perhaps if this town does not work out.* The thought made him grin.

"I know exactly what to say to wipe that off your face."

Chief Smiling Bear had stepped out of her office and directly in his way. Her expression was sociable but worried.

"I don't doubt it," he replied, peering over her shoulder at his desk, twenty feet distant. It might as well have been a mile. "It's one of your super powers."

"BCA here to talk to you."

"Why?" he asked, trying not to sound as appalled as he felt.

"Like *I* know? Go detect."

And whatever it is, he thought, stomping past her as she gave way, all his earlier grace forgotten, *it's got her anxious. Phenomenal.*

The first thing he saw about the Bureau of Criminal Apprehension guy, unfortunately, was not even really part of the Bureau of Criminal Apprehension guy. The first thing was the smart phone. The guy's thumbs were wiggling furiously with the speed and dexterity of a ten-year-old gaming veteran hopped up on Mountain Dew.

Lue watched this for a while, torn between bemused and fuming. Smart phones were the bane of proper communication: all contractions and abbreviations and LOLs and uninvited @'s. No one who loved the spoken Hmong dialects, no one who loved written or oral English, no one who loved any language worth spit, could tolerate one of these. Lue's phone remained stubbornly dumb—or perhaps it was a smart phone after all, and Lue had never bothered to use anything other than the talking part. *Whatever.*

He waited another few seconds before clearing his throat. "You're from the BCA, then?" he asked, perfectly neutral.

The man looked up, and in a flash the device was gone. "Lieutenant?"

Lue was suddenly impressed, even though the man had only said one word. Part of it was the pocketing of the phone, to be sure. But most of it was the BCA agent's demeanor. His features were almost a Gaelic stereotype: reddish brown curly hair, dark blue eyes, pale freckled skin that probably burned and peeled and burned again in the summer, and the stocky, broad-shouldered build of a farmer used to repairing his own equipment. And carrying his own cows.

He looked comfortably rumpled in jeans, a white button-down oxford, and a dark brown blazer. His jaw bloomed with reddish stubble.

He looked solid. He looked *real.*

I should probably talk now. "Yes."

"Lue Vue?"

"Yes."

Lue waited for the inevitable. It would go something like this: *Is that your real name? Your real name is Lue Vue? Really? It is? Because that's one of the weirdest names I've ever heard. Ever! What is it, Chinese? You look Chinese. What did you say—Hmong? What's Hmong? Is that part of China? Because you look . . .*

"Morning," the mysterious hulk said. His voice parted the air, and Lue was certain the windows shook from the proud baritone. The guy could've done radio ads. Except radio guys usually weren't so terse. "Morning." Was it a greeting, or a noun?

He waited for the name play, and blinked when it didn't come. "Can I help you, then?"

"Yes."

Again, Lue waited. He dropped the bag of trail mix on his desk, walked around the mysterious hulk that was the BCA guy, carefully set his tea down on the desk blotter (he took unlimited bull from the other officers for the blotter; apparently they went out with line dancing), and took a seat. His visitor's eyes never left him. There was neither hostility nor friendliness there. "What can I do for the Bureau of Criminal Apprehension?"

" 'Ask not.' "

"What?"

"Kennedy, John F."

"Ah, I see. Well then, you've got it backward." Lue checked under the cup to see if it was blotting the blotter. It wasn't. "JFK would *want* me to ask what I can do for . . . "

"I know. Irony." The BCA agent's hand went back briefly to his pocket, as though he was just remembering to hang up on a call. "I can help you."

"Well, that is super." Lue could see the chief out of the corner of his eye, doing her this-is-a-brisk-walk-to-somewhere-I-need-to-be-which-happens-to-take-me-near-your-desk routine. "How exactly, Officer?"

"Lieutenant."

"How exactly, Lieutenant?"

"McMahon."

"How exactly, Lieutenant McMahon?"

"Lieutenant Art McMahon."

"Is there any more to your name, Lieutenant Art McMahon? Perhaps we can get it all out there right now, because I do not have all day."

Art's arm shot out. It looked almost like a blow (*what kind of cop throws a punch in the middle of the Cop Shop?*), until Lue realized the guy was offering a handshake. He shook, noting the callused palm and firm grip. A man unafraid to use his hands, then. And that *voice*. Wow.

"We can help."

"You and who else?" Lue asked.

"You and I. We can help."

"Whom?"

"Each other."

"Super." Lue didn't know whether to feel irritated at the piecemeal sentences or admire the way this man demanded full attention to every sparse word. It was like the man was dropping ten dollar gold coins instead of nouns and verbs.

"I'm from Bemidji," Art said, eyeing Lue's trail mix with ill-concealed disdain. "Why the grain?"

"They were out of hops." Lue reached for the bag, took a deliberately large handful, and tossed it all down his gullet. "Mmmm . . . I can feel myself getting healthier and more sexually potent by the nanosecond."

Art blinked slowly, like a lizard.

Lue thought about that.

"So," he finally prompted. "The BCA office in Bemidji is interested in all this? Why?"

"Weird murders there."

Lue froze, his tea halfway to his lips, his trail mix stuck halfway down his throat. He coughed, forced it down, then took a big gulp of tea, coughed again, and managed, "What a coincidence. We've had a weird murder, too."

"Yesterday." It was an order: *tell me about it.*

Lue smiled. "I am sure you have already downloaded my report."

"You have a report available?"

"I take pride in filing reports within hours, for all fracases." *Or would that be fraci?*

Closing his eyes, Art seemed to take in the scent of Lue's healthy snack. "Better to hear from you."

He saw the chief accidentally wander by again with an impatient glare.

"It might help to know first: what are you facing in Bemidji?"

"Something similar."

Lue pressed his tongue against his cheek in irritation. "Next time, friendly hint, before you rush on down here, take a minute to shower and change your clothes. Then try a phone call. You will save time."

He heard a telltale crumple and observed with no surprise that Art had grabbed a bag of teriyaki beef jerky from his blazer pocket. "Nnngg?" he grunted with a telltale nod toward, and wiggle of, the bag, which Lue translated as, *Would you like to partake of a portion of my refreshing snack?*

"Taciturn, yet generous. No, I do not want some. If I have to watch you eat that at eight o'clock, I will need more than tea."

"And grains," Art added, standing.

"Was that a joke? What a beautiful friendship this is blossoming into."

"No joke."

"What was I thinking?" Lue saw the man was a good three inches shorter, and maybe fifteen pounds heavier . . . all muscle. Fortunately, Lue was comfortable with his masculinity, and wasn't threatened by a short, muscular, taciturn, barely communicative fellow upholder of the law.

Art put the bag away. "We'll eat somewhere."

"Sure, eventually. Oh. You meant us. Right now." Lue sighed. "Chief Smiling Bear will want to know how well the two of us are getting along. I also want to drop by the morgue, which somehow seems appropriate given the progress this conversation is making . . . and then Saint George's facility. We can get a skillet of something, somewhere in there."

"Okay." The jerky bag crumpled as it was crammed into a jacket pocket.

"You can come with me to see the chief, of course. Let me do the talking. Heh."

"Yes."

"It was a joke."

"Yes."

Despite himself, Lue laughed.

Then he abruptly cut off the sound and studied the man. It was true, this conversation had involved very little open give and take.

And it was also true that some people could *make* you

like them. It was a knack, like being able to raise one eyebrow.

He decided Art could be one of those. The man had said very little (to put it mildly), but Lue could not deny his charisma or presence.

"Come on," he said. "A bit to eat sounds good right now. It will give Meenay at the morgue a bit more time, anyway."

CHAPTER 5

If he had been blindfolded and led to the morgue, Lue would have known where he was at once. It wasn't chilly (unless the AC was malfunctioning, as happened occasionally), and it wasn't too hot. The place didn't stink of rotting corpses, as some assumed. And it didn't smell like a hospital, as others assumed.

It smelled like burnt coffee.

"Disgusting," Lue commented, peeking into the coffeepot and trying to keep his breakfast down. "Who's the victim this time? Brazilian Roast? Columbian Supremo? Organic Rainforest Blend?"

"Not answering," Dr. Meenay muttered, crouched over one of her microscopes. "Tox isn't back yet. Go away. Get some breakfast."

"We just had some," Lue protested. "I had an egg white omelet, while my new partner from the BCA here had an inordinate amount of bacon. We skipped the coffee. And we wish you had done the same."

Art wrinkled his nose. "This is bad."

"You have no idea," Lue said. "She's a maniac about her coffee. Buys the gourmet junk, uses bottled water instead of city water. So the waste is simply astronomical."

"You don't want to know what's in the city 'water,'" the doc replied, still entranced by whatever the microscope was showing her.

"Grinds the beans fresh, keeps 'em in the freezer the rest of the time. Then she keeps the pot on so hot and so long, the coffee is the taste and consistency of motor oil. And at least as expensive."

"Is not. Go away. Had breakfast? Try lunch."

"Hazelnut Crème!" Lue said triumphantly, spotting the telltale evidence in the garbage can below the coffeepot. "Oh, poor Hazelnut Crème. We barely knew you. Dr. Meenay, this is Lieutenant McMahon. McMahon, this is Meenay."

"Mee-nay," Art echoed, feigning social politeness and nodding. Lue noticed that the man knew better than to offer his hand to someone so absorbed. *Uses few words. Reads body language well. Probably a good interrogator.*

"Tox isn't back, chem tests aren't back," she mumbled. "Nothing for you yet."

"You should date her," Lue said, jerking a thumb at the doc. "You two have the same love of language."

"No."

"Why haven't you gone away?" Dr. Meenay genuinely seemed surprised to see them still in her morgue. "Go away. Nothing's ready."

"Well, jeez, what have you been doing all damn morning?" Lue wasn't especially upset. He knew if Dr. Meenay hadn't finished the autopsy, he was sure there was an excellent reason. "Were you catching up on reality television?"

"I loathe reality TV. An oxymoron."

"Fascinating. So what *have* you been doing?"

"Farm accident."

"Oh." That was *not* an oxymoron. While farm accidents were hardly a daily occurrence, as people from big cities assumed, they still happened. When they did, they never happened small.

"Tractor hit a combine."

"Oh."

"Which then crashed through the south wall of the barn."

"Huh."

"Igniting the—"

"You know what? I no longer want to know." When farm accidents did happen, they tended to ramp up the gruesome. "Listen, do you have anything at all for us? A hunch? A theory? A cup of coffee that does *not* taste like hot liquid death?"

"He's very dead," Dr. Meenay proclaimed.

"We should return later," Art announced.

Yes, Lue thought, *the two of them really would make a great couple.* They were both striking (Meenay, with her dancer's legs, spiky red hair, pale green eyes, and bow-shaped mouth, could have been a swimsuit model) with bad dietary habits and a clear dislike for conversation. *A match made in heaven! If "heaven" were another word for "this morgue."*

"Homicide," Meenay continued. She picked up a cup off the counter and took a long slurp. Lue watched carefully to be sure she—yes! She was! She *chewed* her coffee. That's how evil and hideous her hot beverages were.

"So the county's best coroner has determined that our guy a) is dead, and b) was a victim of homicide. Brilliant! Taxpayers, you are welcome."

"When will you be done?" Luckily, Art had the focus of a laser. And perhaps the personality of one.

"Four hours," the hot, creepy pathologist replied. Lue

checked his watch, noting how long this conversation had lasted without eye contact between any two of them.

"Four hours." Art turned on his heel and headed for the door. "Saint George's. Then the crime scene."

"What a wonderful suggestion, Lieutenant McMahon. Yes, by all means, let us conduct some research on the victim's most recent employer, also known as Saint George's Medical Facility, and then revisit the crime scene while Dr. Meenay finishes the autopsy. Then we will be able to . . . what? The conversation's already over? Awwww."

He had to trot to catch up. For a man almost half a head shorter, Art could *move* when he wanted. For a minute, Lue thought of his ex-wife, how she could always—

Now that *is something to think about.*

Or maybe not.

He let it go. It was a weird day in the middle of an odd week and he was tired and stressed.

He put his ex-wife out of his mind, and ran to catch up with the strange BCA agent.

Fourteen Years Ago

Run, run, as fast you can . . .

. . . you can't catch me, I'm a monster!

Evangelina stared down past her two dangling legs, through the twilit grain hatch.

After that fateful day two years ago, she had never been foolish enough to dive in . . . even though she was pretty sure she could always fly out, now. She hadn't come here to swim in corn. She had come here to reflect.

Even as the sky darkened, she could make out the distance to the granular mass below. When she squinted, she could see herself still down there, wriggling in the kernels, kicking dust over her aunt Susan, looking back up at Niffer.

Thinking what she had been thinking.

"Vange, you up there?"

She almost fell in, she was so surprised. Bending back and glancing downward over the edge of the silo, she saw Aunt Susan stepping out of her old blue Ford Mustang, which looked like it had hit 100,000 ten years ago but still ran . . . well, actually, it ran like crap. How had she not heard that car?

"I thought I'd find you here," Susan continued, her voice raised high enough to reach the hatch. "Your mom's worried about you. I know, again. But Jenn's worried too, and no one knew where to look for you."

"I'm okay."

"I can see that. Barely. It's getting dark. Why don't you come down? Your mom has dogs on the grill."

Evangelina sighed, pulled her legs out of the hatch, closed it, and began climbing down. It took a while to climb all the way down.

"Why didn't you fly?" Susan gave her a bemused look. "It would have been quicker."

The girl shrugged.

"C'mere, give me a hug. Gah, that one sucked. Try again. Aaaphh! Better. Vange, tell me what's wrong."

"Billy Brandfire called me a monster today."

"Billy Brandfire? Has he looked in a mirror?"

Evangelina pushed away from the hug, rejecting the joke. "It's true! I'm a monster. Or I'm nothing."

Susan's piercing blue eyes narrowed as she put a hand on the girl's shoulder. "Do you really see yourself that way? I thought you were smarter than that."

"Well, I'm not!" Evangelina's cheeks and neck warmed. "I'm stupid, and I'm ugly, and I scare people."

"You're brilliant and beautiful."

"But I still scare people."

Susan bit her lip in a mixture of laugh and surprise. "Cripes, kid, you don't miss a thing, do you? Yes, you scare people. Some people."

"Like Billy Brandfire."

"Like Billy Brandfire."

"And Niffer."

Susan paused. "And Niffer."

"And Mom."

"That I wouldn't know, kid. I don't know if anyone's seen your mom like that—"

"You're not afraid of me."

Susan turned and pulled Evangelina by the hand toward the car, which was parked as always on a slant, like the owner was in a hurry to have fun and couldn't be bothered to look for painted lines. "No, I'm not."

"Why not?"

"Because no matter how fierce you look, I'm always going to remember how beautiful your rainbow eyes are."

"Do you like me when I look fierce?"

Susan opened the passenger door and spanked Evangelina as the girl climbed in. "Of course I do." She shut the door, but of course it was a convertible, so she could still hear her. "I love you when you look fierce. And I love you when you don't."

"Oh."

She caught sight of Susan's exasperated look in the headlights. "Monster or nothing, you said. So now that we've handled the 'monster' part, you're going to keep pressing on the 'nothing' bit? You know better, Vange."

"No I don't!" Seeing the woman's disdain, Evangelina was truly outraged now. "I can't do anything when I'm like this!" She waved her spindly arms over the dash, linguine with bones. "I can't fly, or run so fast, or do any—"

"Can I do any of that?"

"Huh?"

"You heard me." Susan had opened her own door and slid in. "Answer the question."

"No."

"Am I nothing?"

"Of course not. You're Aunt Susan."

"You're damn right I am. I'm the real thing, baby. Here—hold on to my pocketbook." She turned the ignition and peered into Evangelina's face, like she wanted to mem-

orize her or something. "You're so beautiful, Vange. And so strong. When you're in your other body, sure. But like this, too. You're the most lovely thing I've ever seen."

Evangelina couldn't speak. She opened her mouth to try, and burst into tears instead.

"Now, what's this?" The girl was pulled into the woman's warm embrace. "What's all this? Gorgeous and strong and not too bright sometimes, huh? And you're lucky, too, babe. You think, somebody with your bodies, your abilities, your birthright and your personality and your brains, you think someone like that just shows up every day? Vange, you're one in a billion. The moon can be full or crescent or missing or green . . . it doesn't matter. Because you're one in a billion no matter what. The moon's a big tease, Vange. You're the real thing."

"Thanks, Aunt Susan." She broke the hug and wiped her eyes.

"You're welcome." The car jerked forward, tires squealing. "Let's blast this rocket home. The wolves will eat with us tonight, and I love their songs so much."

"Me too." But Evangelina wasn't thinking so much about the wolves, as she was about what Susan had said.

The real thing. Not a monster. Not a weakling. A real thing. The Real Thing.

After that, when Aunt Susan really wanted her attention, or wanted to show Evangelina she'd done especially well, she called her RT.

No one else knew why.

CHAPTER 6

Saint George's ended up largely a waste of time. First, as Lue suspected beforehand, what hadn't burned down a few weeks ago in a mysterious "accident" was under very tight security. Local law enforcement had never really gotten a crack at the scene, because the Federal Bureau of Investigation, combined with National Guard troops, had swooped in with alarming speed and force, keeping local law enforcement at arm's length. Chief Smiling Bear was still fuming about it.

Now, the federal agents were gone, and only a small complement of National Guard troops remained behind to back up the facility's security force. Cops could get in now; but staff were tight-lipped and fond of saying, "we can't recover that right now, due to the incident."

So it was a lot of: do you have the personnel file for David Webber; and no, we don't have that because of the incident; and are there any coworkers we can talk to who might have shared Webber's last shift; and no, we don't have the shift records because of the incident; and what about any videotape of that incident and let me guess, you can't give me that because of the incident; and thank you for understanding, sir, the incident really has thrown us for a loop; and how about coffee, do you have coffee, or did the incident whisk away your coffeemakers, and at least they got two cups of mediocre coffee that still would have been better than anything Meenay could have scrounged up at the morgue.

Lue dreaded having Art there for this embarrassment. He would have dreaded having any out-of-town colleague see such a shambles, but knowing this stocky, reserved BCA agent was seeing it was somehow worse.

At least, the other detective appeared already to know all about the escape of two inmates, and the destruction by fire of about a third of the facility. In fact, it was Art who suggested moving on right away to David Webber's residence.

It was at that residence that Lue found himself watching Art, contemplating a solemn truth.

All crime scenes are different, and exactly the same.

Lue considered sharing this wisdom nugget with the BCA agent, then reconsidered.

Oh, why not? "I was thinking, Lieutenant McMahon, about how all crime scenes are different, and exactly the same."

Art was squatting on the porch, studying the spot where David Webber had been found, a scowl rippling across his features. "That makes no sense."

"It does if you have seen as many scenes as I have. Get it? *Seen, scene?* Did you catch that clever wordplay? That, my new partner pro tem, is what is known as a homophone. Cue immature snickering." He paused. But there was no snickering to wait through. *Excellent!* "Other examples in the English language would be pear and pair. Not and knot.

Aides and AIDS. Err, air. Aweigh, away. Bred, bread. Sent, cent, scent." *A triple homophone! Oh, lovely day.*

Speaking of scent, Art was . . . was he *sniffing*? He was! He had stiffened and was sniffing the air, like some sort of glowering, tightly cropped Irish setter in brown corduroy.

"David Webber was not alone," Art said.

"Yeah, we figured that, from the way someone killed him. And from the way I saw someone else, or something else, and fired my gun." He pointed to the empty holster under his tweed jacket.

"And someone else."

"You mean a third person? What do you base that on—your sense of smell?"

Art gave him a crooked look, and then pointed to the siding behind some stacked patio furniture. "Good hiding place."

"Great, a good hiding place. How do we know someone actually used it?"

"Look closer."

Lue bent down and finally saw what Art was getting at: there was a series of small, carved marks on one of the panels, as if someone had been ticking off time with something sharp.

"Three sites in Bemidji have those," Art explained.

Lue was, for the first time in Art's presence, thinking too hard to speak for a while. He thought about the coincidence, and what could make marks like that, and whether they in the Moorston police ought to have caught this detail on their own or if that was asking too much, and a few other things, mostly that he would need to take a really thorough look at any Bemidji files Art could offer.

"Okay," he finally said. "So whoever or whatever I shot, was definitely in this spot for a while before David Webber came home and cracked open a beer on his porch. The marks are ticking off the time—maybe minutes, maybe more random than that."

As he spoke, he could see it. He could see Art seeing it. "So David lies down, he has his Mark V with him, but that *does not* matter because his attacker has the element of surprise, is already too close, and has a great angle for a killing stroke. The guy probably deserves some credit for squeezing off as many rounds as he did, given all the disadvantages. So how does all this point to someone else, in addition to the two of them?"

Art's lips wrinkled into a grimace . . . no! It was a smile. "You missed it."

Annoyed, Lue scratched his scalp. "Yes, okay, Detective, I missed the scratch marks. You might consider cutting me some slack, given the fact that you have the benefit of additional crime scenes upon which to draw . . ." *Which I really, really need to check out . . . for the sake of both ego and conscience.*

"I mean, you missed something else."

"Oh."

"Come with me."

"There is nothing I would rather do." *Except have a root canal.*

A few steps off the porch was the small copse of maples that separated Webber's property from the next. The two of them had passed it coming in, as multiple Moorston police officers had walked back and forth past it while investigating the scene not twenty-four hours ago. Art, Lue recalled, had barely paused here on their way to the porch. Yet the man now pointed to something that no one else had seen, including Detective Lue Vue himself.

"Snapped branches. Bark burns. And different scratches." He was pointing at the base of one of the thicker maples.

Lue examined the slender branches in the area Art indicated; several were broken recently. In addition, there was a palm-sized dark mark toward the bottom of the trunk. Getting closer, he saw that the mark was not typical rot, as any casual observation would suggest—but was instead almost certainly the result of a recent chemical reaction. Above the burn were scratches. Unlike what defaced a tiny bit of the porch siding, these marks were wider, less subtle, and more rugged. *What the . . . ?* Something like a . . . a bear might have left them.

Might.

"There's nothing like this on the porch," he admitted. "But this may have nothing to do with what happened last night." Except it looked fresh. He might not have years and years of cop experience, but he'd had a cop's *brain* long before he went near the academy. So he didn't believe in coincidences like that. He hadn't even before he'd gotten married.

"You shot at the suspect?"

"Yes."

"Where?"

They walked over to the spot by the cedar fence. There were still some evidence markers on the scene, but Art didn't look there. He was picking through the grass—not for shells or blood, Lue realized, but for something else.

"Here."

As he bent close to the turf, he saw what his colleague had: several of the blades of grass were not cut short by a lawnmower, but rather burned down halfway.

It was incredible that Art had known to look for these things. Lue comforted his hurt, shriveled, dying ego with the knowledge that the man had simply known what to look for, from the Bemidji scenes. *I've got to look over those files.* He'd been schooled more in the last five minutes than he had in years. And by a man in corduroy!

He shut his eyes and tried to think some more, this time aloud. "So why no burn marks on the porch? Why was this person here at all?"

"Good questions."

Lue sprung to his feet, even though he did not feel energetic. He felt out of his depth. "This is not conclusive. It is still possible that whoever was by the tree, and whoever I shot, was also on the porch."

To his surprise, Art reached out and gave his back an almost tender pat.

"There's no shame here."

"I know that." He tried to sound sharp, but it came out more like a confession.

"Any other knife killings you're working on?"

Lue thought about that. "We have an unsolved murder case about two months old. It's not mine, so I don't know if it's a blade or not. I'm sure Chief won't mind if we look into it."

"You know the address?"

"I can call the station." He was already trotting toward the car.

CHAPTER 7

About an hour later, they were standing in an abandoned house, a small Cape Cod–style, three bedroom, two bath, that the bank was still trying to sell . . . with no luck.

The former owner, Janice Pohl, was a lonely woman who had worked for years at the local grocery store for barely enough to pay the mortgage . . . all this according to the file (Mark, the patrol officer who had irritated Lue last night, had sent PDF files to Art's smart phone).

There had been no witnesses, and the autopsy only indicated bleeding to death through what appeared to be a knife wound. All reasonable traces of the murder would be long gone, Lue knew, courtesy of a repaint job and fanatic cleaning.

It didn't matter. The murder had taken place months ago under mysterious circumstances, and Moorston was small enough where everyone was still talking about it, and so this perfectly nice, perfectly underpriced house with wall-to-wall carpeting and an assumable mortgage at 5.25 percent sat empty. Given the vast numbers of homeless trapped on the planet, some considered that a worse crime than the actual murder.

"And that would be where . . ."

"The body was found," Art replied, tapping his smart phone. He was prowling all over the first floor like an impatient panther.

"There is no way we will find any new evidence here," he protested. "I mean, what you did back at Webber's was impressive, but that crime scene is fresh. All we are going to find here is mouse turds and paint."

"No mice."

Art began climbing the stairs, and soon Lue was following him through the upstairs rooms: bathroom, bedroom, bedroom, a tiny office-which-was-an-office-as-it-was-too-small-and-the-window-was-too-small-to-meet-code-requirements. New paint and new carpet were everywhere.

"Sure, Art, no mice. You know that because, what, no mice in Bemidji, so none can be here?"

"You know that's not what I'm saying."

"Well, what are you saying? That we have nothing but dead ends? It feels like that. We have no witnesses to the attack here, and thus the presence of mice can neither be confirmed nor—hmmm." *Nice view. Come to think of it, this house is a pretty good value.* As a single male in a hazardous, low-paying job with lousy hours, yet excellent health benefits, Lue had been resigned to apartment living for the next several decades—or until he could seduce another woman and charm her into marriage and having children, and even, if they were true soul mates, buying joint property, assuming the interest rates weren't dreadful.

But this place, this pretty little house . . . unlike the average citizen, Lue knew that not only were crime scenes not haunted, the killer rarely returned. They were always a good bargain, for rational decision makers.

It's wrong that I'm thinking about using a horrific neighborhood tragedy to make an offer on a house, right? I should be focusing on the crime and the victims and the suspects, right?

Right, his subconscious agreed. So it was settled. It was wrong. It was insensitive. Maybe even creepy. Okay. Case closed.

"I wonder if I could qualify for a mortgage on my own," he mused aloud.

"Let's try outside."

"There are definitely mice outside," Lue agreed. "But no witnesses."

"I mean for evidence."

"She wasn't killed outside." Of course, Lue knew that reasoning was false. Checking outside was perfectly sensible, given the circumstances. But he simply could not resist twisting Art's tail. Call it a failure of character.

When they found small scrapes on the siding behind the shrubs not far from the back door, Lue didn't know whether to feel relief or deep irritation.

Pohl's neighborhood was more thickly settled than Webber's, so there were no tall cedar fences or maple copses where anything could hide long enough to leave burn marks or anything else. And of course, poring over the grass would be useless at this point.

"Maybe what I saw at Webber's never came here," he mused aloud.

Art kept searching the base of a lone oak toward the back of the property. "That is possible."

"It could be something the person who leaves the scrape marks knows about, it could be unknown to that person, it could be hostile or friendly to that person or people."

"All possible."

Lue took a deep, steadying breath. "So. I have used *what* and *it* quite a few times, and you seem okay with that. Even though most murder suspects are people. So I think we can both agree that *what*ever left the burn mark at Webber's, *what*ever singed the grass there, *what*ever I shot at and *what*ever seems *not* to have been here . . . *it* is not a typical suspect."

He internally cringed, waiting for Art's derisive laughter or brusque comment. But the shorter redhead only nodded as he began to walk back to the car.

Lue let out the breath he hadn't realized he was holding. "Okay. So we *do* agree on something beyond human. That is . . . huge, actually. I thought you would be harder to convince."

Nothing from Art. Lue began trotting after him. "Why are you so easy to convince?"

Still nothing. And it was interesting, wasn't it, how Art hadn't answered?

Don't jump to conclusions, he told himself with deepening unease. *You're projecting.*

But still he wondered. Art had popped up out of nowhere, almost literally. And Lue had the distinct impression the man could disappear from sight as quickly and easily.

Lue was getting tired of playing catch-up all day. There were all sorts of new things in his life now that he knew very little about. Case in point, the Bemidji files . . . and maybe he'd pull Art's folder, too. One of the gals in HR owed him a favor. Knowledge was power, and Lue Vue liked to store it up like a dragon guarding treasure.

Dragons.

Ha.

CHAPTER 8

Detective Lue Vue liked to fancy himself a master interrogator. But trying to unlock secrets from Art McMahon was, he began to think, like trying to pry pearls out of live oysters. Art looked annoyingly unmoved by the other man's threats and hoarse promises of dire consequences if he didn't come up with *full disclosure immediately!*

After watching Art stare back at him through a full thirty-minute "interrogation" in the car on the way back to the station, Lue's shoulders slumped. "Fine, don't tell me why you were so easy to convince about monsters! But I will find out."

"Mmmm."

"I warn you," he warned, warningly. "I am a pit bull clenching a severed limb, in matters such as these."

"So you'll talk less now?"

"Not hardly. You *will* eventually cough up what I want to know."

"Yes. When you take a promise of silence."

"Vow. A vow of silence, you . . ." Lue mentally flipped through a catalog of potential insults. "You know what? The whole vow/promise distinction can wait; we can circle back to the . . ."

" 'Circle' sounds right."

". . . we can circle, all right. First, we need to discuss trust. Partners need to trust each other."

A snort was the only response to his speculation, which emboldened (emboldened! there was a word he hardly *ever* got to use) Lue to continue said speculation. "Once we trust each other, we can focus on the questions at hand: Why is this monster here, instead of in the countryside where monsters belong? Is it targeting victims, or killing randomly? If not random, why *these* victims? But for as long as we have no trust, those questions have to wait."

Lue waited for a brief, unhelpful retort. What he heard instead was, "The victims were not random."

"Not random? So why these victims?"

"Who and why, always seem to be on different sides of the same coin." Art rolled down the passenger window slightly and took in the autumn air. Lue recognized several pauses in Art's cadence. It was a lot like the pause from someone who was learning to avoid a stutter, or speaking English as a second language at their first formal occasion.

Lue waited for another thought from his partner pro tem. *I can wait. To catch this thing, I can wait, I can tolerate anything. A taciturn BCA agent. Polyester boxers. A credit report riddled with errors. Dyslexia. A one-eyed-person-in-the-land-of-the-blind soliloquy.*

"We should talk to your witness."

"Come again?" Lue had begun thinking about the house again—the manageable yard, the numerous closets with floor-to-ceiling shelves, the new cabinetry. If he could find a roommate, maybe they could pool funds, go to the bank and work out a rent-to-own arrangement . . .

"You had a witness at Webber's."

"Yeah, the jogger." *Hey, roommate!*

"I need to talk to her."

"Yeah, me, too."

"I suspect Pamela Pride knows more than she lets on."

"You know that without meeting her? You really should meet her." Lue mentally reviewed his credit rating. It was excellent, since he took paying bills on time even more seriously than he took visits to the gun range. He was what banks craved: a workaholic eager to jump neck-deep into six-figure debt that would take decades to pay off. Ms. Pride could be a check-bouncing victim of multiple identity thefts, and they'd still average out okay. "I mean, meet her first, before jumping to conclusions."

"I read your report. You did not ask all of the right questions."

"Tell me about it." *How long do you plan on staying in Moorston? Is that condo you're staying in a bit too small? Do men in uniform thrill you? Are you willing to give me power of attorney for an afternoon?*

"She has more to tell."

"Broken record, Art, ever heard the phrase? I get it: you need to ask her more questions. That poor woman."

Art closed his window and scowled at Lue. "You have feelings for Ms. Pride."

"I pity her. I pity anyone caught in your monosyllabic crime-solving web. What questions do you have in mind? Maybe I can tease them out into full paragraphs, so you actually appear human."

"We should go there."

"What, to her condo across town? Now? The station is only four blocks away."

Art turned in his seat and leaned in, practically breathing on the driver's neck. "I took you for a man of clearer priorities."

"She works weekdays."

"She may feel traumatized by what she's seen."

Lue let out a long, snakelike hiss. Art was right—many witnesses to murder scenes took a day or two off work immediately afterward, to get their bearings or clear their heads. And if Pamela Pride had more to say, she was their best lead. It would do no good to face Chief Smiling Bear with an impatient BCA agent.

"You could call her, at least."

"Fine." The car veered, and they headed in a new direction.

CHAPTER 9

"Things happen," Art told Lue.

Lue had been poking at the GPS since he hung up his cell from talking to Pamela (yes, she was home, which both annoyed and pleased him). It was challenging to pretend he hadn't already memorized Pamela Pride's address, but he believed he was making a good show of it. Art's statement provoked a crooked smile. "Things happen? Would you care to be more specific?"

"Things you might not believe."

"Okay."

"Things which are true."

"Right."

"Things which appear unbelievable, but are true nonetheless."

"I feel like you may have already covered that." Lue coughed into his fist. Sometimes, there was no polite way to ask: "So, are there pills, or some sort of medication, which you may be due to take today?" *Possibly overdue?*

Art blinked. "I don't require medication."

"Of course not."

"My immune system is excellent."

"Really? You have *never* been sick?"

"I had a slight cold at three years old."

"Huh. So, tell me more about these unbelievable but true things, especially if they have anything to do with the monsters you were avoiding talking about before."

"To help me resolve these crimes, you have to understand."

"About things happening which I might not believe but which are true even if I do not believe them? Indeed! Any other nuggets you want to toss my way? By the way, I think I have my first migraine. And my first duodenal ulcer. Do you believe this is a coincidence?"

"Everyone has a secret."

Lue raised his eyebrows thoughtfully. "Okay, *that* I can understand and agree with. So, Detective McMahon: what is *your* secret?"

Art lowered the window again and examined the neighborhood. "We're here."

"I already knew that. Pick a different secret."

As Lue pulled his dark-brown Caprice to a stop, Art popped his seatbelt off, swung open the door, and was out and up the sidewalk in half a second. He looked primed, he looked energized. He did not look at all confused. About anything. Lue envied him that.

He followed quickly, not because he was hoping Pamela Pride had more info, but because he had to rescue her from the corduroy-jacketed freak striding up her sidewalk.

And ask her for her credit rating.

CHAPTER 10

Pamela Pride answered the door in gray, loose-fitting sweatpants and a maroon sweatshirt that looked at least fifteen years old. Her hair was stuffed into a large pink plastic clip, her eyes were a bit puffy from lack of sleep, and there wasn't a lick of makeup in sight.

Spectacular, Lue told himself. He checked Art for a reaction. The BCA agent stood stiffly, face inscrutable, badge held firmly aloft. *That must be the secret. Art McMahon is a eunuch.*

"Do you think you really need the badge? She knows me, Detective McMahon."

"She doesn't know *me*. Ma'am, may we come in?"

"Yeah." Pamela smiled at Art, winked at Lue, and widened the door.

Pamela's condo was well appointed but sparse. The spare furnishings confirmed Lue's theory that she had not lived here long, and that she had cosmopolitan tastes. The kitchen immediately to their left had all new appliances (Lue noted this glumly, as the house from earlier today had a refrigerator and washing machine that had clearly not been replaced post-murder), and multiple framed prints of abstract art in autumnal tones accented the cream-colored living room beyond.

"Ms. Pride, this is Detective Art McMahon, from the Minnesota State Patrol's Bureau of Criminal Apprehension. He is assisting me with the investigation of the murder of David Webber."

"Okay. You want tea?" She was over by the shining steel refrigerator, displaying a side-door selection of Snapples.

"Thank you. Do you have green?"

"My favorite." She reached in, grabbed a bottle, and slid it across the kitchen island. "Detective McMahon? I've got green, diet peach, diet raspberry . . ."

"No thank you. Ms. Pride, I must ask you questions."

Her grin faded. "Okay. I figured that. Fire away."

They followed her into the living room as she tossed a diet raspberry back and forth between her hands. This time, Lue caught Art watching her backside as she sat delicately on her firm leather couch. *Ah, the secret. The man actually has a pulse.*

"No work today?"

Pamela shook her head as she popped open the bottle. "Didn't sleep last night. Called in sick. Your call woke me up." She looked up at Lue and shrugged apologetically.

"What's your job?"

"Lab tech at Nonnatus."

Art gave Lue an inquiring look. "Hospital," Lue clarified.

"How long have you worked there?"

"Ten . . . no, eleven months. I graduated from Argosy University, and came right here."

"Argosy—right in Saint Paul, right? So you know that downtown pretty well," Lue deduced. "How's the nightlife?"

She rolled her eyes. "Dead as roadkill. My roommates and I always went over the river to party."

"To Minneapolis? Ouch. Pretty conventional." Lue winced. "My ex-wife tells me Saint Paul is better than most think. Lowertown neighborhood is resurging, maybe has some new wine bars. You lived right there and never checked it out?"

"Nope." She returned a crooked smile. "I wasn't the wine bar type."

Art cleared his throat. "Why did you move to Moorston?"

She raised her bottle of tea. "That's where the job was, champ. Nonnatus was the only place to give me an offer straight out of school."

"Do you like Moorston?" Lue asked, ignoring Art's impatient glare.

"It's got its charms. I like that people seem to look out for each other, and I feel safe jogging in the evenings. I've never been in a river town before, and the historic downtown has a great coffee shop . . ."

"General Java's?" Lue guessed.

"Yeah, that's the one!" She looked appreciatively at him. "You go there in the morning?"

He shrugged. "Nah. Shift starts too early. I try to grab an occasional lunch."

"Oh, I'm there *every* morning at seven . . ."

"If we could focus, please."

"Sorry." She slunk back into the couch, and Lue gave Art a reproachful look.

"Please recount what you saw near the Webber house."

Lue pulled his earlobe and clenched his teeth. Pamela spotted this and gave him a warm smile: *It's okay. I don't mind saying it again.*

"I was jogging down Snapdragon Lane away from the river . . . that's south, right? And I heard three or four gunshots. I had my phone on me, so I called nine one one. They said they'd have a car there in a few minutes and to keep away from the scene, so I kept jogging." She shrugged, flicked a hand through her hair, popped the pin, did something with her hair, then did something else and now her hair was pinned back up. "A few seconds later, I saw Detective Vue's patrol car and flagged it down. That's it."

"Did you see anyone else before the shots?"

"While I was jogging? Not on that block, I don't think."

"And after?"

"No. Not until Detective Lue got there."

"Did you go look behind the house, where the shots were fired?"

Her eyes widened. "Wow, no. The nine-one-one woman told me to get away from the scene and leave it to the cops."

"The nine-one-one transcript confirms that," Lue reassured her. "But we had some reports nearby of an unusual shape fleeing the scene. We thought you might have seen something, before or after the call, which might give us some clues as to what it might have been."

"An unusual shape? You mean, like a bear or something? I heard bears were making a comeback in this part of Minnesota."

"Sure, a bear, or anything else that might have seemed unusual. You see anything like that?"

"I wish I had. That would be neat. We certainly didn't have any of those in St. Paul. Maybe the nightlife around Argosy would've been better if we had."

Lue snickered. Art fumed.

"Did you see David Webber at all that evening?"

"No."

"Earlier that day?"

"No."

"Had you ever seen him before that day?"

"No." Her posture shrunk a bit farther into the couch, and she looked nervously at Lue. "I never knew the guy. What, am I a suspect? I thought it was an animal."

Lue chose not to hold back a chuckle. "No. Detective McMahon is simply being thorough. Just answer his questions, and we'll be on our way." He gave Art an obvious warning look . . . and received one in return.

"Has anyone visited you since that evening?"

"No." She took a big gulp of tea. "Should I be worried? I mean, if it's an animal, it's not going to care if I was there, right? Animals aren't that smart, are they? Not even bears?"

Lue considered another comforting statement, but Art's combative stance made him think twice. He was certainly treating Pamela as a suspect, and Lue was worried what might happen if he truly upset her.

"Have you seen anything strange lately?"

She looked him up and down. "Well, *you're* pretty strange. The way you talk and the way you look at me like you don't believe anything I'm saying. If you're chasing after an animal, I don't have any pets and I haven't seen any bears. If you're chasing after a person and think he may still be out there, give me a physical description so I can call him in if I see him."

"What a fabulous idea. I think Detective McMahon has all he needs for now. You still have my card, Ms. Pride?"

She stood and pointed with a well-manicured nail at the steel refrigerator. On the side, a black square magnet with some short saying on it in a thin script, held up a familiar white and blue Moorston Police Department business card.

"You call me if you think of anything else, okay?"

"Yes, Detective. Thank you."

"I am not done—"

"Yes, you are." Lue grabbed Art's elbow as he passed him, barely avoiding whiplash, and pulled him through the kitchen. He caught the thinly scripted words on the refrigerator magnet as they passed: *Hunger is the best cook.*

CHAPTER 11

The moment Pamela Pride's door closed behind them, Art yanked his arm free of Lue's hold, made fists, and growled his question. "What's your problem?"

"My problem? You interrogate like a jackass."

"At least I interrogate." Art stormed down the hallway and slammed through the door.

Lue followed him with an angry stride. "Oh, you dislike my style? *Quel surprise.* Well, perhaps we should compare notes. What did you learn from that interview, about Pamela Pride?"

"I learned nothing valuable, between your interruptions."

"Nothing at all?"

"Nothing new. She confirmed the information in your report."

"Wow. Sounds like a wasted trip then, am I right?"

"It's not a waste to make sure."

"Nor is it a waste when you pick up new information. Which I did, by acting less like a jackass and more like a detective. Did you take *any* training in interrogation technique?"

"Explain." They were in the parking lot now, and Art didn't exactly look like he was listening to any explanation Lue was about to give.

"First, she's lying about attending Argosy University. It's in Eagan, eight miles away. Not far enough away for someone making a false resume to remember, but certainly too far for someone who went there not to correct me."

"Second, she's lying about General Java's. I actually *do* go there every morning at six forty-five, and I haven't once seen her walk in any time close to seven."

Art stopped and leaned against the passenger side of the car. He was listening now.

"Third, she wants to create a rift between you and me. She wanted me to get mad at you for pressing her: she treated me like a visitor, and you like an intruder. You played right into that, stomping around with your blunt questions and swinging your penis around like a billy club . . ."

"My penis is not . . ."

"Nobody wants to talk about your penis anymore. Fourth, she grabbed onto the whole our-suspect-is-not-a-human theory and ran real hard with that one. She said 'animal' at least three times after you simply asked her if she saw an unusual shape. You could have been talking about a man carrying a large sack, or a guy with a wheelbarrow, or a three-foot-tall acrobat. Heck, my *aunt* has an unusual shape when she gets up in the morning."

"Yeah?"

He ignored the interruption. The last thing he needed was Art wondering about his family. "But she went right to animal, stayed there, and tried to drag us there, too. She even brought up the idea of an animal smart enough to stalk . . . a monster, you might say.

"Fifth, she's not afraid of law enforcement. Not even really nervous around us. Had no trouble suggesting our next steps—go find an animal, of course—and even flirted with me, even while you were trying to intimidate her. So she knows one or more people in law enforcement, I'd guess."

Art let him finish, and then got in the car wordlessly. Pissed off, Lue got in the driver's side and slammed the door shut.

"What did you think?" he asked his partner as he ground the ignition. "Because I talk a lot, I have no clue how to listen? You Minnesota introverts are all the same: you think you have some magical Zen property that gives you special insight. You see a person who likes connecting with others through language, a guy who chats and jokes and puts himself out there a bit, and you assume that person is insecure, or too passionate, or disruptive, or boastful. You think that person has no listening skills. Add to that the typical arrogance a state detective will have when dealing with local police, and you get . . . well, *you*."

The car screeched out of the parking lot. Lue adjusted the mirrors, even though he didn't have to. Then his angry brow leaned toward the windshield. Then he sat up to check his gauges. Then, back to the mirrors again.

"What do you think it all means?" Art finally asked.

"Is this you, asking for my opinion? Fine. I think Pamela Pride knows more than she lets on—she probably saw that same monster that night, and probably got an idea that it could stalk her. She would be afraid of it, and would want us to be thinking along those lines, so maybe we would come to our own conclusions. That way, she can keep her sanity."

"What about the lies?"

"About Argosy, and Java's? Well, there may be a sinister explanation for that, but right now we could also assume that she really needed a job in a bad economy, traveled far enough where a lie on her resume might last awhile, and is simply trying to weave a successful story for herself. None of that is a crime." *It does, however,* he thought ruefully, *make her unsuitable as a cosigner on a mortgage or rental agreement.*

"And trying to create a rift between us?"

"That, I can be more certain of: she thinks you suck, and she prefers talking to me. End of story."

"You should ask her out."

"That would be unethical."

"Hurry up and solve the case."

Lue was about to respond vehemently, until he saw the left corner of Art's mouth. "Humor is not your strong suit, Detective McMahon."

"Our best move is to return to the station."

"Where I was trying to take us a half hour ago."

"Good thing you listened to me."

Yes, Lue thought as he turned a sharp corner. *It was.*

CHAPTER 12

"We're not at the station."

"No, we are not." Lue picked up a jar of raw oats and sniffed it. "Lunch time."

"We have work to do."

"The work will get done, Art. I stay late nearly every shift. Now try not to talk too much: my sense of smell requires a quiet aura."

Art looked around in despair. "My sense of smell requires bacon."

"Not bad, for your first real joke." Lue passed the rest of the grains and meandered into pastas and cereals.

"We were talking earlier. About monsters."

"Ah, I see you are finally ready to talk." Lue's chest swelled. *Master interrogator, indeed.*

"Have you ever seen a monster . . . with wings?"

Trying not to look excited at the veritable fire hose of information Art was pointing at his ear, Lue caressed a box of organic oat O's. "Once or twice. Have you ever had wheat germ? You should think about wheat germ."

"Have you ever seen a monster . . . with too many legs?"

That one made Lue think. "Nothing bigger than the size of a quarter. Maybe a dollar bill." He shivered. "*Yuuuuggh.* Squishy. Hey, that reminds me: I could have a tofu dog." He scanned the co-op, glancing over the rows of loose tea, stevia, honey, chai mixes, (real) ginger ale, handmade soap, organic lemon-scented toothpaste, to recall the refrigerated section. "You ever have a tofu dog, Art?"

"No. It sounds delicious."

"That is quite the ironic attitude emerging there, partner. If you would rather not have a tofu dog, you only have to . . ."

"I don't want a tofu dog."

"Your lips say no, but your cholesterol level says *oui, oui.*"

Art whipped out his smart phone, checked something, and put it back in his pocket. "Lunch hour's almost over."

"We came into the store three minutes ago."

"It's twelve forty-nine."

"What, you can only eat at noon?"

"I like to eat at noon."

"No, you like to interrogate witnesses—badly—at noon. It was your choice to hit Pride's place, Art. Lie in the bed you have made."

Art observed the rows upon rows of hostile grains. "I would rather lay somewhere with real food."

"*Lie* somewhere with real food. You *lay* something down. Like a fork, or a gun, or meat, or your dignity."

"My point is, real food."

"You can even lay *yourself* down, on top of meat that you have *laid* down. Once you have *lain* down on the *laid* down meat, you can *lie* to a *lay*person and call it tofu."

"So you have seen monsters."

"Yes. In fact, I saw one at Webber's house."

Art paused. "Actually, you may have seen two."

Lue maneuvered between overstuffed endcaps of Odwalla bars and reached out to open a refrigerator door. "Two? No, there was only one . . ." He held the door open, thought about it, and closed the door without taking anything. "What are you trying to tell me?"

"It's time you looked at the Bemidji files."

Twelve Years Ago

The night Winoka died, its people were saved by the wolves.

Evangelina woke up right away, hearing a song she did not recognize. The howls were discordant and rushed. She rolled out of bed and went to the window. It opened to let the chill autumn inside. Far away, she heard the rumbling of an engine in the sky.

Moments later, her mother was in her bedroom. She was calm but tense, and her words came out as if she had practiced them for this moment. "Vange. Get away from the window. Change shape, right now."

"Why?"

"Something's coming. It might burn. You and your sister might need to protect me."

Evangelina was stunned into obedience. Did her mother actually need protection? She couldn't imagine a stronger force, with the possible exception of Niffer.

As if on cue, a bright blue set of scales wove into the

room and encircled the older woman. "Mom. You and Vange should go to the basement. I need to find Susan."

"I know. Come on, honey."

Her mom grabbed her by the tarsus and pulled her along. In under a minute, they were in the finished basement. The wolves' howling was more fevered than ever.

"What's coming, Mom?"

"An airplane."

"That doesn't sound too scary."

"It's what it's carrying." Her mother seemed distracted by despair. "I guess the rumors were true. The Regiment has come to America. No other power could access the military necessary to pull this off, not with Mr. Elmsmith holding the position he has."

"Mr. Elmsmith is Susan's brother, right?"

"Father, honey. He runs the military. Or did. I'm worried for him."

"Where's Aunt Susan?"

"She's safe."

"Uncle Goat will keep her safe?"

"Gautierre. Yes, he'll keep her—"

Fury erupted everywhere. It felt to Evangelina as if a titan of flame had smashed into the house, blasting apart the tiny windows near the ceiling and tearing down everything it could reach. She saw her mother duck, and she reflexively spread her wings to cover the woman, clinging to her with an eight-legged hug. Debris and dust showered her tough, young back.

I'm saving her, *she told herself with a thrill.* I'm really saving her!

Evangelina found out later that many families across Winoka had perished in that single explosion. Whereas the Scales residence had been on the northern edge of town and therefore was merely leveled, hundreds of homes near the center of town had been consumed by a crater. Evangelina never forgot the sight of it, as the few hundred survi-

vors took flight from the ruins of Winoka. Farther to the west, beyond the familiar old farm and silos that had miraculously remained standing, the wreckage of a bomber smoldered—Niffer had gotten to it a few seconds too late, but Evangelina still felt a swell of pride.

We can save ourselves. And we can fight back.

CHAPTER 13

At Art's insistence, they chose a bar and grill that would serve meat (and, Lue noted slyly, grains) all afternoon. On the way, they stopped by Art's motel, where the BCA agent slipped into his room to pick up a box.

While Lue waited in the car, he spotted something strange: an elderly man leaning against the frame of the office door.

The man pretended not to look at either detective, but it was obvious to Lue that there was nothing else around to provoke interest. He had a cane folded and tucked through the loops of his faded, worn jeans. He had a backpack slung over his other shoulder. The zipper had come a bit undone, and a sinister pastel flash of yarn was peeking out.

He looked run-down and helpless, a step from the gutter. But Lue knew the man could get that cane out and snapped to the pavement in less time than it took to blink. His clothes were old, yes, and meticulously cared for. Not like they were the best he could afford, but like he was fond of them and took care of them, wearing them almost literally off his skin.

But, though he looked interesting, he wasn't causing any trouble, and now here Art was back in the car, with a box crammed behind his seat. "We should go," he said, motioning to the man who had been watching Lue.

"Who is he?"

"Motel manager."

"You trust him?"

Art shrugged. "I know he hasn't been in the room."

"How?"

"I have people watching."

"Cute. You have someone watching me, too?"

"*I* am watching you."

"All right, well, watch me drive to the Suds Bucket and read these files."

They were at the modest downtown corner restaurant less than ten minutes later, in a back corner booth where the box fit next to Art on the seat. Lue ordered the Caesar chicken wrap and minestrone soup, while Art ordered a bacon cheeseburger and turkey chili.

Once the waiter had gone, Lue waited for his partner to say something. After waiting a full minute, he coughed and said something that had been on his mind for some time.

"There is this wonderful graphic novel—Japanese graphic novel, it is called *Crossing Midnight*."

Art grunted. Lue remained patient; now that the files were sitting next to him, he knew he'd get his chance to read them, once his partner was ready.

"One of the characters in it reminds me of you. Reminds . . . ha! Could *be* you." Lue leaned closer, examining the short-cropped hair and auburn bristles on the other man's check. "Are you Japanese?"

"No."

"And/or hundreds of years old?"

"No."

"Mmmmm. I will be watching you, pal," Lue said in a menacing yet tired tone. He leaned back. "Now is the time to tell me if you are an ancient Japanese sprung from a graphic novel like the goddess Athena from Zeus's head."

"No. Some call that Japanese graphic stuff porn."

"Yeah, well, some people consider the *National Enquirer* real news. But it is most emphatically not. And not all Japanese graphic novels are porn."

"I don't care."

"Well, try, okay? You sort of remind me of a character I was reading about last month."

Lue waited, and wasn't surprised when Art had zero to say on that subject. Not many people could resist the "I read a book that reminded me of you" or "I had a really weird dream about you" or "I met someone who reminded me of you," but Art could, and Lue knew why. For Art, there was nothing but the task at hand. No petty distractions. No worries about causing offense or getting off track or stepping on toes. No ego, no . . . *self.* It made him formidable, yet annoying.

"It was from this story, *Crossing Midnight.* One of the characters is a cop named Yamada, and in this story, his lord had been murdered years and years ago."

"Great story. You told it well."

"Pay attention! See, this Yamada, he was really taciturn and it drove people crazy. Taciturn, what am I saying . . . he made *you* look gabby, Art. Gabby!"

"This paperwork." Art was gingerly poking through the printouts Lue had grabbed (clutched, actually) as they sprinted from HQ. "It's disorganized."

"Anyway, Yamada's lord was roundly defeated in battle, but it was not his fault . . . he had been betrayed. And the guy who won, the traitor, he asked Yamada for his allegiance, right? And Yamada, the poor guy is grief-stricken because his lord is dead at the hand of a slimy asshole traitor. So he says, essentially, 'go blow, jerkoff,' or words to that effect."

"There is no Japanese word for 'jerkoff.'"

"How multilingual of you. Listen to the damned story. So the bad guy, the traitor, he says, 'You don't have anything to say? You will not pledge allegiance to me? Fine, from now on every word you speak will cost you a year of your life.' Boom. Curse is laid. Yamada is *screwed*."

"Unfortunate."

"Right! Because no matter how terse he is, no matter how carefully he chooses his words, no matter what he says he is costing himself years of life every single time he opens his mouth."

"Not what I meant."

"My point is . . ."

"I choose my words."

"Right. So . . . what do you think?"

Art glanced over at the other booths, which were empty, and back at Lue. "It's a story."

"You have no soul."

To his astonishment, Art smiled. Lue nearly fell backward off the chair. He didn't think Art's face *worked* like that. Amazing. The smile made the BCA agent look like a real person and everything.

Then, as if finally deciding, Art pulled out the first file. Before he handed over the thick package wrapped in pine green manila, he flapped it loosely in his hand.

"These are not BCA files."

"Of course they—what? What else would they be?"

"*My* files."

Lue squinted. "Is the suspect another BCA agent?"

"It's difficult to explain my concerns."

"I feel the same way, when I look at you."

"That was genuinely funny." The folder flopped onto the table. "Keep this to yourself. Anyone else finds out, I know you told them."

"Very gangster of you. I shall read the file now, if that suits you."

"Please do."

Hours later, as he began the sixth and last file of the box, Lue looked back at the avalanche of impossible papers and disturbing photographs he had seen, and wished he had never started.

CHAPTER 14

"You have family."

"Was that a question, or have you done research?"

It was late that evening. They were still at the Suds Bucket, though they had cleaned up the files and locked them in the trunk of the government-issued Chevrolet Caprice. Lue had called into the station and given Smiling Bear a vague report of progress; he could tell that she could tell he was holding something back. But what was he supposed to tell her?

Hey, Chief, just looked over six super files that contain evidence that dragons are real—and just like us, they apparently kill each other! Secretly, of course. They do everything secretly. Or else people will probably kill them. Which feels ironic.

Or:

Hey, Chief, just looked over six super files that our BCA agent friend refuses to show his colleagues, for fear that someone will kill him to silence him! And now they might kill me, and you, too! No, no need to thank me: you pay me a generous public servant's salary to be this good.

Or:

Hey, Chief, just looked over six super files that make me wonder if I have chosen the right path in life. Because when I look at what has happened here, and then think back to the life decisions I have made, I feel like I'm losing my mind. Hey, why are you calling Saint George's facility . . . oh. Right. Never mind.

He was nursing his fourth beer. Art had stopped at a couple of drinks, he noticed, and was sticking with juice and pop.

"A guess." Art motioned with his glass at Lue's left hand. There was a white mark on the ring finger.

The younger detective raised his hand, his own beer temporarily forgotten. "Ah, yeah. I finally took the ring off, about four weeks ago."

"Dead?"

"She left me."

Art took a careful sip of orange juice. "Why?"

Lue's drink waved back and forth a few times. "Zeet."

It was several more seconds before either spoke again—a contest of wills, Lue soon realized. He motioned the svelte bartender over, who drafted another beer for him. He sipped it. He examined the bottles of rum in the bottom row of the mirrored bar display. Finally, he gave in. "Zeet the Snoring Bee, that is."

"I see."

It was such an absurd claim, Lue almost knocked over his beer giggling. "All right, you win. I shall explain."

"There's no need—"

"Have you ever slept with a woman who snores?"

Art sighed. "No."

"It's a travesty. The smaller she is, the worse the spectacle. My wife was the shortest woman I ever slept with. It was like lying next to an M198 howitzer: quite a show, but don't expect much in the way of sleep." He could see that Art was forging an image in his mind and continued. "I asked her over and over to buy those sticky nose strips, or even get a doctor to prescribe some sort of sleep mask or mouthpiece, but she wasn't having any of it. Finally, after a few months of this, I realized she only snored when she was directly on her back. If she slept on her side, she was fine."

"So you rolled her off the bed, and she left you."

"That beer is sucking words out of you, dude."

"It isn't—"

"Careful, or you'll end up with a paragraph. No, I tried rolling her, but then her body would rebel."

"Rebel?"

"Yeah, her limbs would twitch for about two hours afterward. It was like she was allergic to me moving her, or something. I know: insert joke here. Anyway, I tried more subtle methods—poking and prodding, talking to her, blowing in her face."

"That all sounds annoying."

"So's not sleeping for five months straight when your day job involves firearms."

Art made an abrupt noise. It might have been a chuckle.

"Finally, I resorted to Zeet the Snoring Bee." Lue held up a fist, with the two front knuckles separated slightly. "I discovered that when I pinched her nose gently in mid-snore, she would automatically roll over—but neither wake up nor twitch. It was like magic. Me and my fist."

"Ah, you and your fist."

"Do not be juvenile—I called it Zeet the Snoring Bee."

"It all makes sense now."

"Mock me if you will."

"All right."

"For three and a half weeks, I had bedroom bliss, not even talking about the sex. Which was also fine."

"I don't care."

"Sure you do. All men do."

Art sighed.

"She was a demon in bed, and you are thrilled to know it. Anyhow, just as I think I have the secret to marital success, resistance sets in: a light pinch no longer works. She stays flat on her back, buzzing away. So I pinch her nose harder to get it to work. This keeps up for a few more weeks: she gains immunity, I pinch harder, she relents. You can see where this is going."

Art lifted his empty juice glass at the svelte bartender, who scampered over to refill. "Let me guess. Zeet came to a bad end."

"Alas, he could only sting so hard, before she discovered him. Cue ugly scene. She completely freaks out: why am I trying to punch her in the nose? No, not trying to punch you, honey, this is Zeet the Snoring Bee. What the hell is a Zeet? Not a *what*, sweetheart, but rather a *who* . . . Zeet the Snoring Bee, my little antisnoring buddy, see? Then comes the look, and stop punching me in the nose, and now where am I? Stuck with my right fist and an angry woman."

"I've heard this story before."

"You have no idea. So I try to apologize the next morning, but still she decides not to talk to me. Zeet is some sort of interloper now. In his own home!

"So, I cannot give Zeet up, because I have to sleep. Meanwhile, she develops supersensitivity in the nasal area, so when Zeet comes within half a meter of her face, she wakes up and flips out. Now she says, I *told* you not to punch me in the nose. Again, not punching honey, I want you to stop snoring, go to the doctor or something and we can forget about Zeet, okay? Then we go to, you have to love me the way I am, and why does my snoring matter so much more than who I am, and maybe you think your wife is ugly or not good enough. Holy hamburger, honey, who said anything about ugly? Though I heard they did a study that people who lost weight, snored less."

Art lowered his glass and finally made eye contact with Lue. "A mistake."

"A tactical error. No one can really pin that one on Zeet. But she had gained something like ten pounds in ten weeks, and we were barely married. I was thinking she could be pregnant."

"You thought she was pregnant."

"Yeah, maybe."

"And you suggested weight loss."

"What are you, some sort of marriage expert? What about *your* story, in five words or less?"

"Fewer."

"What?"

"Not less. Fewer."

Lue shook his head. "Did you correct *my* grammar? Because that is not done!"

"Not your grammar. Your usage."

Trying to kick back his barstool, which since he was in a booth was really a bench bolted to the floor, Lue regained his balance. "Hey, to hell with you, man. No one screws with my grammar. Or usage."

The bartender sauntered over. Lue figured her for eighteen—old enough to work in a bar but not drink in one. If she wanted to enlist to defend this country, she'd be considered old enough to fight or kill or die. And yet couldn't be trusted with a White Russian. He was all ready with a rant when she distracted him by talking and being cute and stuff. "You boys ready to pay off the tab?" She made a gesture with her right shoulder. "The old man says you can stay, but he's hoping you pay up before you pass out."

"Give us a second." Lue held his finger up for a long time, swallowing and thinking. "My partner here is telling me how bad my English is. I gotta figure out where we go from here. Also, I am not drunk. Right now. I think."

He couldn't see very much anymore, and he realized how long it had been since he had drunk so many beers in one sitting. *Since that night when I first met her. And a trip down memory lane is the last thing I need right now.*

"She left me, too."

"What?"

"You asked for my story. Five words or less."

"Your story is that my wife left you, too?"

"It's time to go." Art left some bills on the booth table, nodded at the bartender, and slid himself under Lue's arm so he was firmly pulling him along, and out of the Suds Bucket.

CHAPTER 15

This bed is the worst. Saggy in the middle, too firm on the edges. Like sleeping on a badly made omelet. And speaking of omelets, I am ravenous. But this bed! When is she going to—

Wait.

What?

Lue opened his eyes. He was not in his bedroom. He was in another bedroom. From the look of the generic double bed with the generic bedclothes, bad carpeting, worse wall coverings, and poorly bolted door (a developmentally disabled Cub Scout could get through both locks in less than thirty seconds), he was in a motel.

Except since the divorce, and the settlement, he didn't have to sleep in these things anymore. If anything—

Art was in the room with him.

Art was sitting cross-legged on the other bed, which appeared unslept in.

Art was *grinning* at him.

Lue groaned and slapped his hand over his eyes. "If this is the part where you explain we were meant to be, I will need to shoot you."

"No worries."

"Many times."

"Gun's there," Art said, jerking his head toward the bedside table between the double beds. "I was smiling—"

"Grinning. *Leering.* Practically slobbering at the prospect of once again getting your greasy hands on my dancer's body . . ."

"—because you snore."

"I do not!" Lue sat up in a rage, then groaned and clutched his head, and (carefully) lay back down. "Five beers? Ow. *Five* beers? Really? Embarrassing."

"You tried to drink a glass of water," Art-the-heartless told him, "but quit halfway to fall on the bed and sleep. And you *snore*," he added happily.

Lue turned his head slowly toward the nightstand. The digital clock read 6:45 A.M. *At least no oversleeping.* "It was those damn Bemidji files."

"Investigative files made you snore?"

"No, they made me drink too much and pass out in a shitty motel room. Freaking Bemidji, man. No wonder when you got the squeal about our scene you came on the run."

"Fast as I could," Art agreed. "We have to talk about . . . we have to talk about something difficult."

"Is this about your obsession with my long creamy thighs? Because I will try not to judge again and yet, must still disappoint you."

"You wish."

"I do wish." It was true. He did. Because, head pounding or no, he had the feeling Art was about to say something that was unforgettable in the literal sense: he would never, never be able to forget it.

And Art, Lue was quite sure, didn't have a mendacious bone in his body. So what was coming was unforgettable and completely true.

"They're here, Lue. In this town."

"You mean those monster things. Or people who turn into those things, anyway. One of your files used the term 'dragon.' "

"Yes, dragons, here. In *your town*. You saw it last night. You suspected before . . . and you saw it yourself."

"What nonsense. I had no time for a thorough reading, you know that."

"You read enough. You're smart."

Lue cracked a modest grin and took a breath. "Well . . ."

"Don't do that puff-up thing. I hate that and it slows us down."

Lue exhaled and slumped. "I was not—"

"Now I need your help. I've been on this path alone, for too long."

"How long?"

"A year." Art gave the foot of Lue's bed a pensive look. "It's not just Bemidji and Moorston. There are other sites, with fewer cases or less to go on."

"Where?"

Art waved vaguely. "Across northern Minnesota."

"Huh. So, you've visited lots of towns?"

"Almost two dozen. Sometimes, there's one murder. Sometimes, like Bemidji, it's several."

"You got files for those, too?"

"Nothing like these." Art tapped the box on the floor between the beds with his foot. "Most places don't want to hear about monsters. With no witnesses and less evidence, there's not much to do."

Lue spoke carefully, not wanting to interrupt the veritable river of words that flowed from Art. "So when you heard a cop in Moorston had actually *seen* one . . ."

"The transcript of your call-in was all I needed. And

Moorston is big enough, that I suspect more murders could take place."

"We have at least two," Lue admitted. "So if we go back to Meenay and have her do the right tests, you and I agree: Pohl and Webber are going to come up as dragon."

"It's a good bet."

"*Is* there a test for that sort of thing?"

"Yes. That much, I can get the BCA to do. I could have Meenay work with our lab."

"All right, we can do that: but the higher priority is stopping the next murder."

"It may be over, in this town."

"Do you think so?"

"No."

"So you plan to stay in this lovely motel room. Good for you."

"I don't want to be here. I want to be not-here. And with . . . with someone else."

To his surprise, Lue only nodded, and added nothing sarcastic.

"I can't go be with her until this is all fixed. I *can't*. So I need you to fix it . . . to help me fix it . . . so everyone's safe."

Lue sighed, carefully got off the bed, crossed to the tiny bathroom, and began to drink glass after glass of cool water. "You say . . . ggrrggll . . . the sweetest things, Art." Gulp, gulp, gargle, spit. Gulp, gulp. "If only so you and I . . . grrgglle . . . do not ever again . . . wake up in close proximity in a tired cheap motel room . . . grrrggllle . . . do I agree our team-up should continue." Another long swallow.

He stepped around the short wall that afforded a smidgen of privacy, wiping his hands on a towel. "But the thing is . . . the DNA and stuff from Bemidji . . ."

Art waited.

"Well. It suggests that both victims *and* the murderer—or murderers—are . . . well, they're . . ."

"All monsters?" Art prompted.

"Yeah. All monsters. It raises questions, Art."

"You wonder why we should care."

"Actually, I have no problem caring about it. My first question is why you care. Whom are you worried about, Art?" Then, as he flung the hand towel back toward the sink, he rephrased. "Whom did you lose?"

"I believe we've shared enough information, for one morning after."

Lue came back, sat on the bed, stuck his fist under his chin, and thought about this.

"Well. As alcohol-tinged, quasi-homoerotic confession scenes between new partners go, this one went fluidly enough. I appreciate the additional information. Thank you for trusting me with what you have, so far."

"We should hit an Embers, lovingly watch each other eat grains and meat respectively, and then head off to the station, where the chief will be thrilled to learn of this. I still have no idea how to tell her."

"Maybe we shouldn't."

"How conspiratorial of you." Lue slipped on his shoes. As he did, he noticed Art had changed clothes—slightly bluer jeans, slightly less off-white shirt—but had the same brown corduroy jacket. "You know, I should probably drop by my apartment and change clothes, too. The last thing you and I need is a 'walk of shame' joke at the station."

"Don't forget we also need to get to Meenay."

"Right. If she still has no autopsy results, I might dump that expensive coffee-smelling sludge all over her expensive forensic equipment. Now where are my . . ." He trailed off as he saw what Art was jingling at him. "Oh. Lay on, Macduff."

"My name—"

"Shut up, Macduff." A sudden urge took him, and he wondered how he had even lasted this long. "Before we go, I am going to urinate for a thousand years. And you are going to stand there and listen!"

Bemused, Art obeyed.

CHAPTER 16

They were in and out of Lue's place in minutes, and in and out of Embers not much longer. On their way to the station, the dispatcher patched in the 911 call. Neighbors had heard screaming near a downtown residence.

"Closest," Lue grunted, giving the accelerator an admirable stomp. Art braced himself as they took a corner fast enough to scatter a flock of preteen boys. Lue noticed and smiled. "That fried breakfast treating you okay?"

"Just fine."

Lue was disappointed to reach an empty site without anyone waiting for them, or running out of the house screaming for help, or making any sort of noise at all. *Bad news.* The small split-level house had the stale feeling of a home with something dead in it, but they drew their weapons and carefully went through the place anyway.

They found the body first, in the living room between

the large window and the almost-as-large television. The glassy gaze of the woman

monster?

and massive amount of blood already soaked into the carpet tested Lue's optimism, but he stooped and checked for a pulse anyway. Art hovered above him with piece held high.

"'Such a savage, vicious beast as man . . .'"

"*The Brothers Karamazov*," Art replied.

"Right on. What I loathe is, somewhere down the line when the villain has been revealed, this will all make sense. Right now, Art?"

"It doesn't seem to make sense, does it?"

"None. Zero. Zip. Though I think we can save Meenay the trouble of determining cause of death. Sharp edge to the neck, like Webber. Blade . . . or claw."

Art stepped deliberately around the corpse and accompanying mess, crouched in a stance Lue had never seen before. He was almost . . . hunting?

"Yes, it's likely one of those." A glance out the large dining room bay window showed the gawkers already lining up on the sidewalk. There were two or three heavyset women in their twenties, an accompanying male of the same age and body type, one preteens (school hours, so ill or playing hooky), one toddler. Within five minutes, he was sure, more adults and at least one infant would make an appearance. Given the parked police car and gathering sirens in the distance, they respected property lines, and everyone stayed off the grass.

He looked back down at the corpse in time to hear Art's verdict. "Efficient. Vicious. Premeditated."

"Planned or not, the victim still managed to get off a noise. Like Webber. You think the murderer"—the monster, he could have said now—"could still be here?"

"Probably not. Let's finish the sweep."

They cleared the floor quickly and then checked the

basement. By the time they got back upstairs, the next wave of police cars was pulling up outside the living room window.

"We missed her," Lue concluded. He stepped to the back of the house and looked out over the kitchen porch. Half expecting to see another cedar fence with another dark shape clambering over it, he still found the sight exhilarating.

"Art. Keep the new officers away from the backyard!"

After a curious glance, Art went out the front door as ordered to slow down their colleagues' approach. Lue opened the sliding door—plainly, the murderer had time to close it behind him (her? it?)—took one gentle step forward, and then crouched to examine the splatter of blood that lay at his feet.

His eyes traced a path across the broken porch—more spatters of blood, broken pots of soil, a small piece of torn fabric, and dozens of long scrapes, and heaven knew what else was yet to be discovered in the torn turf beyond.

A victim. A murderer. And someone else.

CHAPTER 17

It took the entire morning to poke through and document the crime scene at Amanda Coolidge's home—Ms. Coolidge was, naturally, the victim. Officer Mark Langenfeld was the first backup to show, as he had been at the Webber scene. This time, he was more helpful. So were some of the other officers who made Lue clench his teeth at times.

Must be Art the BCA agent, keeping us all in line.

Mark's report was focused and relevant. "One set of tracks—uneven pacing, possibly a limp, you might want to see if you agree, Detective—heads out through the brush there." The patrol officer pointed southeast, toward the river and center of town. "Then whatever *that* is"—he pointed at the enormous tangle of intersecting turf wounds and punctures—"well, I'm sure you can see where that heads in the opposite direction. Except the entire thing disappears once it hits the road a half block away. It's like the animal—it's gotta be a bear, right?—knew how to use the city sidewalks."

"Maybe someone saw it using a crosswalk," Lue mused aloud. This got a genuine chuckle from Mark.

Another officer came forward. "Detective. We've gotten blood samples off the porch and grass, and at least two fabric samples. We've also laid down markers and photographed most of the scene. I think you may see something that looks like the burn marks you told us to keep an eye out for."

"Thanks, Dave. What about witnesses?"

"Neighbors only heard screams. Nobody saw anything. Michelle and Jim are still with a couple of the chattier neighbors, but I don't think they'll learn much more. We'll see, I guess."

"Thanks again. Detective McMahon may have specific instructions for those samples. Could you please check in with him?"

"You bet."

Mark and Dave trotted off toward Art, as if polite and professional compliance were their watchwords. *That could be true,* Lue realized. *Maybe part of the problem with these guys is me instead.*

Art himself was crouched down by the siding near the porch. Lue knew what he was checking for, and he knew that he would find it: the short, parallel marks of a killer waiting for the right time to attack.

Which one was waiting, and where, and for how long? Which one landed the killing blow on Coolidge? Were they both here to kill her and merely competing for the honor, or was one stalking the other, or were there completely different reasons?

And how many more Pohls and Webbers and Coolidges are there in this town? What are their chances of survival? Do they see this pattern? Are they worried?

They weren't going to find the answers here, Lue fretted. In fact, he was wondering if they were going to find the answers anywhere.

At the station, Lue tried to maintain focus on the things he could control. Mark, Dave, Michelle, and Jim all followed him dutifully as he walked down the hallway toward his desk. Art brought up the rear, in (to no one's surprise) thoughtful silence. He had caught Mark and Dave elbowing each other like kids in a candy store, but put it down to the thrill of the hunt. He doubted they were intelligent enough, or savage enough, to pull off a string of murders the likes of which they had all just seen.

"Dr. Meenay, like every coroner in the country and possibly the world, will incessantly harp about being overworked, but I think if we—"

"There they are!"

Chief Smiling Bear emerged from her office with a stack of papers, jaws moving furiously as she chomped on grape bubble gum. "I was thinking about you guys," she called. "How's the crime scene?"

"It has some interesting leads, but . . ."

She checked his expression and guessed the rest. "You figure they might go nowhere. Well, consider this your first big break. FBI just released a composite sketch of a young woman they say is tied to several murders across the Midwest. You'll never guess what kind of wound she leaves."

"Slicing, on or near the neck?"

"Bingo."

"The FBI?" Art pushed through the other cops and even nudged Lue aside. It didn't feel as subtle to the taller, thinner detective as the BCA agent might have intended. "How are they involved?"

"Jealous, Art?"

Chief Smiling Bear rolled her eyes. "It can't surprise you, Detective McMahon, that the FBI sometimes does things without local or state knowledge. In this case, the source of the information would be witnesses from the Saint George's incident. Here's what they came up with."

Lue reached for the sheet. "Anyone else have this yet?"

"They say it'll be on TV and the web by tonight."

Lue looked. "This is . . . not great."

The chief shrugged. "Grainy black-and-white footage plus bad camera angles divided by freaked-out witnesses equals sucky sketch resolution. Something's better than nothing, right?"

"Ah, there you go, throwing advanced math in my face yet again. This plus this equals that, this is greater than that . . . thanks, Chief Calculus." The sketch actually wasn't too bad. It showed an attractive woman with dark hair and (probably) eyes; pale skin. A sharp nose, a small chin. Wide, clear forehead. More than attractive, he realized after a closer look. Beautiful. "As you said, better than nothing. Take a look, guys."

He held the sheet up slightly so Art and the four cops could all see. There were murmurs among the Moorston police, and another elbow-gut-check from Dave, but it was Art's reaction that caught Lue's attention.

At first, it was what Lue expected: silence. Blank-faced, uncommented silence.

But the more Lue looked, the more he realized it was more than that. The blankness was careful, manufactured. It was more Art than Art ever had been.

Lue had not known the man long, but he knew focus. He knew emotion. He knew poor tempers and the hundreds of ways in which witnesses, victims, and perpetrators cloaked such feelings. He could separate his personal feelings about a person, from how they acted. As sure as he was that Pamela Pride was the hottest witness he'd ever seen, he had no trouble spotting that she'd been hiding something during their last interview.

Well, he was also sure Art was a good man. And he was

equally sure that the BCA agent was absolutely furious at the sketch in front of him.

This woman, he told himself, shivering. *I do not want to be this woman, when Detective Art McMahon of the Bureau of Criminal Apprehension arrives.*

CHAPTER 18

Lue caught sight of her the moment she walked into the bar. This was not difficult, as he had chosen a booth with a direct sight line to the front door and kept looking up from his menu every fifteen seconds.

The sight of her still made him catch his breath. No one else in Moorston dressed like her. Not then, and not now. Her walk through the bar to Lue was purposeful and slow. Her gaze never left his, even while his was all up and down her. It was like being stared down by a sexy laser.

"Still got it?" she asked, as she and her velvet dress slid in loving concert into the booth across from him. When she crossed her short but powerful legs, he could hear the smooth rustle of her pantyhose. There had been a time when that sound would have resulted in an instant loss of at least ten of his IQ points.

"Nancy, you realize you are more than a hundred miles from Minneapolis, right?"

She sniffed and tossed her head. "Don't I know it." The light caught and shimmered in her crystal earrings, or diamond . . . no, they'd better not be, neither of them made that kind of money. And if they *did*, she'd damn well be better off spending it on her education instead of earrings made from compressed coal. "I'm still waiting for this crap town to get a wine bar, instead of yet another hole in the wall like this." She shook her head at the several fluorescent-lit beer signs.

"Snobbish is not a good look for you."

"Liar." She said it with a perfectly devilish smile.

"This is a nice place." He said this loud enough for the svelte, eighteen-year-old bartender to hear, he was pretty sure.

"She's at the other end of the bar, Lue. You'll have to speak up."

"If you hate this town, why are you still here?"

She shrugged. "I'm not ready to leave. Soon."

"Does it have anything to do with—"

"Do you really want an answer to that?" She took out a compact, checked her reflection, changed nothing, snapped it shut. "Is that why you called me?"

"I—I called you to see you. It has been a while."

"What, we're dating again now?"

"Why be like this, Nancy?"

"Like what?" She didn't wait for an answer. "So I've seen you around town with the BCA guy."

He sighed. "Lieutenant McMahon."

"Yeah. So, what did you tell him about us?" She smiled up at Svelte Eighteen. "What cabernets do you have?"

"Um, the only reds we've got are . . . um, I think a merlot, and maybe a pinot grigio . . ."

"That's *pinot noir*, dear. Grigio's not even the right color. I'll have the merlot, if you can find it. My ex will have another beer, and a long look at your ass as you walk away." She turned back to Lue. "So?"

"Funny, Nancy."

"So what did you tell him?"

"I told him nothing—"

"Did you give him the Japanese-Hmong-two-different-cultures bit, or the she-couldn't-handle-my-job bit, or the Zeet-the-Snoring-Bee-control-freak bit?"

He stared into his near-empty beer glass.

He saw her knuckles actually whiten as she unconsciously made a fist. "Cripes, you actually used Zeet the Fucking Snoring Bee. Unreal. He believed it?"

"Parts of it are true!"

"Parts of all three are true. It doesn't make them any less lame when you say them. Of course, I should have known you'd never give him the real reason."

"You cannot be serious."

"What, he'll arrest me?"

"Of course not. He's seen the FBI sketch from Saint George's. You are nowhere near the suspect's description. Not age, not height, nothing. Thanks." He said this last as he reached for a new beer.

"Certainly not my color." Nancy winked as she snagged the merlot out of Svelte Eighteen's trembling fingers. She took a sniff. "Thanks, honey, this is lovely. Add it to my ex's tab. Oh, for heaven's sake, why are you even looking at him to check? You and I both know he'll buy either one of us drinks for the next three years, if we keep the cleavage coming."

"Some of us call that chivalry, Nancy—"

"You're once more staring at her ass as she scurries away."

"Well, stand up in front of her and I will gladly stare at yours instead."

"Ha. So you *do* like the dress."

"Of course I like the dress. There is not a straight male in the history of velvet clothing who would not like the dress."

"I bought it for you."

He snorted. "With the money I sent for your education, no doubt."

"I don't need any more education. I need a spouse who's not a capricious, shallow bigot."

"How many times do I need to tell you I am sorry?"

"Once would have been adequate, if you had really meant it. We know you never did."

"You could have told me about yourself."

"I did."

"Right. After you had landed me and thought it would not matter."

"It shouldn't have."

"It did. Not as much as the deception, though."

They glared at each other over their new drinks. *And so it goes, and so it goes,* he thought, dismayed. He could remember being single and watching divorced couples squabble. He could remember being baffled; even smug. Who was that couple hissing at each other? They had loved enough to pledge their lives, and now divorced over the husband's loathing of fabric softener? Theirs must have been a petty love indeed. *His* love would be different.

And so it had been. But not in the way he thought.

"So, dear ex-husband of mine, you were telling me about the Great Lieutenant Art McMahon—"

"I never said his first name."

"You didn't have to. I know all about him. Most of us do."

"I should not be surprised."

"You just cannot make a contraction, can you? So uptight in your second language. Like you were uptight about me. Uptight about everything."

"What do you know about Art?"

"You're worried about him? You think he's dangerous?"

"I think he might be."

"Well, he probably is. I don't know this from firsthand contact, mind you. He has . . . a reputation."

"He hides things from me."

"Of course he does. Like you hide things from him."

"Nothing I am hiding from him can come back to hurt him."

"He probably feels the same way. I wouldn't worry about Lieutenant Art McMahon." She swirled her glass and stared into the merlot.

"Whom, then, should I worry about?"

Nancy tipped back her head, polished off the merlot, and smacked the glass back onto the table. "Don't call me again, Lue. Stop sending me money. Pretend I'm not even in town anymore. Soon enough, that will be true. What we've seen in this town is just the beginning."

"Beginning of what?"

"You're a detective. Figure it out." As she got up, her dress snagged on something—possibly her own hand—and the lavender ridges rode all the way up her left thigh. Tucked into the hip of her panties, Lue spotted a shining leaf the size of a woman's palm.

She watched him notice, and took her time pulling the dress back down. "I like to hang on to it, even when it's not a crescent moon. Some of us think of it as unnatural, but I like the control it gives me. You never know when I might need to fight back against a killer."

"I believe you have nothing to—"

"Don't be stupid. Do you have any idea how risky it is for me to be around here at all? I wonder how much you'd even care if I were the next body you found."

"I would care a great deal, Nancy."

"Whatever. You're an insensitive bastard, Lue. Guess what—you want to plaster this woman's face on the evening news? You want to pull in the state police? You all want to find her? Fine. I hope you do. I hope you find her in the dark, when she's good and angry about what's going on. And then I hope you find out your clip is empty. That would be justice, like your world has *never* seen."

He yawned. "Keep hiking up that dress, classy-ass."

"Right. Hey, good luck with the bartender. Make sure you turn her over and check her for scales under a crescent moon before you propose. You'll save her a lot of heartache."

Lue had nothing to say to that, so Nancy left.

INTERLUDE

Tonight

She walked slowly, her feet barely making a sound against the gritty linoleum, eyes fixed on the array before her. He watched her while she was still several yards off, unable to get away, holding his breath. Behind him, the face and voice on the television droned about local deaths, a suspect on the run, property damage, neighbors annoyed—always more about the inconvenience than the loss of life—police befuddled.

Police had no role here—not in what she wanted, or what he wanted.

Never looking up, she advanced. She was no more than ten feet distant, but he realized she regarded him as little more than an insect. How could he be anything more, given the circumstances?

She paused and considered her fateful choice.

Trail mix with peanuts, or without?

She reached out and grabbed the mix with peanuts.

Starting toward the cashier, she reconsidered when another salty snack caught her eye, and grabbed a Slim Jim from the end cap display. Then she shrugged and headed for the refrigerated back wall, where multiple shelves of water bottles pressed their labels against the glass doors. She opened a door, grabbed one, and headed back for the cashier. The last two bananas next to a 'FRESH' FRUIT sign looked perfect, but she frowned.

"Are they fresh or not?" she asked, still staring at the yellow crescents. Her voice was honey over ice.

Even though he knew she wasn't looking, he nodded and pointed at the sign. "Says right there. Fresh."

"No it doesn't. It says"—he put down her purchases and made air quotes—" 'fresh.' "

He shrugged. "They taste good. I had one this afternoon, before my shift started."

For the first time since she had entered the convenience store, she looked directly at him. He thought he would keel over. "That would have been over eight hours ago."

"I'm working a double."

"I mean, that's a long time for quotes to keep a banana fresh."

"We've sold, like, twenty of them. Nobody's complained, miss."

The left corner of her mouth raised, and he thought idly of proposing to her. He didn't need this job, did he? Not if he had her.

"I guess I'll take a banana, then." She picked everything back up, used her free hand to pry the bananas apart, and left the slightly greener one behind. A few steps later, she was right in front of him. Right . . . there! So close he could reach out and . . . "Can you let me know if this is over three dollars? That's all I've got."

He looked down at the small pile and did the math in his head. It would be five dollars and twenty-six cents. "You're fine."

As she laid down three wrinkled bills, her gaze flitted up to the television screen and narrowed. The reaction lasted long enough for him to turn . . . and see her face again, this time in an artist's rendering.

"Authorities advise the woman is armed and dangerous. If you see her, do not approach her. Instead, please call the number on the screen immediately."

"Well." Behind him, the honey was gone, and only ice remained. "That's unfortunate."

PART TWO

Art

CHAPTER 19

Art breathed slowly on the convenience store countertop, and then inhaled even more carefully. He was starting to get a headache.

Stress. It has been stress. Nothing but stress. For years. And the closer I get, the more stress.

"Say, Art—come check this out."

Lue Vue, the Clever Detective Who Loved to Talk, was over by the bananas. That seemed quaintly appropriate.

"Seriously, come on over."

"You're five feet away. I can see you fine." In fact, Art was already scanning the fruit stand for clues.

"Says here 'fresh' fruit."

"Yes. You're hungry?"

"No, look here. 'Fresh.' " Vue made air quotes with his fingers. "Why do they do that? What are the quotes for? Are they kidding about the 'fresh' part? If fresh is not the right word, what word do they mean? 'Aging'? 'Rotting'?

I mean, tell me what you mean with your ridiculous sign, am I right?"

Art squinted. He wasn't sure if the headache was getting worse. Lue was . . . unfathomable at times. Before Art had come to town, Lue, like every other cop in this country, had a staggering case load. Yet here he was, talking and talking and talking and talking and—

"I do not understand why people don't use quotes correctly. We all learn how in fifth grade. It is not like you need a graduate degree."

—talking and talking and talking and—

"Oh, forget it. Okay, Mr. Alvarez, you say this woman"—Vue held up a copy of the artist's sketch they'd been running in the media. "This woman was here in this store? You saw her? Mr. Alvarez?"

The lanky college student behind the counter, who had been staring at Art ever since the officers had arrived, noticed Vue with a visible start. *Skittish,* Art told himself. *Teenaged. Easily startled. No real situational awareness.* "Yeah. Um, yeah. She was here."

"How sure are—"

"It was her, man. She saw herself on the television, and she booked."

"You got that good a look?"

"You kidding? I couldn't take my eyes off her."

"She came in, you stared at her, she watched herself on TV, she left? This is your accounting of the evening's events?"

"No, man. That's not what I said. She came in like any other customer, spent a few minutes picking up some things, paid for them—"

Art held up a hand. "She paid? Cash?"

"Yeah." The teenager popped open the register drawer, riffled through the ones, and picked out three of them. "I bet you'll want them, to see if you can get any evidence off them."

Lue held out a plastic bag. "You have done this before." *Or you watch far too much prime-time television.*

Alvarez shrugged as he put the money in the bag. *Look where I work.*

"You are sure these are the bills she used?"

"Yep. The most wrinkled, tattered dollar bills I've ever seen. The last ones she had."

"She told you that?" Art frowned and rubbed the bridge of his nose; the throbbing of his headache seemed concentrated there. "And you believed her?"

The student straightened, as if considering for the first time that he may have been taken. "Yeah. I mean, she looked desperate enough. And it's not like what she bought was that expensive. What, you think she lied to shave off a couple of bucks? That doesn't make—"

"How long ago?" Art interrupted.

Alvarez almost jumped. "What, man?"

"How long ago was she here?"

"Dude, she left, I called, you showed up. You figure it out. Maybe ten minutes?"

"Not ten minutes."

"What, I'm a liar? Don't they, like, write down the time when someone calls nine one one? Dude, I called *you*. Why are you busting my balls?"

Art pointed a meaty finger at the register. "You dug."

Vue caught on. "Right. Also, leave your balls out of this."

"Those bills were not on top. So other customers have come in since she was here. With it being so late, and not everyone using cash, and even those who do not always having singles . . . how long has it been? An hour? Two?"

"Geez, dude. What's the difference? She's gone. I doubt she's hanging around the parking lot. The TV spot said to call, I called. Dude!"

"My name is Lieutenant McMahon."

"Fine, Lieutenant McMahon, what's your problem?"

"She got to you."

Alvarez's lips quivered. "What do you mean, 'got to me'? You think I'm trying to help her, man?"

"No. Not trying." The corner of Art's mouth twitched. "Just helping."

Vue gave his partner a quizzical look. "What do you think happened here?"

Art scanned the store—the flickering fluorescents above the bottled water, the ungrammatical sign that still smelled of banana even though none were left, the crowded yet tired rows of packaged dry foods, the screen still blaring over the kid's head. "She came in to eat. Met this moron. Paid half price. Saw the TV. Realized he recognized her. Thought about killing him. Chose another path."

"You threw a lot of words out there for consideration, Art. Thanks for breaking it all up into tiny sentence fragments so I could follow it well enough."

A look: *I've got a tiny sentence for you.*

"Okay, so you say she chose another path. What do you mean—she convinced him to lie? How? Paid him—she had no money. Seduced him?"

Now Art couldn't help but laugh.

Alvarez sputtered. "Hey, dudes. I'm *standing* here!"

"No need. She ordered him." Art turned to Alvarez. "Didn't she?"

The kid's eyes flashed all over the place. "What do you mean, ordered—"

Art pounded the counter. *"Speak!"*

"Cripes okay she saw the TV and looked at me and told me not to say anything for a while and give her two hours so she left and I gave her two hours and what's the goddamn big deal anyway—"

"Quiet."

As if from a tightened faucet, the words stopped.

Art saw Lue's mouth open in slight surprise; but this was not the time or place to explain fully. Even if it was the appropriate time and place, he wouldn't have been inclined to explain fully.

So he did what he did best: he abbreviated.

"I know the type. So does she. Nothing more here."

"Well, we could use the security tape."

"Go for it. I'll be in the car."

He felt his partner's careful gaze on his back as he left the store.

CHAPTER 20

"What?"

"Nothing."

"You're staring at me while I drive. Would you rather be driving again?"

"No, Art. I am . . . admiring your driving technique."

"It unnerves me."

"I doubt that. Nothing unnerves you."

Trying to execute a right turn without looking back at the face fixed on his, Art sighed. "You don't trust me."

"I trust you. I wish I knew more about you."

Art glanced down at the gauges, over at the mirrors, looking for something that would help him with an answer. Lieutenant Lue Vue was a good man, he knew. Perhaps it was time to be more forthcoming.

"You want to test my DNA."

"What? No!"

"I understand. It's on file. You can call Bemidji."

"I would never . . . I mean, I assume it is, with you being a police officer. I have no intention of checking that. The Bureau of Criminal Apprehension speaks for itself, Art. You have nothing to explain to me."

"You lie well. Check it, when you can."

That got Lue to look somewhere else, at least, for the remainder of the trip back to the station.

Once there, they got another surprise. Chief Smiling Bear sat up against Lue's desk, and another woman stood straight facing her. The second woman had vibrant orange curls that bounced lightly off the shoulders of a sharp navy suit. As the chief's gaze wandered to catch the oncoming detectives, the bright curls whipped around and revealed a tornado of freckles surrounding hazel eyes.

Art let himself drop slightly behind Lue, to earn another moment to collect himself.

"Lieutenant Vue. Lieutenant McMahon. I'd like you to meet Special Agent Mercy March. Federal Bureau of Investigation's Minneapolis office."

The stranger stepped toward them, arm extended fully. "Lieutenant Vue. Chief Bear's been—"

"Smiling," Vue said, because he lived for the coming conversation about the chief's name . . . yep. She was already mock glaring.

"Oh." Agent March faltered, then tried a tentative smile. "Chief Smiling—"

"Both words are considered my last name," the chief explained, "like MacMahon would be for an Irishman . . . I'm not Chief Mac or Chief Mahon, I'm Chief Smiling Bear. Except what Lieutenant Lue Vue didn't mention is that I'm used to confusion around my name, as I'm sure you're used to foolish men and 'Miss March' jokes."

"A pleasure to meet you," Agent March said, and then her tentative smile bloomed into the real thing. "Yeah, I do get that from time to time."

"Would've been even worse, if you'd been old enough before the Internet kinda made *Playboy* moot."

"Perhaps we should change the topic." Lue took her hand and shook it firmly. "I take it we have an interstate pattern now." He turned to Art and winked. "So, BCA is not in charge anymore. How devastating for you. Where shall I send flowers?"

"I'll recover." Art swallowed and extended his own hand. "Special Agent."

"Please, call me Mercy."

He nodded. "Mercy. Lue. Chief. We should find a room."

She looked him up and down—he may have been the only one who caught that—and nodded at the chief. "You have a conference room the four of us can use? This may take some time."

"Sure." The chief looked down at the thick briefcase stuffed with folders that lay at the agent's feet. "We've got most of Lue's case spread out on one of the walls anyway. You can add to what we've got." Like any good cop, the chief was horrified at adding to a complex mess, while thrilled at the chance to get more intel on the bad guys.

Two hours later, they had three walls full, and part of the conference table. The chief's assistant had just dropped off their intricate coffee and tea orders (along with Art's simpler order of water).

"It's an impressive run, if it's all true," the chief noted as she walked the length of the room. "Minot, North Dakota. Turtle Lake and Green Bay, Wisconsin. Pierre, South Dakota. All over the quad cities in Iowa and Illinois. And now Bemidji and Moorston, Minnesota. Our girl's been busy."

"For years," Mercy said. "I've been lucky; I work for a group who thinks about the long run."

"A group who can afford to," Lue interjected.

"Yes, of course." She nodded respectfully. "I wasn't trying to play nyah-nyah with our national budget. But my point is she's been doing this a long time, all over the place."

"There's no sequence," Art observed. His voice startled them; it was the first time he had spoken since Mercy March laid out the evidence she had compiled.

"I take it you mean," Mercy replied, "that our suspect did not follow any geographic pattern over time. That's not entirely true. There are multiple murders at each of the sites. In all cases, Ms. Scales 'cleaned out' an area before moving on. She spent anywhere from a week to two months in each city."

Lue was flipping through the file marked "Scales, E." "Are you sure about the name?"

"The Saint George's incident confirmed what we'd suspected. The destruction of that building matches with the more violent scenes at residences in the Quad Cities, and in Pierre. Ms. Scales doesn't always take the building down with her—sometimes she's more surgical."

"You're sure she's acting alone?"

"Excellent question, Lieutenant McMahon."

"You are so good at those," Lue piped up, grinning. "My hero."

Mercy betrayed irritation at the interruption, but quickly recovered. "Yes, we're sure it's just her. You've likely seen this in the Bemidji cases, and it's true across all these instances. There's never any other foreign, unexplained DNA or other trace evidence at any of the scenes. All the DNA matches correspond to her sequence, and she leaves plenty of it. She's not careful at all. It's like she *wants* us to find out she was there."

"She wants us to follow her," Art asserted. "She's daring us."

Lue pulled a flash drive out of the folder. "What's on this?"

"I'll show you." Mercy pulled a laptop out of her briefcase—it surprised Art after everything else that had come out of there—opened it, and plugged the drive in. A few moments later, a video appeared on the screen.

"This was taken by a college student about two blocks away from a murder scene in Green Bay, that same night. Fortunately, the kid didn't have the presence of mind to send this viral before law enforcement on the scene got a hold of it. We haven't released this to the public, for what will be obvious reasons. Detective Vue, based on the transcript of your call a few days ago, this should look familiar."

Watching the screen was both difficult and stressful. The shakiness of the handheld camera didn't help. Four teenagers—maybe five—were crammed into a vehicle a smidge bigger than Lue's childhood moped. The young women had bare arms featuring plastic bead bracelets over tanned wrists; the young men had wispy facial hair and wild looks in their eyes; everyone, including the driver, had a beer bottle in his hand.

They were whooping and hanging limbs and heads out the window and flashing passersby. Whoever was holding the camera (likely a smart phone, given the resolution) had a particular affinity for the redheaded woman to his right, in the backseat. The sky outside was dark, punctuated by the occasional streetlight and neon bar sign. She called out to every person they passed on the sidewalk and asked if they knew "a really cool place to party." Every guy had a different recommendation.

Suddenly, one of the girls in the car screamed. Two seconds later, something slammed into the right side of the car, tilting it wildly, forcing the driver to slam on the brakes, and almost making the cameraman drop his phone. The picture veered to face the cause, and for a moment the surroundings blackened. Then the dark corona passed, and the assailant came into full view through the open window.

The reptilian head seemed as surprised to find the car there, as the occupants were to find it scraping the edges of the passenger door. Coal scales gleamed, and a claw braced against the window opening, inches from the screeching redhead. Instead of the two slit dinosaur eyes one might expect, there were multiple bulbous clusters, each glistening an array of primary hues.

"Bobby, hit the gas! HIT THE GAS!" someone yelled, and the car lurched forward. An awful sound resulted—Art guessed an axle was broken—and then Bobby ditched the car in a rather nonchivalrous fashion. The camera view jerked about, showing random views of the broken car's panicked interior. The device left the car and documented some speedy pavement shots, followed by a more conscious attempt to film what had run into the car.

Two black, leathery wings covered the car roof. Wisps of shadow trailed off the beast's crest and wingtips. Above and between the wings, the previously seen reptilian-insectile head opened its mandibles and howled an unearthly sound, blasting green and black spittle across the road.

Here the cameraman lost his nerve again, and the video ended as he turned to run.

Mercy rolled back the video slowly, until they could see the clearest frame of the monster clutching the wrecked car, maw wide open to consume the chilled evening.

"Spirits save us," Chief Smiling Bear muttered. "What *is* that?"

Art was watching Lue carefully. Lue was watching *him* carefully. Neither one of them showed an iota of surprise. *Interesting.*

"It's a dragon," Mercy replied matter-of-factly.

"That's impossible," the chief insisted.

"Was anyone hurt?" Art asked, without breaking eye contact with Lue.

"You mean from the car? No. A few witnesses nearby suffered some scrapes as their drunk friends pushed them down and ran away. The only fatality was the murder victim two blocks away."

Lue grinned at Art. "I guess I should count myself lucky that it was heading the other direction when I showed up at Webber's."

Art nodded slowly and kept the staring match going. "Special Agent March. Have any federal agents engaged her?"

"Not yet. Frankly, we're not sure what kind of firepower is necessary to subdue her."

"Subdue her," he repeated. "I doubt that's possible."

"We'd prefer to bring her in alive, of course." Mercy seemed not to notice that neither man was looking at her. "The research possibilities alone are staggering."

Chief Smiling Bear snapped her fingers several times. "Excuse me, did no one else hear the word *dragon*? What you're talking about is impossible."

Lue finally broke away from Art's gaze. "Chief, dragons are not impossible. Do you remember that video from Winoka, couple of decades back?"

She shrugged. "I always figured that for a hoax."

"It was not a hoax," Mercy assured them. "Susan Elmsmith faithfully recorded what she saw. While it's best if the public chooses not to believe her, we in law enforcement don't have the luxury of illusions. Dragons are rare but real. This one is particularly nasty. Her name is Evangelina Scales . . ."

"Back up." The chief raised her hand. "These things fly around in the streets, breathing fire and eating livestock . . . and we've never seen a video of one until now?"

"Well, technically, you saw a video of one twenty years ago," Mercy pointed out. "You chose not to believe it."

Art smiled; he couldn't help it. What this woman brought into the room, helped him think better. Interestingly, it also calmed the headache.

"Nice wordplay, Special Agent: but there were at least three movies that came out in theaters that same year and featured dragons, which I also chose to believe weren't real."

Mercy shook her head, tumbled curls flying. "I was younger and more impressionable, I guess, because I never doubted it. Not for a second; not for part of a second."

"That would be a nanosecond," Lue piped up helpfully.

Mercy was still shaking her head, but more slowly. The vibrant curls seemed to be flowing in slow motion. Art was having a difficult time not staring at her. "I remember being terrified to sleep for weeks."

"I don't know if I'll sleep myself, anytime soon. But you didn't really answer my question. How can they stay secret, given their size and . . . appearance?"

"These dragons are not simply large lizards," Mercy answered. "They're shape-changers. On a normal day, they look like you or me. When conditions are right—conventional wisdom is that the crescent moon brings out the change—they change into true form."

Art kept watching Lue. The man was not sweating, but he was plainly uncomfortable in his chair. And his silly jokes . . . they seemed to have a somewhat forced quality. Perhaps it was these rigid plastic seats.

"And the eyes? They all have eyes like that?" The chief shuddered. "They look like flies, or locusts."

"Ah. Yes, that's a complication," Mercy admitted. "Evangelina is *not* like most dragons. Unfortunately, Chief Smiling Bear, dragons are not the only species that can adopt a human form."

A pencil slammed down. "Of course they aren't . . ."

"Sorry," Mercy said, smiling. "The fun isn't over yet. While rarer, there are also reports, confirmed by forensic evidence accumulated over the last two or three decades, of arachnid shape-changers as well."

"Arachnids? You mean spiders, don't you? *Don't* mean spiders as a personal favor, okay? Please tell me you're screwing with me." Then, in a tone of curiosity, amazement, and horror: "How big are these things?"

The FBI agent reached into her briefcase—again!—and

threw something on the table. The chief cursed as she kicked her chair and backed away from the table. Lue pushed away himself. While the gesture surprised Art, he was able to keep his calm.

He wondered if any of these people had ever hunted for their food. He doubted it. Of course, they never would have hunted this . . . more likely the reverse.

The leg segment—Art figured it for the lower third of a foreleg—was bent to fit in smaller spaces (like this woman's briefcase), but straightened it would be the width and length of a man's arm. Clearly preserved with formaldehyde, it bristled with thick, brown black hairs of uneven length. The tarsus at the tip appeared coated in a dark green substance.

"You carry that around with you?"

"I don't normally keep it with me, Detective Vue. I brought it with me because I didn't know how many law enforcement personnel I'd have to convince. You wouldn't believe how stubborn some people's belief system can be."

"The video was sufficient."

"Also, it's good luck. I took it to Vegas last weekend and killed at keno." At their thunderstruck gapes, she held up her hands, palms out, in a placating gesture: "Kidding!"

Art reached out and grabbed the segment. The preserved hairs were stiffer than they would be in real life, he knew. And, fond as he was of her on short acquaintance, he wondered how he would feel if Special Agent March had flung a severed human limb across the table—which, in a way, she had. Or how she would feel if *he* did it. He stood and handed the tissue specimen back to her. "The thing that hit that car had both legs *and* wings."

"Correct, Detective McMahon." Mercy nodded appreciatively at the return to topic, as she took back the segment. "We believe what hit the car—again, her name is Evangelina Scales—is a hybrid. If you look closely here"—she pointed at a shadow above the hood of the car, and then the roof—"and here. You'll see multiple leg segments. More than the dragons of western descent typically possess. She's got the skin, wings, tail, and mass of a dragon; and the eyes, mandibles, and legs of a spider."

Art touched Lue's shoulder, bringing him back to the table. "You saw her at Webber's?"

Lue nodded.

"How can you be sure it's a *her*?" the chief asked Mercy. "And how can you be sure of her name? Have you seen her as a human?"

"No one we know who's seen her has lived."

Lue rubbed his nose. "That would be one way to cut down on witnesses."

"The closest we came was actually here in town—when she self-admitted to the Saint George's facility. Unfortunately, in the devastation that followed her arrival, all decent visual recordings were lost. We know her gender and name, only because of a single audiotape that survived the incident. Security handed it over directly to the FBI on the scene. We've had it ever since."

"It might be nice to hear that tape," the chief suggested icily. "Especially since that facility is here in Moorston, and the killer is still likely within town limits. I don't suppose you have *that* somewhere in that briefcase?"

"Actually, it's on the flash drive. Of course, Chief, I'll be happy to play it for you. In fact, you can have the drive when we're done here." Mercy leaned forward, her expression intent, her tone respectful. "I hope you understand I had nothing to do with how we received the information. Had I been on the scene, I would have insisted on leaving you a copy in the first place."

Mercy smiled apologetically, and Art felt himself wanting to smile back. This woman radiated integrity, and he liked that. Even if she did store gruesome limbs in her briefcase.

"Anything else on that flash drive?"

Mercy shrugged and motioned around the conference room. "PDFs of all the stuff I've got hanging on the walls. Also, a composite sketch we've been running in the area, based on survivor accounts from Saint George's."

"Yes, we saw that," the chief said. "It's everywhere, now."

"Survivor accounts," Lue said, and shook his head again. "Not much."

"Exactly . . . we're not sure how reliable the sketch is, but it's all we've got."

Lue and Art looked at each other. Lue spoke first. "So no other audio or video."

"Nope. Audio recordings are rare in this day and age, of course, and video—well, cameras are all over the place in this day and age; but her sketch isn't the sort of thing you can search effectively for, among civilian populations. How would we know who she is?"

Art saw Lue smile for the first time in a few hours. "Special Agent, we are about to make your day."

CHAPTER 21

"You're sure this is her?" Mercy had barely moved during the replay of the convenience store video, and even now she could have been talking to the screen.

"It's her," said Art.

"How can you be sure?"

"Try looking at her. Then look at your sketch. Rinse and repeat."

Then, though he didn't know why, Art stuck his tongue out at her. Her reaction was a fabulous reward: a mixture of shock and humor.

"We have a witness, Agent March," Lue confirmed, oblivious to Art's gesture. "The store clerk is a bit dim, but he was watching your sketch on the television while she was in the store. She practically gave him a confession before convincing him to give her a running start."

"Gentlemen, this is huge." Mercy hit some keys on her laptop, and a few moments later the video was uploading to her regional office. Her fingers were almost a blur; speed *and* accuracy, not to mention all the resources of the FBI backing her up. "I think you just accelerated my inevitable promotion. Let me buy you lunch."

"He only wants granola," Art pointed out.

"Lies, scurrilous lies! I had granola for breakfast. I now require Tofurky."

There was a distinct rattling bark as the chief cleared her throat. "Children. It's a little early for celebratory food . . . especially sins against nature like Tofurky."

"It is *never* too early for—"

"Perhaps we should find the suspect and bring her into custody before celebrating," she pointed out dryly. "You know. In case the FBI has maintained its high standards of case closure. Wouldn't you agree, Agent March?"

"Agreed, Chief. Thanks for bringing us back down to earth." Mercy's grin was a winning expression, and Art found himself admiring how she related to the difficult personality Smiling Bear presented. He wondered how many others this woman had won over.

"You think you can capture her?"

"I don't see why not, Detective McMahon." The redhead puffed a curl out of her face with a quick breath. "Dragons are not invulnerable. They can be hurt, even killed."

Art's eyebrows arched. "What are we talking about, exactly?"

When Mercy responded, it was with an even tone and a level gaze. "We are talking about bringing her in, dead or alive, preferably alive. It would be best if she stood trial—in a confidential tribunal, of course—and I imagine she would serve out any sentence in a secure research facility."

Art thought that over and opened his mouth, but Lue beat him to the punch. "So, Special Agent March. You and your FBI colleagues have never watched a movie or read a book, am I right? Either that, or the head of this research facility is a mortal enemy of yours."

"I beg your—"

"Because in the books and movies, the authorities always figure they can study the monster or harness its power for the betterment of science or society or whatever, and then whoever is in charge of the supposedly secure research facility where staff are studying that monster always dies. Always."

"Detective Vue. Is that a threat?"

"I thought it was a movie review. Or possibly a book review."

She was giving him an odd look. "Is it your position, then, that we should kill Evangelina on sight, before giving her a fair trial?"

Lue snorted. "Of course not."

Abruptly, the chief spoke up. "Actually, I'd be okay with that."

Three pairs of eyes widened slightly. Lue waved his hand in front of her face. "Chief Smiling Bear? Suddenly not feeling so smiley, are we?"

"This thing . . . this 'Evangelina,' if she really has a name . . . has already killed at Saint George's. She has killed at multiple residences—"

"Allegedly killed, Chief."

"—at multiple residences in this town. More are sure to follow, based on the pattern we've seen from her. Just here, never mind what she's done other places.

"I think it's adorable, Agent March, that you think you can put a bridle on this beast and ride her like a pretty pony into the nearest hair-braiding facility. What I expect you'll find, is that you'll have to empty that Beretta you're carrying into her eye clusters if you want to slow her down, much less stop her."

Mercy rolled her fingertips over the table a few times. "You sound pretty sure of yourself, Chief."

"I've been at this awhile."

"Longer than me, of course."

"I'd noticed."

"You must think me to be some sort of young incompetent. Maybe I get assigned cases like this because I tested brilliantly at the academy, but I'm too book smart and know nothing about the street. Or maybe you think I get cases like this because I have political connections. Or maybe you're wondering if I slept my way into this high-profile assignment . . . and I need an older, less slutty woman to guide me along . . ."

"Whoa, hey . . ." Lue stood up with arms raised. "We need to keep this civil, people . . ."

Art leaned back and chuckled. Chief Smiling Bear looked like she had been poleaxed.

"Let me assure you," Mercy finished, "that I am an experienced and capable operative, who can and will lead this investigation. Our entertaining theories on what it takes to stop her are irrelevant. If Evangelina Scales, whatever form she's in, presents a clear and mortal threat to my safety or the safety of other peace officers or civilians, I will be bringing her in dead. Otherwise, I will be bringing her in *alive* to stand trial. We call that due process." She looked around the room. "You *do* process due process here in northern Minnesota, don't you?"

Art licked his lips. "We do."

"Well, there you have it, then!" Mercy slapped the table and leaned back in her uncomfortable plastic chair. Her Midwestern accent thickened as her stress level rose. "I guess we won't sneak up on her, then, and empty a clip into her eye cluster with a Beretta after all. Chief Smiling Bear, if you want your Detective Vue or any other officer under your command to be on my team—"

"Aw, man . . ." Lue thought about moving his arms, laced his fingers behind his head instead, and gave his boss a pleading look.

"—then I'm gonna have to tell it straight. We're peace officers, not assassins. You see this? All this?" Mercy gestured to the chaotic conference room. Papers everywhere, cups and napkins everywhere, shocking, terrible pictures erected on boards, theories, scribbles; the working chaos that already seemed weeks old, even though they had erected it in a single afternoon. "Call it a war room if you want, but this isn't a battle plan. This is an investigation. Only a qualified judiciary can judge Evangelina Scales."

"Oh," Chief Smiling Bear said pleasantly. "Thank you very, very, very, very much for setting me straight."

Art's eyebrows climbed. The jovial atmosphere had vanished from the war room. He liked Chief Smiling Bear, but that voice hid knives, especially for the FBI agent. As for how he felt about Mercy, he wanted to get to know her better, immediately.

Her philosophy, her passion, her mix of professional and profane . . . she was intoxicating. Art thought of himself as a leader, an alpha, a captain among men. Neither Lue Vue nor Chief Smiling Bear made him feel any different. But this woman . . .

. . . well, he didn't know if he could *follow* her. He would certainly stick close to her. Because of all the things she was, there was also something she was *not*.

She was not boring.

Ten Years Ago

Bored bored bored bored bored bored bored bored.

Like this: bored.

And this: BORED.

And this: ***BORED****.*

And these: bored bored bored. Bored! Bored! Bored! Bored! Bored!

"Seriously with this?"

Evangelina looked up. Aunt Susan had come from nowhere . . . it was so weird the way Susan could sneak up on her like that . . . even when she wasn't trying to do it, she did it. Susan claimed that because she'd grown up with Niffer, some sort of dragon camouflage power rubbed off on her. That was ridiculous. Right?

"This is why your mother is home schooling you?" Aunt Susan had picked up the notepad and was flipping through the last couple of pages. "At least you changed the font size a few times. Very creative for a fourth grader."

"I'm waiting for—"

"I know. She asked me instead."

Evangelina's heart fell. "She canceled again. We were supposed to go into town for a movie."

"I can take you."

"It's not the same." She knew those words would sting, but she didn't care. "She never does anything with me anymore."

"You know she's busy. Making a new home takes time. She's the leader."

"I thought Mom was the leader."

"Well, there are some things your mom can't do."

"Like what?"

"It's not my place to say. Hey—granola bar!" The woman pointed at the shiny packet lying near Evangelina's hip. "May I? I'm starved."

Evangelina shrugged, so Susan plopped herself down on the ground and snagged the bars. They both stared down the wooded hill at the shimmering, hundred-acre lake. Loons called softly to each other. The wolves, they knew, were still about.

What few remained.

Evangelina finally spoke. "So, what, I'm not going to see her again for another two or three months?" She looked at her "bored" notebook, normally for science, and slapped it shut so hard and fast she ripped the cover in half. "There's nothing to do here!"

"On the bright side, you get to do nothing with me and your mother. That's not so bad, is it? I'm like the substitute sister you never wanted."

"You're more than that. But there's no one my age around."

"What about Billy Brandfire—"

"Billy's a dork! He stares at me and never says anything. He creeps me out."

"You have the wolves."

This provoked a thoughtful silence.

Susan patted her shoulder. "Do you want to stay here?"

They both took in the woods around them, and the dozen or so cabins behind them up the hill, barely visible through the maples and pines. This remote location, virtually on the edge of the Boundary Waters, had been home for the past two years. Winoka's survivors had scattered, some into small groups like this on the edges of Minnesota, others completely vanished.

"No. I want to go. We never get to go anywhere."

"You know how dangerous it is in town. That's why this is special, right?"

Evangelina looked Susan up and down. "So what if someone recognizes us? Who'll protect me?"

"Protect you?" Susan laughed as she rose and dusted off the buttocks of her jeans, and Evangelina couldn't help smiling. "Honey, you're supposed to protect me."

I can do that.

CHAPTER 22

Art cleared his throat. "Detective Vue."

He observed Vue swivel in his desk chair. Left, right. Stop-with-right-toe, left. Left again. Stop-with-right-toe. Left. Left.

"Look!" he stage-whispered to Art while scribbling notes on the blotter (when he spun close enough to it), listening to the person on the other end of the telephone, and gulping seeds and dried grapes while occasionally tapping on the computer keyboard. Art had seen many amazing things in his life, and this one might have made the top ten. "I can keep the spin going three times, see?" Left. Left. Left.

"Amazing." Art meant it, but not for the reason Lue thought, and not for cynical reasons either. He admired Lue's ability to multitask. This might be a silly example of it; but it was representative, and it reminded him of what he valued in the agent. Spin while you talk while you eat while you whisper. Investigate while you mock while you revisit while you learn. Interrogate while you smile while you trap while you listen.

Yes, Art was glad that Chief Smiling Bear decided to back down in front of Mercy. The two had come to an arrangement: Mercy would take the afternoon off and settle in to the AmericInn about a mile away; and the chief wouldn't draw her piece and try to blow apart the young whippersnapper's freckles.

It was nearly six o'clock now; Lue had stayed to write up a few reports, and was therefore at his desk when the call came.

Lue whirled past his desk blotter, dashed another note in a language Art did not read (something arcane called quickhand or smallhand . . . the man had an odd fear of people stealing his notes), and said, "Yes, of course. I can understand that . . . sure . . ." Oh, Lue was quite good at this. Art knew he could learn from the talkative man, as much as extroverts could annoy him.

He continued to study his new partner. He had spent some time the last couple of days chatting up Lue's colleagues, looking for insights on the unusual detective. Earfuls had resulted.

Oh, hey, welcome aboard, what brings the BCA to . . . oh, that guy? He's a trip and a half, man. Scary smart, Art heard from a patrol officer so intense she was almost vibrating. *Some of the guys, you know, they don't like him much—I don't think that's his fault, though. Vue doesn't want to play the game. Good for him.*

And from another: *The V-man? Look, he's not the warmest guy in the world, okay? But he's aces with me, he's aces with my partner, and if you have a problem I'll crack your jaw. I've been in a jam or two with him—we've got a meth lab or two to bust in this town, and speed of all things is back, and even one or two gangs have tried to make inroads around here. None of it fazes him. He sticks at your side, he stays focused, he gets the job done. That's all I care about.*

And: *He's a prick. And a show-off. And he never. Shuts. Up.*

And: *Aw, he's okay, once you get past the ego problems. He's always running around correcting grammar and stuff, which he wouldn't need to do if he had any self-confidence. I think because of his family. You know about his family?*

And: *Well, sure, his family! You probably already know, they're Hmong refugees. And they landed in not entirely friendly countryside when they got here. I wouldn't exactly run over to the chamber of commerce with this, but people think of Minnesota as this wonderful laid-back place where it snows half the year and everybody gets along, which it is. Mostly. But we got more Hmong than any other state except California. And a lot of people—it's tough to admit it in this day and age, but a lot of people would change that if they could. Lue's the kind of guy who's going to change that kinda thinking, someday.*

And: *Well, he decided he had to take care of his family. And he was so young . . . I think it did something to him. Taught himself English, taught his folks, helped them acclimate, all that. Can you imagine doing all that, in goddamn second grade? I don't know that I'd have been as good at it. I think that's why he's so . . . um . . .*

He's an ass.

He's a saint.

He's brave.

He's a genius.

He's stuck up.

He's okay. Once you get to know him, anyway.

Art didn't quite know how to process all of this. It wasn't what he was raised to do. He was a hunter, pure and simple. That didn't mean he was stupid or even simple. It meant complexity made him uncomfortable.

"No problem at all," Lue was saying. "It will take only a few minutes . . . stay in the condo, and open the door for no one until we get there." He hung up and practically leaped to his feet. "Pamela Pride wants to talk to us again, *yes-ssss!*"

"Why so excited? She lied to us."

Now he was scrabbling through paperwork and desk drawers. "Where is my lucky granola? I cannot fool and beguile anyone on a diet of hot tea and commercially made granola . . . what did you say? Oh, the lying. True. However, we cannot forget two simple facts: first, she is incredibly hot; and second, she still has information that may be helpful to us."

"I don't know about the hotness."

Lue froze, hand halfway into a desk drawer. "What did you say?"

"I said, I don't agree that she's that attractive."

"Oh." The hand withdrew, and Lue sat back in his chair. "I see. You are one of *those* guys."

"What guys?"

"I mean the kind of guy that can afford to be choosy, even to the point of ridiculousness. Your burly shoulders, your rugged stubble, your piercing eyes, your strong-but-silent attitude . . . you make the girls swoon. They want to understand you, solve the mystery that is you, make you admit to them and them alone what a small and frightened child you are, deep under all those pectoral and other assorted muscles."

"You're being foolish."

"You prevent antilittering fines on the highway by catching the panties that these women throw at you from speeding automobiles. So you can have these stratospheric standards. A woman like Pamela Pride comes along, someone who may have a troubled past but could fry bacon on her own breasts, and you say, 'Meh.' 'Meh,' you say, and again I say that you say, 'Meh.' You throw off the curve, man. You throw off the whole freaking curve, and the rest of us have to live with the consequences."

"And those consequences are . . . ?"

"The more homely and wispy among us can hope for no more than 'good friend' status, where we listen to the woman we lust after pine after *you* as we shop for shoes together and drive them to the airport."

This may be my favorite conversation with him so far.

"Whatever. I can cry into my trail mix." Lue seized a large Baggie from the open desk drawer and stuffed it into his jacket pocket. "It is, you will be awed and impressed to hear, my own recipe. Granola, cranberries, banana chips. And my own secret ingredient, which I would not tell you even under hours of torture. Okay, I will give you a hint: cinnamon. And no, you may not have any."

"I don't—"

"I can see the urgent lust for a healthy snack in your eyes, Art; you are not fooling me. I bear witness here and now, to one of the secrets that the most special among your harem of jilted would-be lovers, whoever she may be, will come to learn once you stop keeping her at arm's length." He sighed. "Come on. I might even let you drive, if you promise to make a videotape of the eventual consummation."

"I won't."

"Drive, or consummate?"

"Won't." Art figured that was safe enough.

"There is something wrong with you," was the cheerful answer, and in that tone and expression Art thought he saw the Lue many other cops didn't: Lue liked the strange, the different, and the bizarre as long as he was in the driver's seat.

It was a quality Art knew he could use . . . it was also a quality that might have let them eventually become friends.

A little shocked at himself, Art shoved that last thought far, far away. He was here for a specific purpose. He was not here to find a new bar buddy, a police chum, and/or a fishing pal. When his work here was finished . . . well, then, so was Art.

Anything else—even thinking about anything else—was worse than a distraction. It was a betrayal not only of his life's work, but everything he was, wanted to be, and would be.

It was also very, very dangerous. Not just to his job. To . . . to everything. Art wasn't afraid to die, but he hated the thought of dying in disgrace.

"Come, my taciturn pomegranate, and we shall save the maiden in distress. You will look upon her," Lue promised, jangling his keys as he led the way, "and you will declare her to be fair. Or I shall stuff your handsome, half-shaven face full of cinnamon-laced granola, and you will finally not look so hot to the fairer sex . . ."

"Should we call Agent March to meet us there?"

"Hell, no. Chief said she had the afternoon off. We act now, share later. Like the feds do."

The thought of not seeing Mercy made him sulk, and the realization of why he was sulking made him sulk more. Lue, chattering about everything in the world on the way over, didn't notice.

CHAPTER 23

"I'm so sorry to bother you. It's just, you said if I needed anything . . . even if to talk . . ." She sniveled and wept into a dish towel.

Art looked for the "gorgeous." He guessed he saw it—there was a lot about Pamela Pride that many men found conventionally attractive. There was too much about her, he felt, which was not genuine. Not necessarily dangerous—women in leggings and sweatshirts generally didn't come across as perilous—but disingenuous.

She's trying to play him, Art observed. For pity, attention, protection, company, whatever it was, he didn't care. He was at least glad that Lue was not blind to her deceptions, and that the two detectives agreed that those deceptions were likely harmless.

"We were so glad to hear from you," Lue was saying. "Right, Detective McMahon?"

Art shrugged and nodded simultaneously. He began to

examine the banal framed prints in the living room. Leaves, trees, forests. *Original.*

"Okay, this will sound silly . . . but I think someone's following me." Before either of them could comment, Pamela rushed ahead: "I know, it's all in my head, right?"

"Right," Art said, realizing too late that this was out loud.

"Except I don't think it is. I can almost feel whoever it is. Behind me, you know, when I'm going to the store . . . or the gym . . . sometimes when I come home, I can tell someone's been in here. Like I barely missed them. Like if I got home five minutes earlier . . ." She shivered and rubbed her arms.

Pamela took a shuddering breath. "And I think . . . I think . . ."

Without saying a word, Lue invited her to continue. The expression on his face was rock-solid Please Tell Me Everything And Do Not Be Afraid. *He should teach a class,* Art thought sincerely.

"Well, I think about what you and Detective McMahon said about an animal, except maybe one that's smarter than the average animal. Like a monster! You remember that?"

"I remember that coming up," Lue said meticulously.

"Well, I don't know if it's that, or if it's that sketch of that woman they're running on the news now, but whatever it is, I'm sure it's following me."

"Have you ever seen it?"

"No. I think whoever or whatever it is, is staying secret. Disappearing when I turn around, hovering near the windows . . ." She rubbed her arms again. "I think it may have even been in the condo last night."

"What do you base that on?" Art asked, losing patience. *This is a waste of time.*

He didn't really listen to the answer, and from Lue's expression he could tell he was missing nothing. The conversation continued between the two of them for a while longer. Everything about her annoyed Art—the fluttering eyelids, the damsel-on-stage routine, the breathless recounting of shadows on the second-floor balcony. Here was a woman who got her way in everything: good looks, a body that fit into any yoga shirt or bathing suit she desired, a career through lying about her school, and above all the attention of men.

Not this man, he resolved as he walked through the living room into the hallway that led to bedrooms. *She's not my type.*

He reflected on the type that *did* attract him. A few minutes later, he found himself frustrated: he kept thinking about Mercy March.

That makes no sense. Think of the differences between you. Think of the challenges. Think of the way she tossed that disgusting spider leg across the table at you.

Lue's patient voice overlay his efforts. "Try to go through each event of the last twenty-four hours," he was telling her . . .

Try as he might, it kept coming back to this for Art: Mercy would not leave his mind. They were both leaders, both hunters, both focused minds.

"Okay, good start, Pamela . . . what else?"

He chided himself. *Distractions! Perilous detours! This is not your mission! This is not your goal! This is not your promise!*

Perhaps not, another voice inside of him answered. *But it could be my destiny.*

"Yeah, he creeps me out sometimes, too. The way he stares into space like that. A harmless tic. Detective McMahon cares as deeply about your protection as I do, Pamela. So, you were saying . . . ?"

He took a few more steps down the hallway, out of their sight. Surely Ms. Pride would not mind if he looked around the place and made sure there were no stalkers hiding in the linen closets . . .

"Hey! Where are you going?"

She bolted across the living room and down the hall. Before Art realized it, she had grabbed him by the upper arm and was twisting him to face her.

"Ms. Pride, I'm—"

"You can't go down there! That's my bedroom!"

He raised his hands in apology. "I meant no offense. I thought ensuring the security of these rooms . . ."

"W-well, ensure it somewhere else!" Her face reddened, and she began to stammer. "I d-didn't call the cops so th-they could flip through my underwear drawers!"

Uncertain of what to do next, Art looked at Lue. Lue, standing, shrugged back. "Um, Ms. Pride, we might feel better about leaving you here alone, and so might you, if we could take a glance in each room. Nothing invasive. You could be with us the entire time."

Something must have occurred to Pamela, because she abruptly let go of Art's arm and looked down. "G-geez, I'm sorry. Th-that was stupid. You g-go ahead and look, Detective. I don't m-mind."

"Sure. Thanks." Antennae perked, Art sidled down the hallway, keeping one eye on the first bedroom door and his other on Ms. Pride. Lue casually walked up behind her, and Art appreciated the subtle support. He pushed open the first door to find an empty bedroom. Behind him was the second door: a guest bathroom.

The third door was at the end of the hall. No doubt this was the master suite, and the location Ms. Pride would be most sensitive about.

Already ajar, the door beckoned to him. He stepped forward, pushed open the door with his left hand as his hand hovered over his holster . . .

He had no time to flip on the light switch: the enormous shape was lurching toward him from the back of the bedroom. In an instant, his Beretta was in his hand and he had pumped three bullets into it.

Then he froze. "In the name of the sacred . . ."

"What?" Lue called from down the hallway, his own gun drawn now, still backing him up in case Pamela freaked out again. "What did you shoot? Is anyone hurt?"

"I don't . . . this can't . . . how is this . . ."

Finally, Lue pushed past Pamela and stepped up next to Art.

"Wow. No kidding." He turned back to Pamela and pointed. "You did all this?"

"Y-yes. First day I moved in. Ugh. I'm so embarrassed . . ."

"No, no, you should be proud. This is . . . wow. Art, will you be okay?"

Art could not look away. The entire room was a pastel nightmare—soft pinks and creamy yellows and foamy greens. Unlike the rest of the condo, which was painted stark autumnal colors with sparse furnishings, in here there was barely room to move or see or think. Nearly every square inch of wall was covered in unicorn prints—framed, matte finish, ornate pastel frames. Pillows had stitched unicorns gracing their softness, laughing unicorns danced across the (pink) duvet cover, and the entire back corner of the room had been trampled over by a floor-to-ceiling herd of stuffed unicorns that remained hovering over the far side of the bed. No, it wasn't a herd: it was a unicorn mass, a pink and white tumor with poofy horns protecting all angles, an infinitesimally slow-moving invasion from a parallel universe where stuffed unicorns who ruled space and time had depleted all natural resources and were now invading this world for precious bedroom space.

There were three holes drilled into the middle of this mass, each blowing apart the fabric of a different grinning unicorn and blasting its stuffing across the faces of the others, like blood splatter on innocent bystanders.

The BCA agent slumped his shoulders and hung his

head. "I deeply regret the property damage, ma'am. We can . . . we can reimburse you for any monetary loss."

Lue put on a game smile. "See now, Pamela? You feel better, right? More secure?"

Pamela choked back a sob, ran past them, and slammed the door shut. "My unicorns and I are very upset! I hope you're happy, Detectives! Good night!"

"Wow, man." Lue clapped Art on the shoulder as they let themselves out. "This report is all yours, partner."

CHAPTER 24

"So, what do you think *her* upbringing was like?" Lue poured more sunflower seeds down his gullet. "By the way, nice grouping."

Art, who was driving, grunted.

"Maybe we should put a patrol car outside the building for a night or two."

Art grunted again, and flipped on the radio.

"Oh, come on. Have some compassion for her. She plainly has had a hard life. And now her unicorns are dead."

"She doesn't need our help."

"So the whole 'protect and serve' mission . . . feels voluntary to you, does it?"

"I am protecting and serving, by solving this crime."

"Well, the good news is: this is not really up to you. The chief will be happy to assign a patrol car."

"Your chief is too busy mocking Agent March."

Lue put down the granola packet and stared at his partner for a full two blocks.

"You have a crush on her."

"I have a what on who?"

"A crush. On Special Agent March."

Art brought the car to a screeching halt.

"Hey, no offense intended . . ."

Reaching out and grabbing Lue's collar, Art gritted his teeth. "I don't have a crush on her."

"Geez, if you say so. Fine, she would be horrible for you. She comes across as way to bossy. She talks too much. And the chief hates her. There! She must be Queen of the Vampires, Evil Incarnate. Bring on the wooden stake and gigantic hammers."

"The headache is returning."

"Good! What, wait—you have a headache? You need an aspirin?"

"The cure is less of you." *And possibly, more of her.*

"Oh, nice. I offer you medicine, and you give me crap. See that? See that over there?" Lue pointed wildly.

"Grass and benches?"

"The park where I will kick the shit out of you if you don't take, oh my God I used a contraction." He pawed at his tongue as if there were a live cricket crawling in his mouth.

Art winced; the headache was getting worse. "Special Agent March is in a difficult position. That's all."

"Yes, Art, it is referred to as law enforcement. The same job, you may have noticed, that *we* have."

Art flicked a sideways glance at him. "She faces some additional complexities within the FBI."

"How do you know that? Are you a big FBI expert?"

"I know the agency well enough. I know the culture."

"Oh, Art McMahon is a big organizational culture expert, now? Did you write a paper on the topic, maybe? Was it longer than a sentence?"

"You're annoyed because she embarrassed your chief. I understand."

"You *understand*? Are you a psychiatrist now, Mc-Mahon? Is that what you are?"

"You should talk to Agent March about it. Maybe the chief, too. They could help you with perspective."

"Are you . . ." Lue nearly choked on the fresh outrage. "Are you *patronizing* me? You, the cedar block in brown corduroy and red hair . . . trying to patronize me? I do not need soothing!"

The BCA agent shrugged. "Seems like you have a lot on your mind."

"What do you think I have on my mind, Detective?"

"An investigation that's been co-opted twice by higher authorities. A police department that's 92 percent white. A failed marriage you blame yourself for. A hot jogger that could've been your rebound girl. The number of contractions I've used in the last ten seconds. Perhaps more you're not telling me."

Lue's mouth tightened in a tense frown. "You . . . you think you know me. You think you can drive around with me for a couple of days, talk to a few other Moorston cops, kill a couple of stuffed unicorns, and BAM be an expert on the life of Lue Vue."

"I didn't say that."

"You think you can make fun of people like me, because you have no trouble with women like Pamela or Agent March. They want to like you. Everyone wants to like you. You radiate control effortlessly. It was never a challenge for you . . ."

"That's not true."

". . . you always had it easy . . ."

"That's not true."

". . . you have everything you want . . ."

"That's not true."

". . . and when you finish your work here, you can go and you will never have to deal with these people again!"

"I admire what you do here."

"You patronize me again, Art, I swear on all that is holy, I will knock you through that car window."

"Okay." Art rubbed his beard and pointed in Lue's face. "Here's something less patronizing. I think you're an underachieving control freak who uses inappropriate humor to shield the fact that you think you've made one mistake too many in your life and career. You push people away who you think might exercise control, good or bad, over the decisions in your life. You won't let others lead. And you won't lead yourself. There. Was that patronizing? You want to take a swing? Fire it off."

Lue blinked. "Good heavens, Art. That was amazing."

"How so? You think I was accurate?"

"No. Well, maybe. But that was like, what? Seventy, eighty words all at once? Are you going to be okay? Is the headache coming back? The offer of aspirin still stands."

His creeping smile was contagious, and Art found himself chuckling.

"Our first lovers' spat," Lue remarked as Art put the car back in drive and slammed the accelerator. "I hope Agent March is not the jealous type."

"Stuff it, Lue."

As they settled into comfortable silence for the rest of the drive, Art found himself wondering what Lue Vue was like as a child, and what kind of friends he had.

Eight Years Ago

Evangelina loved the pack.

Still fewer than their last days in Winoka, the wolves who remained with the Scales family had replenished their numbers somewhat over the years. There were always some on patrol around the camp, but that still left a dozen at any time resting near the Scales cabin. On warm autumn afternoons, there was nothing Evangelina liked more than to lie near them.

She usually did so in her dark form, to match their beast shapes with her own. It reminded her that they all had a different side, a different skin, something the world would accept more readily. That side was less necessary here, far away from towns and cities.

Rolling over to let her other side absorb the rising sun, she sighed. Even the camp seemed empty. Niffer was here less than she was away now. Mom was preoccupied with efforts to locate other camps. And Aunt Susan . . . she hadn't been the same since her father died.

Her thoughts drifted to her own father, a man who had died around the time Evangelina was a newborn. Susan had told her he had been outgoing and humorous, a swirl of extroverted emotion who offset his more reserved, disciplined wife. "He was a dragon even when he wasn't," she had once said. Evangelina had liked that.

One of the wolves began to snore, and she smiled. Did it matter what form any of them were in? They were dragons when they weren't, humans when they weren't, monsters when they weren't, strong when they weren't. Who was the rest of the world to tell them what they were, at all?

CHAPTER 25

The next morning, Art got to the station early. Mercy was already there, which gave them a great opportunity to sit next to each other and work awkwardly in close proximity for at least half an hour before Lue showed up.

There were FBI files from crime scenes in other states to examine, witness testimony to interpret, undiscovered patterns to ascertain, and petty arguments over who would run out for coffee (or tea, or water).

When Lue came in, the sounds of laughter followed, and he looked both amused and nervous.

"What's up?" Art asked.

The young detective wouldn't look directly at them. "Oh. Nothing. What are you guys working on?"

Once he was caught up on their work thus far, Lue was a valuable contributor. Not only did he have insights into possible connections and clues, he also magnanimously provided to Mercy and Art, starts to at least three different conversations ("Would you like some frozen nondairy soy milk from the co-op, Art?" or "Guess what English homonym is the source of most usage mistakes?" or "Mercy, did you know that Art has no clothes that are not jeans, white shirts, and corduroy jackets?").

Right about the time he began a fourth ("So do you like romance novels, Art?"), Mark burst open the door to the war room.

"You gotta hear this," he said, motioning to all of them.

They followed him to the dispatch office, where they were playing back a call.

"This is less than five minutes ago," he explained, motioning to the dispatcher to play the 911 sequence again.

"Police, may I help you?"

"They're all dead."

"Sir, what is your name?"

"Everyone is dead. I think you can take your time getting down here, but I thought you should know."

"Sir, your name and location, please?"

"Triangulate already. I'll leave this phone on at the scene; my own is dead. Everything's dead. I'm not staying here."

"You're saying people are hurt?"

"No. I'm saying they're dead."

"Are you hurt, sir?"

"No. I might be the only one. I'm leaving now. Good luck—this is a mess down here."

"So how did I get stuck with the backseat of a Moorston police vehicle?" Lue wanted to know.

Art kept his eyes on the road, refusing to look in the rearview mirror or at the red-haired passenger.

"And now no one answers my questions. Perfect."

"We'll be there in a minute and a half," Mercy said with

an apologetic grimace. "I'll switch with you on the way back."

"No, no. Not necessary. I can see this is how it is, now. I get it."

"Let him sulk," Art advised Mercy. "He could have taken a separate car."

"You could have taken a separate car. *Your* car."

"I would have done exactly that, had you not snuck into it in the station parking lot upon your arrival this morning and crammed it full of plush unicorn toys."

"You can *not* blame me for that," Lue objected, staring at the window with tightly pursed lips. "At least not me alone. It took at least two third-shift patrol officers to buy the toys at Wal-Mart and carry all those things out of the store, another officer to arrange for overnight storage in the evidence room for all of them, and two first-shift patrol officers to keep an eye out for your vehicle and give the rest of us the all clear."

Mercy giggled. "Quite the coordinated strike force."

Art didn't know whether to fume or smile. He settled on, "I'm glad you're getting along better with your colleagues."

"Yeah, well, nothing like an interfering pair of higher authorities to make us all close ranks. Whoa, you missed the turn there—just catch the next block."

"Keep your eyes open for her," Mercy advised, getting serious again. "We may get an unexpected opportunity."

"Evangelina will be gone by now," Art predicted.

"Attaboy, Art. Think positive—ow!"

"Sorry for that. The curb jumped out and attacked my tires on that turn."

"A fine partner, to try to batter me to death with the backseat of a police issue automobile!"

Art grinned in the rearview, showing a great many teeth. "Wouldn't try. Would just kill you."

As they screeched into a narrow driveway, they noticed

bunches of neighbors keeping their distance from the split-level. Two other Moorston police cars were already parked there, and yellow tape was going up.

Three dead bodies were inside. All had vicious slash wounds to the throat. The cell phone that had made the 911 call was in their midst.

"This breaks the pattern," Art noted as they learned the IDs of the victims. This had taken some time, as one of them was a minor and had no license or anything else helpful. "These people are not related."

Lue recapped the address information. "Two of them have residences elsewhere in this town. Art, this *is* weird. The boy has no parent with him in this house, yet here he is with two unrelated adults. All of them now dead. We can assume the blood tests for Mr. Thomas Martin"—he motioned to the male adult victim—"will come up dragon. But what if Ms. Tina Mares and young Mr. Randy Hahn come up different? I have yet to see anywhere in the BCA or FBI files, a case where a scene like this included civilians."

"It would be new for Evangelina, that's for sure," Mercy agreed. "I suspect they're all three dragon, though. Maybe she came here for one of them, but the other two showed up unexpectedly."

"Unexpectedly? They each had packed bags in the garage. They were going somewhere together."

"Just because they expected each other, doesn't mean Evangelina expected them."

"What about the man on the phone?" Art pressed.

"The victim that got away."

"Or the murderer."

"The murderer?" She raised her eyebrows at him. "Do we doubt who the murderer is, here?"

"Due process, Agent March."

"Yes, I get it. But you can't argue with the pattern we're seeing . . ."

"This breaks the pattern."

"You can't seriously think she wasn't here."

"I see no evidence."

"Not yet. I don't get it, Detective McMahon: you've been hunting her down for what, two years now? Why are you so ready to give up on her after one odd scene?"

"I didn't say that," Art snarled. He saw Lue out of the corner of his eye, watching them bat the conversation back and forth like a heated tennis ball. No doubt the other officers milling about would also be listening. "I want the investigation to follow the facts."

"It will." She turned to Lue. "Make sure your officers take careful prints of all available surfaces. We'll see Evangelina's prints, I'm sure—matches to evidence from the Saint George's site and the convenience store."

"The fingerprints on that cell phone will be even more interesting," Lue replied.

"Bag and tag it all. I'll meet you guys back at the station; I'm going to get a ride from one of the patrol officers . . ."

"You don't have to do that," Art insisted, and then looked embarrassed when she smiled back.

"It's okay. I'm not angry, and it's not just for Lue's sake. I need to look into something back at the station, and I need to update the Minneapolis office on this development. Don't worry—I'll be sure to keep it fact based." She wrinkled her nose, winked at him, and left.

"How come you guys are still skulking about?" one of the lab techs said a few minutes later, shuffling through the scene and pulling out a small digital camera. "Like that, Vue? Skulking?"

"Your word of the day toilet paper is working wonders," Lue replied pleasantly.

"Seriously, how come you're still here?"

"Despair led to stagnation."

"Okay," the cute, pale tech replied, not a hair of her

fluffy head out of countenance. "Good thing, too, because I've got a present for you." She waved a sample case at them, sealed and ready for analysis at the lab. "This hair was in Mr. Martin's hand. Color doesn't match any of the victims."

Art snatched it from her, nodded at Lue, and they left together.

CHAPTER 26

After they dropped the sample off at forensics, they met up with Mercy in the war room and came up with a plan for the rest of the day.

"We have to find Mr. Hahn's parents," Lue suggested. "Patrol officers found no one at his listed address, and their voice mails have gone unreturned. Similar story with Ms. Mares: according to last known information and all the pictures up in her house, she has a dashing young husband. In fact, I *know* her husband: he reported a B&E about two months ago."

"Related?" Mercy asked.

"Doubtful. They broke into the Mares's garage and stole some power tools. Anyway, none of the neighbors have seen him in the last twenty-four hours. Mark called me from the scene; he tells me it looks like they buttoned up the place for a long absence."

"Like the packed bags at Martin's."

"Right on, Art. I think these families knew each other. And I think they were leaving."

"Why?" Mercy asked.

Art shrugged. "Wouldn't you, if you were a dragon in this town?"

"An interesting thought. We don't know yet if they're all dragon, of course."

"Whether they are or not," Lue mused, "we might want to look for patterns of disappearances in the other towns."

"Missing persons investigations should be easy enough to check," Mercy noted.

"Not all of them will be officially 'missing,'" Lue guessed. "Some of them may have even told neighbors that they would be away for a long time."

Mercy whistled at Lue, then turned to Art. "Bright partner you have here."

"Yes." Art winked at Lue. "Bright indeed. We should also widen the interview circle. Check online social networks for friends, see if anyone else has gone missing."

"You savvy enough on the Internet to do that, Art?" Lue teased.

Art whipped up his smart phone. "I'm doing it now."

"You stud. How is the headache?"

Art refused to look directly at Mercy. "It's fine. Thanks for asking."

Lue turned to the FBI agent. "He had a headache yesterday. It gets worse when he spends time with me, but it gets better when he spends time with you, Agent March. You two should track down the networks for Martin and the other victims. The chief and I will get a manhunt going for Hahn's parents. If nothing else, they deserve to know what happened to their son."

Mercy grinned at Art, who stared at the table red-faced. "That sounds like a plan, Lue. Thanks."

* * *

Their new plan paid off more than they ever could have guessed, they realized as they checked in over lunch at the Suds Bucket.

"Mr. Martin had 187 Facebook friends," Mercy told Lue as she and Art sat across from the Moorston detective in the back corner booth. "Of those 187, a dozen are on missing persons reports across the upper Midwest. Another six called their local law enforcement, informed them they were on extended vacation, and requested occasional police patrols of their property. Another three match up with murder victims at sites in Rockford and Moline."

"We got similar hits off Mares," Art added. He worried that Lue would notice how much Mercy's body sidled up to his own, but there was nowhere else for him to go, being trapped inside.

"Wow. You guys had more luck than I did. Hahn's parents appear to have vanished. I interviewed twenty neighbors and friends personally, this morning alone. Not a single interview lasted for more than five minutes." He held up his notepad and recited some quotes, exaggerating a Minnesota twang as he read:

"I think they had vacation."

"I have not one idea."

"They were helping their eldest move to college, I think . . ."

"His mother-in-law needed help moving to the rest home, I heard . . ."

"I dunno, they keep to thesselves, I don't like 'em."

"Maybe they couldn't pay the rent? Economy's terrible around here."

He looked up at the two of them. "It reminds me of a greatest hits album by some punk band called the Amazingly Unhelpful Interview Faction. The good news is, we have preliminary test results rushed back from the Martin scene. That hair sample from Martin's hand has no known match. The fingerprints off the cell phone used for nine one one is for a Dean Caligiuri, a Moorston resident. He has disappeared like everyone else. We should add him to the Facebook list."

Art flipped through a printout. "He's one of Martin's 187, and Mares's 205."

"We're going to find out these people all knew each other, aren't we?" Mercy's fingers were trembling. "They were all dragons, and they've all gone missing or dead in the last couple of years. Evangelina's killing them. Why?"

"Facts first, theories later," Art suggested. "Bacon now." He motioned at the waiter across the room, who hurried over.

CHAPTER 27

An afternoon's worth of investigation later, the story was even more clear. They presented it to Chief Smiling Bear, who frowned incessantly at Mercy while the younger woman spoke.

"So each town starts with a murder," she explained as she pointed to a map of the upper Midwest with several dozen pushpins of different colors poking out. "That's the red. In small towns, of course, you'll see only one or two pins, and nothing else. In bigger ones"—she pointed at the Quad Cities, and Sioux Falls, and Bemidji—"you also see some green. That's residents who have been missing, either officially or unofficially, since the day of the first murder within twenty-five miles. You'll notice the green blooms are larger than the red; that's because—"

"I'm red green color-blind," the chief interrupted.

"Huh." Mercy paused and considered that. "Is that, like, an age-related thing? Kicks in around menopause, or . . . ?"

"Your sharp wit notwithstanding, Special Agent March, I don't see how this gets you closer to Evangelina Scales."

"Whether it does or not," answered Lue nervously, "it certainly gives us a better picture of what is happening out there. And the more we tap into those social networking sites, the more easily we can see where dragon networks still exist . . . and predict where the next murders might be."

"That means we catch the murderer more quickly," Art finished.

"You seem awfully enthusiastic about that prospect, Detective McMahon. I hope you plan on following Special Agent March's explicit procedures for *nicely* bringing in unstoppable mass murderers."

"Chief, I think revisiting that conversation will only . . ."

"I plan on cooperating with my partners," Art replied, "as long as it gets me what I want."

"And what is that?"

The BCA agent pointed up at the map and did not try this time to hide his fury. *"That has to stop."*

"Agreed," Mercy chimed in. It seemed as though Mercy's hair acted in direct accord with her emotions, because her curls seemed to all be standing up and waving, like sea fronds. "And it will. Thanks to what your staff have accomplished, Chief Smiling Bear, along with Detective McMahon. We're so unbelievably close now."

"We still have some filtering to do, Agent March." Lue lifted up a sheaf of papers he was still going through. "These networking listings expand exponentially. Those 187 friends of Thomas Martin turn into thousands of friends of friends, and millions of friends of friends of friends. I had no idea *I* was three steps removed from nearly everyone in town, after only a few months here. Most of the police force is two steps removed. Including you, Chief." He winked.

Chief Smiling Bear didn't return the sentiment. "So it

doesn't sound like you're really getting all that close to useful information."

"The friends list is still great stuff—we just have to dig through it. And friends of friends can bring up some interesting tidbits, too. Here, Agent March—look who lingers only two steps from the Hahns." He made a mark with his pen and slid the relevant paper across the table. Then he started flipping through a few more piles.

Mercy looked down at the page and her eyes widened. "Oh. *Oh.*" She showed Art.

"Huh."

"Yep, here she is again. And two steps removed from the Martins." Lue flipped some more, then gave up. "You know what? A computer will do this faster. Here, check this out while I warm up the laptop . . ." He slid the new pages over and turned to his keyboard.

Mercy saw the name again, and again. Art saw her lick her lips. "See if you can find an address for her."

"I doubt we will. Maybe we can get an e-mail at least." He tapped at his keyboard for about thirty seconds, which Art actually found more fascinating than he would have thought under different circumstances. "Nope. Her profile is minimal. I guess we should be surprised she even dares to have one."

"She could be a nerve center," Mercy guessed. "An outreach method."

"So soon?" Art asked. "It hasn't been very long."

"She was pretty important to Evangelina," Mercy pointed out. "This may be why."

"If you want to learn more, a warrant will be necessary."

"Right on, Detective Vue. Detective McMahon. Chief." She winked at the last. "I assume I can safely leave you in charge. I have a judge to bully."

After she was gone, the chief breathed, "What a bitch."

Art restrained the impulse to spring at her.

Six Years Ago

Evangelina crouched, ready to spring.

The woman opposite her switched from a "roof" to a "tail" stance, the blade gliding downward and back.

"Are we going to circle each other all morning? I have flu shots to administer to the camp."

"You've been talking about patience all week, Mom. I'm trying to be patient."

"Yes, well, there's patient, and there's catatonic. If you—"

Evangelina shot forward, six of her legs propelling her while the front two reached out to strike. Her timing would be perfect—her mother was in front of a large oak and had no space to retreat.

The fifty-year-old woman collapsed smartly and rolled forward, spinning under her daughter and leaving the girl to crash into the thick tree trunk . . .

"Ooomph!"

. . . then stood up and smacked her tail with the flat of her sword.

"Hey!"

"You're down a tail. Pretend it's lopped off. No using it. Also, try to simulate loss of balance and a general feeling of bleeding to death."

"Funny, Mom." One of Evangelina's tarsi came up to rub her scaled forehead ridges.

"Honestly, you're fighting like you only have two legs, maybe four. You have eight, dear. Eight! *Plus two wings and mandibles and, until recently, an elegant yet snappable tail. How are you not kicking my ass?"*

"Were you this chatty when you fought my biological mother?"

The older woman paled and took a step back. "I never fought her. I told you, we barely met before she died."

"Jenn told me you slugged her on a hospital roof."

From the expression on her mother's face, Evangelina knew the truth even before the admission came. "Oh, that. Well. She deserved that. But that wasn't fighting, not like I thought you meant it. That was more of a . . . territorial spat."

"Hmmm." She watched her opponent's stance form: the "ox," blade held high and horizontal.

"What's coming for you—for all of us—is more than a short dispute. It's a fight for our lives."

"I know, Mom." It felt weird to say that in the strained, preteen tones one generally reserved for replies to more traditional motherly concerns like:

Bundle up, it's cold outside.

No running in the house with those scissors, now.

The Regiment is coming to kill you, dear.

"So you need to worry less about the past, and more about the future. And how to use eight legs."

"I know, *Mom!"*

"Yes, yes, you know, you know, you know. All the things

you know, Vange, I could stuff a sack with. And the sack would smell like crap." Her mother was smiling, but her emerald eyes were not quite glittering. "I've heard it all before. From you; from your sister; heck, I said a lot of it to my own mother, back when I knew nothing but attitude. Stop telling me what you know, and start showing me. Then I'll be impressed. So. You ready to keep going, dear? We can stop if your tail stump hurts too much."

The sarcasm, the humiliation, was too much. Evangelina felt blood boil inside. It felt different from when most people said it. True heat burned something inside her, near the base of her skull. The resulting dark gasses poured from her ear cavities and formed a dark corona, shrouding her entire head. She could still see . . . but what she saw looked different from before. What had been uncertain was now clear, and what had been clear was now dim.

She hissed and pushed off the tree trunk with her hindmost leg pair to assault the warrior.

This time, she used the next two legs forward to stop her trajectory the moment she saw her enemy begin to swing, the pair in front of those—her strongest—to spin her own body around in a shadowy flash, and the front two to swing.

The warrior was quick enough to recover and parry to the left, but the right landed across the chin, and Evangelina felt a thrill as the defender's head spun. She followed up with the four front legs—two to extend and twist the sword arm until the blade fell, one to catch the opponent behind the knees, and the last to push the chest downward and back.

"Unnh!"

Now the same four legs, all driving at the fallen defender's face.

"Arrrgh!"

Her mother's cry broke the spell, and the corona vanished. The aging woman had blood over her face, most of it streaming from her nose. Evangelina scuttled backward, falling over her own tail.

"Evangelina!"

It was Niffer's voice. She twirled and swallowed. It was *Niffer! She had seen everything!*

Evangelina scrambled to her feet, turned, and began to run. The corona reasserted itself, giving her incredible vision of her surroundings and making her reckless rush a navigable speed. The tree trunks and low branches whistled near her head, and her footsteps thundered in her own ears.

She stopped after a few minutes; and some hours later she returned home to find her mother was more embarrassed and wistful than injured or upset; and days after that the bruises faded from her mother's face; and when a couple of weeks had passed the two of them finally sparred again, each more ready for the other than before; and by six months afterward, Evangelina was sparring two, three, ten opponents at a time, until the entire camp, including the wolves—her whole world, really—was taking her on, and losing.

For some reason, she and Niffer never fought. Not even for fun, not even for practice.

CHAPTER 28

"Thanks for responding to our message."

"Whatever." Susan Elmsmith had a gravel whisper and tired face for thirtysomething. Her clothes were simple and faded, and she sat low in her seat. Two bony hands clutched a murky glass of iced tea.

Upon their arrival, she had not moved her backpack or jacket from the booth seat next to her, so Lue and Mercy had crammed themselves opposite her, while Art found a chair from a nearby table and positioned himself at the end of the table. Even from his position, he only really had a good look at her shoulders and head, both shrouded in dark curls that had lost their shine.

Mercy began. "My first impulse was to dig deeper, locate your address, and have federal agents pick you up. Detective McMahon pointed out that having you meet us, might generate quicker results."

Susan looked at the man Mercy had indicated. "You're McMahon?"

He nodded.

"Detective McMahon, are you aware of the nature of the federal agent you're collaborating with?"

He shrugged and smiled at Mercy. "She appears to have a very results-oriented nature. Our investigation is going well. We're learning a lot."

"How wonderful for you. Have you watched her kill anything yet?"

His eyes narrowed as he looked back at Susan. "No."

Mercy cleared her throat. "Susan, what have you been up to since Saint George's?"

The woman squinted, and a finger rose to twirl a dusty black curl. "Is that why you wanted to meet with me? To bring me back there?"

Lue put a hand on Mercy's shoulder and didn't let her shake it off. "No! As far as anyone beyond the three of us knows, this meeting has not happened. Frankly, from reviewing your file, the reason for your initial commitment is unclear."

"*She* knows."

Art turned to Mercy, who showed frank surprise.

After a few moments, the woman continued. "Special Agent Mercy March is a federal agent. But not just any kind of federal agent. She's the same type that brought me in the first time. They said I was making too much noise, that I needed someplace quiet. So they kept me quiet."

"Wow," Lue observed. "You sound really paranoid."

The worn-looking woman showed her teeth. "Who was it who said 'perfect paranoia is perfect awareness'? Someone *was* out to get me, Detective. And get me they did."

"Until you broke out," Art offered.

Her blue eyes settled on him. "Someone broke me out.

You're not asking me anything you don't already know. Get to your point."

Lue cleared his throat. "What can you tell us about the woman who freed you?"

"How do you know she's a woman?"

"We have substantial audio recording, and limited video—"

A college-aged waiter with a blond crew cut approached the table. "Ma'am, it looks like the rest of your party is here. Can I interest you in our all-day super-day breakfast specials? Our omelet of the day—"

"I'll stick with the tea."

Lue held up a finger. "Egg white omelet, veggies only, two slices of wheat toast with no butter, and ice water."

"Very healthy." This earned Art a stuck-out tongue.

"You, sir?"

"Coffee. Bacon. Then more bacon."

"Ooookay. I'm guessing nothing in the coffee."

Lue groaned. "I can actually hear your cholesterol convening in your aorta."

"You cannot."

The waiter laughed, then paused his scribbling long enough to turn to Mercy. "And for you, ma'am?"

"Nothing for me, thanks." She turned back to the interview as the waiter darted off. "We know that Ms. Scales is tall, in her late teens or early twenties. Her hair is probably dark, unless she is using dye or a wig. She appears athletic."

"My, my. What a whole lot of nothing."

"Ms. Scales is dangerous," Mercy continued. "If you know where she is, it's in everyone's best interest for you to tell us so we can bring her in safely."

"I've noticed the police always think their best interest is everyone's best interest. Which is hilarious to me. Besides, I doubt she'd think it was in *her* best interest." Another sip of tea. "In fact, I'm pretty sure she knows her best interest would be if you'd all leave her alone and stop stalking her like criminals yourselves."

"Watch your mouth," Art snapped.

What happened next startled Lue and Mercy into reaching for their guns, though Art remained in his chair with hands folded. The woman's head snapped sharply to the right, she bared her teeth, and her fist came down two inches from his folded hand.

"You're a little young to be minding my manners, Muscles!"

Art stared at her, and she stared back. He could not shake the feeling that he had done something wrong here, but he resolved he'd be damned before backing down.

"Um, Art, do you want to go up front and check out their pie selection?" Lue suggested, leaving his gun in its holster.

"I'm fine here." He stared right through those blue irises, peering at what was beyond. It was she who looked away first.

"Next question."

"You have no idea where Ms. Scales is?" Mercy tried, lamely to Art's ears.

"I didn't say that."

"You won't reveal her location, then?"

"I didn't say I knew it to reveal."

"We don't have time for this . . . and I can't imagine you do," March said.

"Ms. Elmsmith." Lue tried a charming smile. Art had to admit: it felt like their best shot. "You agreed to meet with us. Surely you want to share *something* with us, or you would have refused in the first place."

This inspired a long sip of tea. "You have all three heard of dragons by now, I assume."

They nodded.

"And the Regiment."

Before Art could answer, Mercy frowned. "What does a regiment have to do with any of this?"

"*The* Regiment has everything to do with it. Far more than dragons."

"Oh, good. It would be a shame to worry *just* about dragons."

Elmsmith went on as if Lue hadn't spoken. "In fact, if the Regiment were not here in Minnesota, you would have no investigation at all. Ms. Scales would mean nothing to you. Susan Elmsmith would never have visited the Saint George's facility, which would still be standing. Like my hometown, and my father. Remove the Regiment, and you solve the problem."

Art remained passive and Mercy sighed, but Lue leaned in. "Tell us more about this Regiment."

"It's a specially trained cadre of soldiers—"

"You mean beaststalkers. We've heard of those. Gifted athletes with weapons training involving lots of swords and bows and dead dragons."

"Yes, but more so. There's schooling to become a beaststalker. Above and beyond that, a select few gain the notice of certain authorities. They enter the Regiment, and receive special preparation."

"Preparation for . . . ?"

Susan raised her tea at Mercy. "You're seriously not going to break in here and tell your colleagues what you are? What you do?"

Art watched Mercy carefully. The woman shrugged. "Ms. Elmsmith, I will gladly tell you and my colleagues what I am. I am a special agent for the Federal Bureau of Investigation. My office is in Minneapolis, which means I investigate federal crimes across a broad swath of the upper Midwest. My most recent case is a string of murders tied together with some circumstantial evidence. If you require my job description and/or salary, you can find it through the Freedom of Information Act . . ."

"Anyway," Susan said with a roll of her eyes. "Members of the Regiment don't just kill things as a hobby after they come home from their regular job. Killing things *is* their regular job. Regiment agents are specialists in search-and-destroy missions. They tend to be better armed than your traditional beaststalker. They're not afraid to use guns, even though it still seems counterintuitive to fight fire-breathers with explosives, but what do I know? As Regiment ranks have grown, we've heard of some agents specializing less on destruction, and more in fields like infiltration, security, interrogation, or even public relations." She jerked her thumb at Mercy. "Maybe she's one of those PR gals."

Art saw Mercy flush. "Enough about the Regiment," he said. "Tell us about Evangelina Scales."

Susan gave him another look. "I imagine she's exactly where she wants to be. Somewhere you can't reach her, Detective McMahon. Somewhere being dragon is not a secret felony, where she can stretch her wings under a crescent moon, where she can hunt with the packs of newolves, where she can fall in love . . ."

Pushing back his chair, Art slapped the table. "I may look at those pies after all."

Lue held up a hand, distracted. "Hold on, Art. Ms. Elmsmith, you said a phrase in there . . . 'new wolves'?"

Susan looked tentative, as if she had slipped in giving more information than she had intended. "Newolves. One word. Sometimes we just call them 'wolves,' though it's easy to spot the differences."

"What is a . . . newolf, would that be singular?"

"Yes." She looked nervously at Mercy. "I'm not sure I should say any more about those."

Art hissed impatiently. "You obviously *want* to talk about them. Talk about them!"

Mercy rolled her eyes at Art. "I don't see how it's necessary to badger the woman about something as silly as wolves, Detective. Besides, if she doesn't want to share, I know enough to catch you and Lue up on the topic."

"Really?" Susan's eyes sparkled. "Educate them. I'd love to hear your take."

If Art was any judge, he would have guessed Mercy relished the chance both to contribute to the conversation, and keep Susan engaged. The topic was already boring to him, but he had no choice but to wait if he wanted breakfast.

"Newolves were once companions to dragons, though few now believe any exist. They used to live in and near a long-lost Minnesota town called Pinegrove, as well as several other dragon strongholds masquerading as 'real' towns."

"As opposed to holographic towns?" Susan asked politely, and was ignored.

"According to the few remaining beaststalkers who personally witnessed newolves—no one under sixty has ever reported seeing one, and not even those who have reported have any physical proof of their existence—these creatures had exceptional senses and reflexes, making them fine sentries."

"But what are they? Or *were* they?" Lue corrected himself, glancing at Art in apology for his interest.

Mercy shrugged. "As Ms. Elmsmith has suggested, they are most likely a type of wolf. Rumors abound: that *newolf* was a cross between a wolf and something bigger, like a bear; that *newolf* was rather like a werewolf, except the normal state was a wolf and only a crescent moon could bring out the human shape; that *newolf* is some sort of romantic myth based on two lovers who mated for life, despite the curses flung their way, including banishment to animal form; that *newolf* was a purposeful evolutionary experiment by dragons driven by godlike impulses; that *newolf* is really a shortened version of *neo-wolf* or *neo-evolutionary wolf* . . ."

"I've heard that one," Susan interrupted with a smile. "The neo-evolutionary thing. It formed part of my interrogations at Saint George's. You guys in the Regiment believe they can rapidly evolve, more quickly than anything has *ever* evolved, with significant mutations every one or two generations instead of the gradual process Darwin explains. They stand like humans, turn bulletproof, jump over cities . . . I love that explanation the best! It's a bird, it's a plane, it's a . . . newolf!"

Art slammed his coffee cup in disgust. "Enough! You're playing games with Special Agent March."

"And with Detective Vue; and with you, Detective McMahon," Susan said, stretching her arms over her head and yawning. "I know you're not going to bring me in. I know my capture and my escape was kept quiet, and any chance that my recapture might hit the press—and I assure you it would—can only complicate an investigation that is already confounding law enforcement. *How are these dragons dying?* you ask yourselves. *Why does Evangelina Scales keep chasing them? Where are the missing ones going?* All fascinating questions, and you all have better things to do with your time than process paperwork on poor little Susan Elmsmith, who's obviously not a dragon at all!

"So instead of wasting any more of your time," she continued, "I'll make the next step in your investigation easy for you: have an honest discussion with each other, about who you all really are."

They all looked at her, and at each other, each confused for different reasons.

"Look. Maybe none of you are as bad as I think you are. But I've seen a lot worse, going back to my teenaged years, from people I thought were good. Family, friends, authority figures. It all stemmed from dishonesty and keeping secrets. So hear me when I say: *until you have the guts to admit the truth to each other, no other truth will find you.*"

She got up, dropped a couple of bucks next to her tea glass, and left. Art, Lue, and Mercy watched her go, unsure of what to say to each other next.

CHAPTER 29

It took a new crime later that day, for them to begin truly talking to each other again.

Lue had begun wheedling for something he called "second breakfast" when they caught the squeal.

"Got to be, got to be," Lue chanted when they heard the dispatcher. Not that there were many options in a small town at this time of the year—the small children tucked away in small schools, the older children out of town in big schools. Still, he understood why Lue's chanting sounded more hopeful than anything else.

Art responded by wrenching the wheel to the left to beat the light. But Mercy, driving her own car this time, beat him anyway—by three full car lengths.

All three of them were quickly out of their cars and up the sidewalk. Art spotted Evangelina immediately, and a second shape in the distance. He went for Evangelina, barking orders he wasn't sure anyone else would truly understand.

As Lue would tell them later, it was a nightmarish replay of the Snapdragon scene . . . time enough for a glimpse of a large black shape, time enough to realize they were seeing enormous black wings, time enough to realize no one was going to catch her, time enough to feel adrenaline shift to gloom.

Art didn't care. Though Lue's lanky shape remained a few steps behind Art's stout sprint, Mercy stayed panting but abreast. They raced up the driveway, passing a fire hydrant and kicking up a blizzard of fallen leaves. The black shape reached the warped pine fence lining two sides of the backyard, curled, flexed, and began to leap.

"Freeze!" Mercy shouted, but Art saved his breath now. He lunged . . . the black shape got even wider . . . and then he smashed against the cedar fence ringing the (presumably dead) victim's yard.

The world actually went away for a moment, then came wavering back along with Mercy's, "Art? You all right? Hold up, let him get a breath. Art?"

He sat up, shook his head, coughed. Lue and Mercy were looking at him with concern; worse, there were at least half a dozen others on the scene by now.

"Dammit, dammit!" Lue was saying . . . shouting, really. "This rerun is getting old, boys and girls!"

"Not exactly a rerun," Art said, still trying to focus. "Did anyone go after the other one?"

"What other one—another dragon?"

That would be a big "no, we didn't, Art." "Not a dragon. Not that shape, anyway. Fast human. Was about thirty yards ahead of Evangelina. Probably male. About six foot four, wearing dark pants and Windbreaker. Minnesota Twins baseball cap, turned backward." He rubbed his forehead. The wooden fence had cracked, but not broken. Fortunately no one seemed to think anything of it—or assumed it had been already cracked.

Mercy was still breathing hard but put up her gun. She

made a motion and two patrol officers trotted past them and beyond the fence. "I doubt anyone can catch either of them now. We'll try. Geez, Art. You really committed on that jump."

She reached out and felt his forehead. There would be a lump there. He loved the feel of her fingertips on his brow, even though she was pressing too hard. The headache wanted to grow, but she kept it at bay.

After a few seconds, he realized what he was letting get away and batted her hand away.

"She's not that far," he said. "Let's go."

Mercy frowned. "You're in no shape to keep running, Art."

"Don't tell me what I can and cannot do." He got up dusted himself off, trying hard to keep his balance.

"Art, a footrace is not the way to go here," Lue suggested. "You made a door in a fence with your face. There are two patrol cars trying to cut them off a few blocks away. We can join them. There are plenty of officers here securing the scene. Come on." He took Art's arm, which was both annoying and welcome. "Let me drive."

That was a good enough compromise, and Art nodded.

Back in the car, Lue traveled a block or two before opening his mouth again. He kept searching out the driver's window as he did so, scrutinizing the alleys and backyards and copses they passed. "Hey, Art. You, uh. Said some weird stuff on your way through that yard. Nothing I could really make out. What were you saying?"

Art rubbed his temples. "I said, get the other perp."

"Really? Because I figure what you said would have sounded more like 'look over there, get the other perp' than what I heard."

"What did you hear?"

Lue didn't answer. Art didn't press.

Through radio contact, they felt Evangelina and the mysterious "other" slip away. No one was seeing anything.

Every report came back negative. They tightened the cordon and began searching door to door, but within thirty minutes it was clear to both of them: the net had holes in it, and both suspects had slipped through.

Not only that, whoever was back at the house was almost surely dead.

"We should go back there."

"Fine," Art answered listlessly. The pain from the fence bump was gone, but the headache remained. He cared about whoever was at the house, but he cared even more that Evangelina was gone, oncc again.

It's not fair. She shouldn't get away. Not after all this. Not after getting so close.

Next time, I won't let her. No matter what.

CHAPTER 30

Back at the crime scene—the Enrickson house, according to Lue's knowledge of the neighborhood—he and Lue passed two patrolmen, one of them vomiting, one of them with a gray green I-just-puked expression.

The public thought throwing up at crime scenes was such a shameful thing, that cops crept away to do it away from all eyes (and, one hoped, away from any critical evidence). The reality was, if a scene was bad enough to make men and women who scraped corpses off pavement throw up, you did what you could to comfort your fellow officers, even if it meant a shoulder pat while he or she advertised his or her stomach contents.

"Karl Enrickson was in Martin's network," Lue pointed out as they entered. "Young bachelor, lived alone."

Art paled as he looked around the kitchen. "Looks like he should have left town, too."

This was more horrendous than any previous scene—

here in Moorston, over in Bemidji, or anywhere in the files and photos Mercy had tacked up in the station war room.

First of all, the interior was in ruins. It looked as though the stove had exploded or there had been a severe microwave mishap. It was more than those appliances, however, and things hadn't just exploded. They had smashed . . . *been* smashed. They had been torn and shattered and destroyed. They had been wrecked and splintered and hammered. Some of them had been split and some of them had been wrenched and some of them had been set on fire.

Second was the smell. All of the things that had been ruined, gave off fumes as if they were still smoldering . . . which they probably were. Burnt plastic, wool, and hair were only the top notes in the odors assaulting Art's sensitive nasal passages.

Third—third!—was the gore. It was hard to believe it was only one body at first, but here was the proof: only one arm and leg over here, plus one leg over there, plus a second arm way over there, still only equaled one corpse. Karl Enrickson was spread from the kitchen down the hallway into a study, and—

Wait.

This victim wasn't male, he realized as he came to the eviscerated torso (and, a few feet away, the head). It was a female. Blonde. The head was still facedown; this scene was complex enough that everyone was waiting for photographs before touching anything.

"Art. Look." Lue was pointing to the lower torso, where the buttocks barely existed anymore. A flimsy fabric, probably the victim's underwear, was soaked in blood save for a small corner.

Three pastel unicorns seemed to be dancing away from the advancing blood.

"You don't suppose . . . ?"

Art looked more closely at one of the arms. The broken

hand was holding something shiny. He minced through two steps of gore and crouched down.

It was a small brass unicorn, with an incredibly long, shining, blood-flecked diamond horn.

"Lue."

"Yes?"

"I think we have a murder weapon here."

Lue maneuvered into a place where he could have a look. "You think Evangelina did all this"—he motioned around them, and then pointed at the unicorn—"with that?"

"No. Lue, maybe this isn't the murder weapon for this scene. Maybe it's the weapon for all the others."

"So. You think Pamela Pride was not here to, what, recruit a jogging partner?"

"Probably not invited at all."

Lue exhaled and gave a sickly smirk. "Whew. I guess I had a chance with her, after all."

"That's pretty awful, Lue."

"Cop humor, my friend. We laugh to avoid crying." His face did get more serious, now. "We should have seen this coming, Art. In fact, you suggested it when I said she was lying about her school. I blew that off."

Art saw where he was going immediately. "We can't be sure yet, Lue. We'll run tests. I might not be right."

"You'll be right. I can feel it."

"It doesn't matter. This is not your fault."

"It is. I thought she was a harmless attention grabber. I let her play me, even while I thought I was playing her. If I had been more objective, I could have stopped her before she killed Martin, and Mares, and the Hahn kid." He looked around in despair. "And absolutely before this."

Art stood up, stepped through the gore, and grabbed Lue by the collar. "Don't you dare," he hissed. "This is not your fault. I didn't see it coming either. And I have more reason to."

"What the hell does that mean?"

Flustered, Art let him go. "I know the type."

"You mean beaststalker."

"I mean Regiment."

"You think Pamela Pride was Regiment?"

"If I'm right, wouldn't it start to look like that?"

"So who killed her?"

"Isn't it obvious?" Art waved his hand, feeling as helpless as he ever had. "Evangelina did. Like Loxos at Saint George's. Just bloodier."

"What about the other guy—the one you saw running away ahead of her?"

"I don't know. With any luck, it was Karl Enrickson."

"Who was . . . a dragon?"

"Sure, why not? Lue, I don't know how many more answers I have."

"No, I get it. This is seriously screwed up, Art. Susan Elmsmith was trying to tell us that Special Agent March is Regiment. If Pamela Pride is Regiment, and so is Mercy: Art, *what if Mercy has something to do with all of this?*"

Art said nothing.

"Art. Look at me, man. My ex-wife, Nancy. Her name is on Thomas Martin's network list, if you know what I mean."

"Yeah. I figured."

"The last I saw her was a couple of days ago. She leaves calls unreturned, and no one I know has seen her. I want to believe she escaped, Art. But with a federal agent trailing her . . ."

"Oh, my God."

Mercy was standing by the kitchen door, staring in at the remains. Neither Art nor Lue had noticed her arrival, but Art didn't think she had overheard Lue. At least, he *hoped* she hadn't.

He tried not to notice her rebellious curls and pretty (yet professional) blouse, and the shape she made as she stepped gently into the bloody room.

"No luck on catching Evangelina or your second suspect," she updated them. "They're taking down the net. She got away again."

"Not exactly," Lue said. At Mercy's inquisitive look, he presented the room. "Does any of this look familiar to you, Agent March?"

It was a more aggressive tone than Art might have used—bordering on accusatory—but he couldn't blame the Moorston officer.

Mercy didn't seem to understand the tone herself, but she looked around anyway. Her face was like glossy printer paper, and sweat began to dampen the curls closest to her cheeks. When she craned her neck to examine the hallway, she quickly withdrew.

"I'm not . . . excuse me." She took a stumbling few steps back out the porch door, leaned on a railing outside, and took several deep, steadying breaths.

Art and Lue looked at each other. *Not exactly conclusive.* They both had felt the same way, and some officers were still outside recovering themselves.

Thus began a long afternoon, and all three of them stayed at the crime scene—partly because they wanted to learn everything in real time, Art knew, but also to keep an eye on one another.

He was actually glad for the sedate excitement that came with processing a crime scene. There were other eyes here besides his own; other people looking, and being careful about what they showed on their faces. That was always a good thing and, right now, was a wonderful thing. Because even with all the cops and techs, Art felt exposed, stared at. He almost wished Mercy *had* thrown up . . . it would have been yet something else for everyone to look at.

It wasn't just the gore. It wasn't the square footage, which was admittedly impressive for a nonvehicular homicide. It was the sheer malevolence of the scene, a sort of gloating *I . . . got . . . youuuu.* There was no attempt to hide anything, to misdirect, to cloak in shadow.

He had never seen this from Evangelina before. It was terrifying, and the last thing he wanted to show the other cops was how terrified he was.

"So anyway . . ." Mercy said, taking a careful step toward him. They were almost beneath what was left of the living room ceiling fan, now hanging by a bare wire with all blades broken off. "You look unusually pensive."

He tried to smile at her but knew it came off as fake. "There's a lot here to think about."

"Yeah, what a mess," she whispered sympathetically.

"Lue figures you might have known Ms. Pride." He didn't know any other way to put it.

Her reaction was satisfying, either in that the idea took her aback or she was a phenomenally good actress. "No. That name is new to me. Though the face over there isn't exactly recognizable. If it turns out I know the face under a different name, I'll happily speak up." She bit her lip. "Let me guess. You both figure Ms. Pride for the other crimes in Moorston, and maybe more?You say to yourselves, what kind of sick person would do this? And you hear about this thing called the Regiment, and you listen to Susan Elmsmith talking about the Regiment, and you say to yourselves: hey, maybe Mercy March is Regiment. And then you figure: maybe Mercy has a room full of stuffed unicorns at the AmericInn, and crazy unicorn panties, and a brass unicorn in that big briefcase of hers. Am I close?"

"Yes."

She looked around. Since the body parts were in the kitchen and hallway, most of the officers and techs still on scene were out of eyesight, and the two or three they could see were busy examining evidence and consulting with each other. She turned slightly and pulled her suit jacket up and her pants down a bit.

"See? Normal underwear."

He coughed. "Ms. Pride's neurosis was likely singular."

"Likely enough. Plus, I've done a lot of thinking about the dangers in my job, and what kind of underwear I want the coroner to see. So we're back where we started. I could be deranged, but in a different way."

"I don't think you're deranged."

She smiled genuinely. "You're sweet. Look, lingerie aside, I'm not going to be able to convince you what I am or am not, here in this house. Or in a day. And what I am or am not part of, doesn't matter as much as who I am and what I do. My honest feelings, my honest actions, right?"

He nodded.

"I'm sure you want to be judged the same way, right?"

He nodded again.

"Then I swear to you: you have nothing to fear from me. I am not involved in this crime, save as the principal investigator. I want to find out who's murdering people, and I want to stop that person."

"Maybe Evangelina just did."

Mercy snorted. "Pamela Pride did not destroy half of the Saint George's Medical Facility and kill Professor Loxos."

"Separate crimes, separate suspects, separate motives."

"And so is this crime, and if nothing else, Evanglina is still a suspect in her first murder, if you really want to be that naïve. Look, Detective: we can parse this all night long, and we probably will. I want you to be as sure of me, as I am of you."

"And how sure is that?"

She chuckled, and the color returned to her face for the first time since she had entered from the kitchen porch. "Not one hundred percent. But willing to learn."

Four Years Ago

"Everything is going to change soon."

Silence.

"When I was a kid this place terrified me. I think it goes back to a game of hide-and-seek that went kinda wrong."

Silence, broken by the rumble of thunder.

"Do you remember that day?"

She didn't expect he would. She wasn't even sure he had been there. But that didn't matter: he was here now.

It was going to rain. It was going to storm, which was even better. Evangelina loved the way the air felt before a storm, the way her body seemed almost in tune with nature's bitchiness. The crack of lightning could have come from her mind's core.

Outside, it began to sprinkle, and the wind picked up. It wasn't yet raining hard enough to hear inside the barn.

"We can't stay here forever, you know. We're hours from home." She turned to look at the boy who'd been standing

behind her all this time. He had followed her when she'd flown to the barn, had been right behind her as she checked the outbuildings and slipped past the grain silos into the barn. He'd felt no more than one big step away the entire time . . . the reach of someone's arms.

To put it another way, as Aunt Susan would have said, he was only a hug away.

"Home," he repeated, and she expected him to keep going, but he didn't.

"They'll be expecting us."

"But this *is home," he said. "Or it was, long ago. Wasn't it? Why not stay?"*

"We can't stay." She felt her irises swirl, the way they did when she looked at him and only him. She knew he would lose himself in them. "Not for long, anyway."

She reached out. He came to her at once: yes! He had been a hug away. And now he was not. Aunt Susan, so wise when not being a wiseass. It was a quality she admired.

Evangelina smiled down at this man, who was older than her but still felt so young. His sculpted flesh trembled beneath her fingertips.

"Everything will change," she said again, and sighed.

He shook his head. "I love you. Nothing will change that. Ever. No matter where you go, I will follow."

Pretty words. Almost stalkerlike. But pretty.

She was neither cruel nor a liar, so she kept her thoughts to herself and instead held the boy's hand. Her fingers slid down to his wrist and felt the slow steady beat of his pulse.

"I believe you," she finally said, and kissed that part of his wrist, and felt his heart on her lips.

CHAPTER 31

"Okay, boys." They were back in their Suds Bucket booth. None of them had ordered food, but tea and juice was enough of an order to keep the waitstaff at bay. Besides, it was late afternoon, so the shop was deserted. Mercy looked at Art and Lue expectantly. "What do we think happened here today?"

Lue, whose concerns about Mercy Art knew had not subsided, chose his words well. "The picture changed dramatically, Agent March."

"How so?"

"Well." He sipped his tea. "We learned the difference between a crime scene Pamela Pride leaves, and a crime scene Evangelina Scales leaves."

"That's a bit of a jump, Detective. I'm surprised you'd rush so quickly to conclusions. The same murderer can use different tactics in different scenes."

"Is it your position that Evangelina Scales borrowed

Pamela Pride's supersharp brass unicorn for a few days, before returning it in spectacular fashion today?"

"Of course not. I'm warning us against sloppy logic. There's a much simpler explanation."

"Which is?"

"Evangelina Scales and Pamela Pride are collaborators."

Lue didn't respond, and Art mulled that over. "It fits most of the facts we've seen so far," he admitted. "Two suspects appear at most of the Minnesota scenes."

"And elsewhere," Mercy added. "I had the Minneapolis office send agents out to recheck those crime scenes in other states. We've only heard back from a couple, but they did indeed find those parallel scrapes on the exterior of each house. It was like Pamela or Evangelina was marking the house before entering it and killing the victims."

Art continued. "One could be lookout, the other the killer."

Lue rubbed his chin. "Hmmmph. But then, why the fighting? We saw it before today, too—the blood spatters at the Martin residence, and fabric tears. I imagine we'll find out those samples match up with Pamela."

"Criminals fight each other all the time. Dividing spoils, petty jealously, suddenly divergent goals . . ."

"I can think of another explanation," Lue offered. "Evangelina is innocent of the crimes Pamela Pride committed."

Mercy couldn't hide a snicker. "Then why be at each crime scene?"

He shrugged. "She could be a stalker. She could be trying to learn what Pamela's up to. She could even be trying to stop her."

"Stop her?" Art interjected bitterly. "If so, she's done a lousy job of it."

"Okay, I can see my theory is a minority opinion. Give it time. We should track how many people get their throats cut under mysterious circumstances, in Moorston or anywhere else, over the next few days."

Mercy gulped some ice from her glass and began chewing. "I suspect this won't be the last murder, Detective . . ."

"Not if the Regiment has another Pamela Pride to spare."

The ice crunched. "What are you implying?"

"Nothing."

She stiffened. "Seldom has *nothing* so clearly meant *everything*." She swirled the remaining ice in her mouth, swallowed, and tried to relax. "Okay, I'm going to try to stop channeling my mother here and approach this in a more friendly manner."

"You could try showing him your underwear," Art suggested.

"Brilliant. Thanks for that, Detective Vue. Lue. Have I done or said anything that makes you believe I am part of a murderous regime?"

He raised his glass. "The week is young."

"You can't be serious. If you have suspicions about me, you should report me to my superiors." She rifled through her purse. "I'll give you the direct line to Director Jorstad at the Minneapolis branch; he's my supervisor and would want to know if—"

"Ah, but if the Regiment exists, then he would be part of it as well."

"Detective, this is ridiculous. There is no defense against a speculative accusation regarding a supersecret organization of dragon killers. I could suddenly pronounce that you and your Chief Smiling Bear are the devious kingpins of a secret circle of vampires, and that Pamela Pride was your newest, slightly off-kilter recruit. You would have no way to defend yourself, since I have what you would consider overwhelming proof: guilt by association."

"What association?"

"According to Detective McMahon, you had a thing for her. Male fantasies being what they are, I'd guess today wouldn't be the first day you've thought about her in that unicorn underwear. Maybe you've even *seen* them before."

Speechless, Lue glared at Art, who returned an apologetic look. "I never really said I had a *thing* for her . . ."

"Look, you two: all three of us have trust issues. We're not being entirely forthcoming with each other. I can accept that if you can. Here's what I know: I'm your friend, here. And I think of you as *my* friends. I don't let friends down." She extended her hand. "Shake on it?"

Lue cracked a grin as he took her hand. "Most murderers would not consider a handshake a binding contract."

"I guess we're both screwed, then. Okay, where were we—we had two theories about Evangelina Scales. I'll respect yours if you respect mine."

"Fair enough. We can agree, I think, that Evangelina is a suspect for today's murder. We can further agree that Pamela Pride is at least a suspected collaborator in the scenes prior to today."

"Agreed."

Art relaxed. It surprised him how much he wanted Lue and Mercy to get along. *This is hard enough.*

"So, remaining questions," Lue continued. "First, what motive might Evangelina have had to kill Pamela today? Second and obviously related, what was their true relationship? Third, if we think the murders might continue, how can we stop them?"

"Last question first," Art suggested. "We finish our work on social networks. Warn the rest."

"If any are even left," Lue agreed. "Okay, we can get to work on that today. What about the Pamela-Evangelina relationship?"

"It will help to learn what Pamela *is*. That is, dragon or not."

"Yes. And today's scene will probably have more surprises for us, which may detail a motive. If she has always wanted to kill Pamela, we would have to figure out why she waited so long."

"It could be she finally had her chance," Art suggested.

"And if she finally decided to kill her today . . . well, same question, why the long wait?"

"And it may have the same answer."

"Fair enough."

Their waitress sitting at another booth, tossed them a bored "you okay?" glance, and they all nodded. Her phone buzzed, and the willowy blonde nearly dropped it, clutched it, and breathed, "So did you like see a dead body over there or anything like really gross?" into it, in the same two seconds.

They all rolled their eyes, and Mercy continued. "I already have the FBI checking records for a Pamela Pride. Of course, she could have changed her name: but if she doesn't come up FBI or dragon, then what?"

"She could still be Regiment," Lue insisted.

Mercy tried to laugh off the suggestion. "Right. The Regiment: we're here, we're there, we're everywhere." She pointed her finger at Lue and croaked, "*We're you!*"

"Yes," Lue said. "I would love more chai."

The waitress was standing over them, dark eyes sparkling, nervously wiping both hands on a towel, cell phone nowhere in sight. "You guys hear? Someone like got killed all *over* the place!"

"We did hear." Mercy sighed.

"All over the place," Lue said, nodding. "She sure did."

CHAPTER 32

Art approached his motel door. The small wooden (mostly) building was on the edge of the small town, which he appreciated for obvious reasons. The property manager, whom Lue had noticed when they had been here together to get the Bemidji files, generally made little noise and no demands. Better: he noticed everything, and never asked questions.

It shouldn't have been so difficult to work the lock and open the door, recently painted lizard (ha) green. Art knew he lived in a world of miracles, many of them right under his nose. And today he was too damned tired to care about any of them.

"Detective McMahon?"

"Yes." A silly question, but the old man valued politeness.

Pushing off the wall where he had been leaning, the manager pulled his cane out from behind his back with fingers so gnarled they were like bent old branches. Then he picked up a small backpack, slung it over his shoulder, and tapped the cane in front of him as he approached. Art never stopped being amazed the man could zip his fly, never mind tie flies for local anglers and pick up dimes in dark corners. "Careful. That lock still sticks a bit."

As he said this, Art finally got it to turn and the door swung open. He squinted in the near gloom, fumbled for a light switch, then heard the *click* as the lamps went on.

"I'll finally get to fixing that tomorrow, if you like."

"Thanks."

"You mind if I join you? I could use some company."

"Come on in."

The old man stretched out a hand, found the chair situated by the coffee table near the bed, slid it around, and eased into it. "Art. Take a close look around. Make sure you have everything you left here."

"Why?"

"I heard some odd noises close by your place while you were out."

"Can you be more specific?"

"Not much. I was in the bathroom by the office for a few minutes. When I came out, I heard people leaving, doors closing—a bit too much going on to be sure. I'm pretty sure they were leaving this room."

Art took a few moments to walk around and scan the room, including the closets and bathroom. When he was done, he sat down in the other chair next to the coffee table. "Everything looks all right, Remy."

Remy shrugged. "If you say so."

The old man reached down into the backpack he had dropped by the chair, rummaged, then whipped out a gorgeous, intricate baby's blanket crocheted in cool blues and yellows. He produced a crochet hook, like a magician yanking a rabbit out of a hat, and went back to work as he talked.

"Ms. Kennealy tells me the due date is upon us."

"She and her daughter are lucky to know you. This will be her first grandchild, yes?" Ms. Kennealy, like many of the older women in town, adored Remy.

"Indeed. They've already asked me to set aside time to babysit, for the occasional Sunday afternoon. I told them I thought I could do two or three Sundays if the kid comes right away . . . I'm glad the Anderson and Schultz kids are growing old enough not to need me much anymore."

"Quite the double life," Art complimented. "A motel manager *and* a day care provider."

Remy pursed his lips. "Sticking around that local cop has sharpened your sense of irony. Good for you." A few loops later, he continued. "I can't hang around this place and keep an eye out for everything and everybody, Art. My ma, please God she rests, had a saying: 'weave your own destiny.' Mine won't stay in Moorston for much longer, I'm afraid."

"I understand."

"I hope the Kennealys, Andersons, and Schultzes do as well. I love those babies. I think they love me, too. I can always tell when they're gonna cry, even before the baby does. There ain't a jar of baby food I can't sell to one of those kids, with enough time and patience. That reminds me, Ms. Anderson came by with a pumpkin pie. I can't stand pumpkin pies; you can come by the office if you want it for yourself."

"Thanks. Perhaps tomorrow."

Remy kept shaking his head. "Poor babies. Can't help but think of them as my own."

"They will have to make their way without you."

"Yup, I guess it's a lesson we all learn. Say, what do you make of that March girl?"

The question caught Art by surprise, and Remy laughed. "Ah, you think I don't catch on to things like that. Mercy March is a name we are all getting to know, Art. I have to say I haven't yet come to a judgment on her, myself. I'd value your opinion."

"She is what she is."

Remy licked his lips, still smiling. "Ah, so she is. That's what has so many people worried. But then, you are what you are—and look at what you overcame. Look at the two of us, sitting here, talking to each other as if we're best friends. As if we're both *people*. That couldn't have happened, I'll guess, years ago."

"You're probably right."

"Of course I'm right. Right as I am when I claim this blanket I'm knitting is blue and yellow. Don't need to see in the conventional sense, to know that."

Art cleared his throat. "Mercy March has sound principles."

"Such as?"

"Honesty. Patience. Humor."

"That's a good start. Interesting, that those would be the qualities that attract you . . . now."

That made Art frown. "What do you mean by that?" he growled.

"You know what I mean. Now don't take offense. Young pups like you are always hot to argue, but I'm just an old man and I don't intend any harm. I think Mercy might make for a good chapter, in the story you weave. Maybe even play a role in your destiny."

"We're a long way away from that."

"Closer than you'll admit to me tonight, I'll bet."

"I haven't known her a full week."

"Love works in strange ways."

The word *love* untwisted something inside Art, something that had felt twisted since the first moment he had spotted Special Agent March at the Moorston Police Station. What was it he had felt that morning—was it love?

It had felt more like guilt.

Maybe it shouldn't.

"Remy," he said, and then he stopped.

"Yes?"

"Do you think she would be okay with it?"

"She? You mean—"

"You know who I mean."

Remy's chuckle made the knitting needles dance up and down. Then he turned more serious. "Forgive me, Art. I don't mean to hurt you. The sad truth is, she's gone. It doesn't matter what she'd think."

"Don't talk like that!"

"You asked my opinion. I'm sorry for your loss, Art. It's time to move on."

"You've said that before."

"And I've asked you before: why are you even here? I figure the BCA doesn't even know you're here. This is about *you*, not her or Mercy or anyone else. So I ask again: why are you here, Arthur McMahon? Why do you hunt Evangelina Scales? Is it a search for closure? Some sort of hope to settle a score?"

"I still don't have an answer."

"Well, you should try to find one. You can't start a new chapter without finishing the old one."

"You and your metaphors. You'd like Detective Vue."

"I'm sure I would. Say, is that rain I hear outside? Heck, that's the fourth time this week . . ."

They sat and talked like that, with Remy knitting away in his chair while Art sat across from him. He got up only to open the window and let the cool air and sounds of raindrops in. A healthy, meaty fragrance from the Happy Chef across the highway edged its way into the room, but Art remained patient.

About an hour later, Remy finally sighed and put the knitting back in his backpack. "Well, it's good to see you again, Art. In a manner of speaking. Wake-up call same time tomorrow morning?"

"Please." He didn't need it, but he knew Remy would call anyway.

"All right then. No, don't get up. I can show myself out. Don't forget to bolt and chain the door, though. No telling what's creeping around out there." He chuckled at his own remark as he tapped his cane, pulled his pack on his shoulder, and shut the door behind him.

Art listened to the cane and Remy's steps as they faded down the walk. Once the office door had opened and closed in the distance, he rose from his chair, walked across the room, and went back into the bathroom. Whoever had left the message had been clever enough to know that Remy might try to come in the room and find a paper or envelope; instead, they had written the message directly on the mirror. Art would have thought the move clever enough for Remy himself; but he didn't suppose the man carried lipstick in that backpack of his.

The handwriting was vaguely familiar, in a bold script:

She will need you, before the end.

He stared at the words for some time, listening to the rain, feeling the autumn chill, and thinking of Mercy.

If only the woman would admit she was Regiment!

INTERLUDE

Tonight

The rain made very little difference to her, as she watched.

In fact, Evangelina had learned long ago that she enjoyed inclement weather—and the more unusual, the better.

Mom had told her she was born in a gentle snow under an aurora borealis. It was more complicated than that, of course: having a spider in your bloodline never made things easy. Her biological mother had died that night, and her mom had taken over from there. Elizabeth was a faithful parent, learning as much about arachnid heritage as she could, to stay true to what Evangelina was. That was hard, given how few arachnids there were left in the world.

The dragon half—from her deceased father—well, that was easier to pick up. Dragons weren't numerous, to be sure: but there were enough of them to make a go of saving them from extinction.

Extinction due to natural causes would be hard enough

to avoid, for any species that didn't thrive on skyscrapers and automobiles and sewage.

Extinction due to Regiment causes, was even harder. That's where Evangelina came in.

She thought back to her teenaged years—if it seemed like yesterday, that's because it almost was. She had barely turned adult when her sister had turned to her for help.

"I wanted you to have your childhood," her sister had told her. "I never really got to finish that, and I wish I had. I can't wait any longer, to ask you for your help."

"What do you need?" Evangelina had asked eagerly. She would have done anything for her sister.

*"I can't be everywhere at once. Only I can do what I'm doing, to create and protect a new world for our people. I can't simultaneously stop the Regiment out in this world. They're murdering us, Vange. Soon there won't be enough of us left, to bother with a new home. We—*you*—have to save those who are left."*

"How?"

"You will bring them to us, Vange. You will go out and find them—Mom and Susan have done lots of that work already, so they can point you in the right direction—and then when you have them, you'll tell them we're starting over. They'll come with you, Vange."

"How do you know? What if they say no?"

"They won't. When you come, they will follow you. You'll bring them to the entry point. Then you'll go find more. You'll be their angel, protecting them and delivering them. Only you can do it, Vange. Only you. Will you?"

It had been such a thrill to hear those words. She had accepted.

Evangelina tried to recapture that feeling, as she lay in the copse of maples with raindrops splattering off her wings and crest. It wasn't the rain that depressed her. It was everything that had followed that single decisive moment. The years since had been few, but they felt horribly, painfully long. Saving their people had cost her innocence, youth, and even love. She had succeeded more than she had failed, but the failures hung heavy on her.

Worst of all had been today, which she had thought would be her best day. Killing the Regiment assassin had been traumatic for her, far more than the horror at Saint George's. That had been bad enough, killing in the midst of a rescue mission where eliminating Collin Loxos had been a necessary evil, cleanly executed.

This, however, had gone very differently. She had gorged herself on the violence, pummeled her opponent into submission, and could have left it at a single dismembered arm. Her enemy had clung to the stump, defenseless, sobbing, and begged for mercy.

Instead, Evangelina had unleashed everything within her that hated the Regiment, that despised what they had done, and that resented the cost to herself. She had torn and slashed, and the more she had, the better she felt.

She had been raised to learn that revenge never really made a person feel better. What then, did it say about herself, that she felt so good during and after? What did it say about her, that she was hoping the Regiment would send another assassin, before it was all over?

"It will be over soon," her mother had told her about a month ago. "There are only a few left to save. We will keep the way open for you. When you return, it will all be over. No one will need to fight them ever again."

It was a lovely thought. Evangelina hoped it was true. It still would not save her: what she had lost because she said "yes" to her sister, she would never get back.

No love.

She still would not have made any other decision.

PART THREE

Mercy

CHAPTER 33

When Mercy March woke up the next morning, her first act was to warm up the laptop. She pulled on her blouse, went into the bathroom to fix her hair, freshened her makeup, spotted the time, and hurriedly sat down at the small desk near the television to call up her videoconferencing application.

The grainy image on the other end was of her living room at home—well, the only place she ever felt like calling home, anyway. Leaving Woolstone was probably the best decision she ever made, but the place still haunted her.

She could see the built-in bookshelves in back, still crammed with the same tomes and sheaves of papers that had been there when she was a teenager. It was maybe a little messier now; one of her chores had been to tidy up this room after her mother's research.

The computer was set up on the coffee table, she could tell. The camera looked up slightly at two overstuffed chairs. One of them was occupied.

"Hi, Dad."

A few moments later, his smile registered. "Hey, Chip."

She tried to hide her irritation at the nickname. "Where's Mom?"

"In the kitchen." He looked behind him and shouted, "Val, she's on."

"Finally, I've a lecture in an hour." Mercy straightened in her seat as her mother's elegant shape entered the camera's view. Valera (never ever ever call her Valerie) March was dressed in a stunning tweed suit, and her auburn hair had been professionally done. She balanced her tea on her lap and gave the camera a perfunctory smile before casting a worried look at her husband. "Honestly, Michael, this is never as easy as you claim it's going to be."

"Lecture in an hour?" Mercy asked, confused. "It's Saturday."

"Yes, well, some of us don't get weekends off, dear. The Humanities Council at Oxford set this up; the Chancellor's likely to be there." Each capital letter was well pronounced. Valera squinted at the screen. "Where *are* you, Picklechip?"

She winced again. *"Chip" was better.* "AmericInn in Moorston, Minnesota."

A mixture of disdain and pity scrunched her mother's face. Her father, meanwhile, brightened.

"Hey! You're not too far from where—"

"We're all well versed in geography, Michael." Val took a gulp of tea. She even gulped elegantly. "It takes twenty-five minutes to get to Oxford and they want me there fifteen early, so let's skip the sightseeing, shall we? You're in Moorston. I've heard nothing from anyone else. And there's no monster tied up on the hotel bed behind you. So the case can't be going very well, Picklechip, can it?"

"You know I can't talk about an investigation, Mom." Mercy immediately regretted the words.

Val's eyes widened. "Oh, goodness, I'm sorry dear, I

forgot my place. I didn't realize what you did was so exclusive, you couldn't even clue in a Regiment Proctor. Why, without these wonderful video chats, for which you are consistently late . . ."

"I was, like, thirty seconds late."

"Late is binary; you either are, or you aren't. And you were. But back to your charming rules . . .

"*My* charming rules?"

". . . I don't know *what* I would do for information, if you kept your mouth shut about an ongoing investigation. What connections could I possibly exploit, to determine the status of the most important mission our organization has undertaken in decades? Hold off, I've a memory. I could call Director William Jorstad, your boss. Bill, after all, took my call when I was first researching internships for an energetic but slightly dim teenaged daughter some years ago . . ."

"I got this job *myself*," Mercy hissed, standing up and leaning toward the laptop camera. "Like I impressed him on that internship *myself*, and got into academy *myself*, and I graduated top of the academy class *myself* . . ."

"Trousers, dear."

Mercy looked down at her bare legs and muttered. "Flip a dip . . ."

"Or perhaps that's how you go to work, in which case I should probably give you more credit for your career advancement than myself."

"Charming, Mom. Call me an office whore, in front of Dad no less."

Her father cleared his throat. "I don't see how doing it behind my back would make it any better."

She gave him a wan, ungrateful smile.

"Val, I know you're nervous, but take it easy on—"

"Stay out of this, Michael. Special Agent March here was just about to cover her privates, and then tell me off with how professional and secret her work is."

Mercy sat down again, feeling blood rush to her face. What was it her father told her once? *Your mother always finds the right words to say, even for the exactly wrong reasons.*

She considered faking a bad connection, but that would just postpone this unpleasantness for a day. She reminded herself why she was out here, pantless in Moorston, chasing after a tireless killer: *unfailing courage, everlasting honor, swift justice*. It was a corny motto, like all mottos were. But she had bought into it, from the moment Director Jorstad had taken her under his wing.

She sighed. "Vue has doubts about Evangelina."

"No one cares what a local police officer thinks."

"McMahon may agree with him."

"Well." Val sat back slightly. "We might care about that, if anyone even knew who this McMahon was or where he came from. Set that aside. What do *you* think, Picklechip?"

Mercy bit her lip. "A woman named Pamela Pride was found murdered at a residence not her own. There's plausible evidence that she's been committing, or collaborating on, some or all of these crimes. Actually, Mom, I'm surprised you didn't already know that."

Val looked faintly taken aback. "And from whom would I learn such information?"

"Well, maybe 'Bill' would have let you in on that."

"Watch your tone, young lady. Bill knows better than to call too early on a Saturday morning. So this woman . . . Pamela . . . ?"

"Pride."

"Yes, well, what do we know about her? Is she another dragon?"

"Not confirmed."

"Well, there you go. The investigation is moving at light speed. At this rate, Evangelina Scales will be a distant comet before anyone assembles enough evidence, courage, and wherewithal to bring her in."

"That's not fair, Mom . . ."

"Did you join the FBI for the fairness of it all? Did you accept admittance into the Regiment ranks for the fairness of it all? Do your job, dear, and finish this hunt. Then you will find that things are perfectly fair, after all."

Mercy refrained from wiping her eyes, and willed her tear ducts to close.

Her father waited for the pause to last, and then reentered the conversation. "So, Chip, are you still liking Minnesota?"

Mercy let out a mirthless burst of laughter. "Yeah, Dad, I like it fine. I have an apartment in Minneapolis overlooking the river, the job Mom thinks she lined up for me is great, I just met a great guy, blah blah blah. Is that what you want to hear?" She simmered at the sight of the two of them, sitting separately in chairs, close yet separate, hard to say which one she hated more.

He shrugged. "I want to hear that you're happy, if that's the truth."

"Oh, the truth. Well, the truth is: I'm usually happier before these chats, than afterward. Good luck with your lecture, Mom."

"Thanks, Pickle—"

Mercy slammed the laptop shut.

CHAPTER 34

"He is not one of them."

"Huh?" Mercy's attention did not break from the computer screen that loomed beyond the rim of her water bottle.

She was analyzing the evidentiary reports coming in from the Enrickson scene . . . but thinking of her mother's Oxford lecture. Which would be brilliant, of course. Groundbreaking and dazzling. Dozens would rush the platform, men and women, all equally besotted, and her mother would handle them all like iced royalty, cool and majestic. Really, it was so—

"Art. His DNA came up clean for dragon, and clean for arachnid."

Mercy turned to face Lue now. The man held a sheaf of papers out, grinning proudly like a kid with an A+ on his science project. "Of course Art's not a spider or a lizard," she said patiently. "I knew that the moment I saw him. You should have, too."

"You have to admit—a Spider-Art would look pretty cool." He held up another piece of paper. "Look, I did a conceptual drawing. Still not convinced?"

She swallowed, feeling the heat rise through her neck and cheeks. Why was she getting so upset at him? "Lue, weren't you listening at the Suds Bucket yesterday? I might as well ask if you have the wrong DNA. Would you like it if I went behind your back and ran a few tests?"

Lue shrugged and held up another sheath. "I did it for you. Chief actually ran it herself, for objectivity."

"That's not the point, Detective." Now Mercy could feel crimson seeping around the freckles on her nose and forehead, for the second time today. She stood up, briefly checked herself for pants (whew!), and entertained tossing her water into Lue's face and all his damned paperwork. "We're a team. We trust one another. That's how this is going to work."

"Okay, but before we enter Mercytopia, where everyone is super and secrets are of no consequence . . ."

She ground her teeth together so hard, she almost felt a molar crack. "Mercytopia?!"

". . . I want to point out that they did find something strange in the DNA. It will take some time to . . ."

Mercy sighed and rubbed her forehead. "Beaststalker."

Lue's head jerked forward, his eyes widening. "Beaststalker?"

"Don't act so surprised, Detective. You saw him at the scene . . . he should have left his brains all over that fence. Instead he was out for less than a second and then right back on his feet. Does Art strike you as the sort of man you'd like to engage in hand-to-hand combat?"

"I guess not."

"When under stress, has he breathed fire, or spun any webs, or done anything else that causes you worry?"

Lue paused, and Mercy wished momentarily that she could see into his brain. "No."

"So put it together: trained law enforcement, complicated DNA, comfortable with hands-on combat, relentless focus on a killing monster . . . you'll get the same results from me, Detective. In fact, you probably already have."

"You know local law enforcement cannot access DNA files for FBI agents."

Mercy shrugged and held out her arm. "Take a sample. Run it."

After what appeared to be a pause of temptation, he sighed and put down his papers. "Okay, I see your point. We all trust each other, blah blah blah. Your naïveté will be the end of you, Agent March. I cannot believe Art the Beaststalker likes you."

"He does? Really? Why? What did he say?"

Lue stared at her. She shook herself and blinked. "Wow. Junior high flashback. Sorry, Lue. Please ignore everything I just said."

"I usually do anyway," he assured her, amiably enough.

Her smart phone registered a new text. The number was blocked.

Special Agent March. We need to meet.

Intrigued, she showed Lue the message, and then typed back:

Who are you, and why meet?

The answer came almost immediately, as if they had anticipated her questions.

I have a message from Evangelina, and others. I want to look you in the eye as I deliver it. And for you to look in mine.

"Sounds creepy," Lue contributed when she showed him the message.

Where and when?

Lion's Park. Fifteen minutes.

"Get Art," she told Lue as she jumped to her feet. Her balance felt unsteady. *Should I call for backup? The person didn't say, "Come alone." Do they care?*

"Anyone else?"

"No."

CHAPTER 35

Lion's Park was not the worst park in Moorston, but it was not what Mercy (or anyone) would call attractive. It exuded the carelessness of a dwindling city parks-and-recreation budget, mixed with the dreams of low-income children that would struggle to come true. The park had more blacktop than greenery, and most kids, Lue told Mercy and Art, didn't like to play here. It was as though they sensed something bad had happened some time ago, and something bad could happen again with very little provocation.

Art and Lue gave the area a visual sweep, but Mercy did not bother. She could tell immediately who had called them here.

The woman was in her early sixties, and unlike most sixty-year-old women she made no attempt to hide her age. Rather she embraced it, which made her all the more beautiful.

Her shoulder-length white hair was probably blonde

once, as with so many Minnesotans. Her eyes were brilliant green, and her spine stayed straight as she rose from the park bench and strode toward them. Smiling was not how Mercy would put it, though the corners of the tall woman's mouth were slightly raised. She barely looked at the men, gaze fixed on Mercy as she extended a lean, gently wrinkled hand.

Negotiator, Mercy deduced immediately from the handshake. "I'm Special Agent Mercy March. This is Detective Lue Vue from the local police force, and Detective Art—"

"I know who you are, Agent March. Detective Lue. Detective McMahon." She nodded curtly at the other two. "I'm going to leave in sixty seconds, so I recommend you listen carefully. I have three messages for—"

"Excuse me, ma'am, but who are you?"

Mercy looked impatiently at Lue, as the woman continued. "Fifty-five seconds. I have three messages. First, Susan Elmsmith has nothing more to offer you. Stop harassing her."

"Harass?" Lue yelped. "That is rich."

"We have no further plans to call on Ms. Elmsmith, Ms. . . . ?"

"Good to know. Second, your investigative hunt is misdirected."

"Our what?"

"Your suspect in the series of murders that interests you so much is not trying to kill. She is trying to save."

"So who's the murderer?"

Mercy rolled her eyes, then instantly heard her mother's voice: *How worldly.* She made herself stop, then said, "Honestly, Lue, let her finish, and then we can . . ."

"If you want to know who's behind it, ask *her.*"

Mercy flushed at the woman's gesture. *What does she mean by that? How on earth would I know who's behind it, beyond the obvious suspect? And why would she—?*

"Third, you need to take a message back to your superiors in law enforcement—official and otherwise.

"Here it is: We get it. You don't like us. It was foolish of us to hope, I suppose, that Winoka could end up any way other than how it did. We've spent two decades in exile, and since we don't expect anything to get better anytime soon, we're going to part ways. You won't see us again. All you need to do is let us leave. No one else has to die."

Over Lue's and Art's silence: "That would seem to be up to Evangelina Scales," Mercy retorted. "She's the one who strewed Pamela Pride's innards all over the interior of the Enrickson house."

This earned her a familiar expression that hovered between maternal and disdainful. *Maybe she and my mom are in the same bridge club.* "Agent March, you're probably very bright, and you probably put up with a lot of crap from people who underestimate you."

"Aw, thanks."

A warmer smile this time, a real one. "I'm going to guess you're also one of the best field agents in the region, so assigning you would make sense to everyone, especially yourself. I'm also guessing at your most important quality: you don't ask tough questions—or at least, not big-picture questions."

"Thank you?"

"You're more of a sharp-on-the-details sort of gal, I suspect. That may get you into trouble someday, but right now you're impressionable, and your masters likely hope they can shape you in the right direction. Put it all together, and you're perfect for this assignment . . ."

"Wait a moment," Lue interrupted. "Winoka? Smoking cats, Winoka! You said Winoka back then, right? You come from there! Your picture was all over back then, you were the mayor—Elizabeth Georges, right?"

For the first time, the woman stopped paying attention to Mercy. "Detective Lue. My surname hasn't been Georges since I married my late husband."

"Elizabeth Georges Scales," Art filled in.

The woman bit her lip. "Your sixty seconds is up. Tell your masters, they win. You can all have your dragon-free world—though I suppose I can't guarantee we'll get to everyone. The few left behind will have to find an altogether different way."

"Ma'am, I'm afraid we can't let you leave." Mercy stepped back into the negotiator's field of vision. "Your probable relation to Evangelina Scales, and your obvious knowledge of her activities, suggests you have more information regarding this case. You need to come with us, please."

A big, warm, terrifying smile. "You are adorable."

"Agent March." Art cleared his throat. "Perhaps a business card."

"Are you kidding me? No, we do this by the book. An obvious link to our prime suspect walks up to us in the park, and you're suggesting we let her go with a phone number?"

"You're not 'letting me go.' I'm leaving."

Elizabeth turned and took two steps before Mercy caught her by the upper arm.

Elizabeth looked down at the hand on her arm and raised an eyebrow. "Okay, less adorable now . . ."

"Ma'am, I can bring you in on suspicion of aiding and abetting, if I have to. Let's not get violent."

Elizabeth laughed. "Not get violent? Oh, honey, you're working for the wrong people. I've been preaching that message for years, and of all the people who don't listen . . ."

Mercy felt her ears warm. "The FBI is not—"

"I'm not talking about the FBI and its majority of true patriots. I'm talking about the virulent strain of murderous contagion infecting its ranks, and the ranks of this country's otherwise honorable military. You know this plague as the Regiment, I believe. Take your hand off me."

"Ma'am, there's no such thing as the—"

"Take your hand off me."

Mercy felt Art's hand on her shoulder. "Take your hand off me!"

"Don't be foolish. There's no way she's alone—"

"Foolish?!" Mercy's warm feelings for Art iced over. "You've got a big mouth for someone who speaks in small sentences, mister . . ."

"Hey, Art, Mercy, everyone, how about we all calm down?"

Art glared at Lue. "Take your hand off me."

Whether it was the distraction of having the detectives interfere, or her own underestimation of this woman, Mercy suddenly felt movement and didn't react quickly enough.

The movement turned wretchedly dizzying. By the time her middle ear was done swirling, she was on the asphalt facedown with an arm twisted behind her back. Something whistled through the air, Art hit the ground with his hand grabbing something stuck in his neck, and then she heard Lue grunt.

"Ms. Georges Scales, you are assaulting an FBI agent. This is a—owww!"

Five seconds later, she was restrained in the middle of the park with her own handcuffs, disarmed with her firearm tossed casually to one side, her two partners unconscious several feet away, while the elderly woman who had taken her down grabbed her chin and squeezed.

"My elder daughter, her husband, and I are going to be a lot nicer to you than you or the Regiment would be in our place."

Mercy had a brief vision of her own mother, which she quickly pushed away. *What would she think of this? "Oh, Picklechip: you definitely don't want the suspect's relations to restrain you with your own cuffs. That's bad technique. You'll not get far, I fear . . ."*

"If you persist in your investigation of my younger daughter, I can't guarantee we'll be as considerate next time. Call it off, Agent. While you can."

She let go of Mercy's chin, then grabbed her scalp and smashed her nose into the pavement. Through the subsequent pain, blurry spots, and taste of blood, it was difficult for Mercy to discern if there ever was a daughter or son-in-law on the scene, or what route Elizabeth Georges Scales took as she left. Just the thought

. . . about this . . . she can never ever find out . . .

kept cycling through her brain.

A minute later, under the uncertain eyes of several civilian gawkers, Mercy saw Art come around. He hissed, sat up, dropped a needle from his hand, and assessed the scene.

"She had backup."

"Apparently. Find a girl a key?"

"Sorry I called you foolish," he said as he groggily searched the pavement.

"I'm sorry I was short with you. A few feet to the left . . . there, you see it."

He uncuffed her, and she immediately picked up her piece. Doing her best to ignore the gathering crowd, feeling her face flush hot with anger and humiliation, she motioned to Lue. "Did he get shot, too?"

"No. Something crept up on him." He pointed to the bruise on Lue's temple.

"I've heard they can do that, sometimes. Camouflage. Must have been her daughter, or son-in-law. So one snuck up on him, while the other had a bead on you from a distance. I didn't see anyone else around, so the shooter must have had cover." The images flashed through her brain and the words poured out of her mouth, but she could not shake the anger she felt. *She beat me. That old woman. And she never changed into anything else.*

Ow.

Those stories about Winoka—are they true?

Ow!

Art was looking around, farther away. "Tree line's one hundred yards away."

"Nice shot, to find your neck from there. Could have gone into your eye." Neither of them stated the other obvious fact: *it could have been a bullet.*

She was brought back to reality by the slow stream of blood that had now reached her chin and was dripping onto her front and shoes. Art reached into his corduroy jacket and handed her a handkerchief for her face.

"Thanks."

"You're welcome. We should leave."

Art scooped Lue into his arms, and they trotted toward the car.

CHAPTER 36

"Bad day yesterday, Picklechip?"

"I guess." Mercy squirmed uncomfortably; how could her mother always spot that? The pavement face-smash had barely left a mark, and Mercy had gotten up early specifically to cover the small scrape with makeup. She resolved to pop open a self-reflecting window on the video application next time, so she could analyze what her parents were seeing.

"Probably not much progress, then." Already, Val began to sound bored.

"Investigations take time," Michael insisted congenially, smiling at his wife. "Give her more than a few days, Val. She'll win yet."

"Dad, please." Mercy found his eternal optimism irritating. *Why is he even on these calls?* "I'm beginning to think there may be more than one explanation for these murders."

"Is that so." It wasn't a question. Val set her tea down on the coffee table, hard enough that Mercy flinched at the sound. "What other explanation have you arrived at that ties Evangelina Scales to each of the murder scenes?"

"That . . ." Mercy trailed off at the sight of the older woman's hard stare. "Never mind. You don't want to hear it."

"No, but I do! You are the special agent in charge of this investigation. I am four thousand miles away, as the dragon flies: you are my eyes and ears. Tell me what you see and hear, please."

Not entirely convinced of her mother's sincerity (*a sad thing to ponder*), Mercy continued. "I've considered that Evangelina may actually be trying to protect the victims from a third party."

Valera March narrowed her eyes, picked up her tea, and glanced at her husband. "Well, if that's the case, she's certainly doing a substandard job, wouldn't you say? Tell me, Special Agent. What evidence have you procured, that is setting the investigation in this dazzling new direction?"

"The murder of Pamela Pride—"

"Is another murder that Evangelina Scales has committed."

"Evidence at the scene included a potential murder weapon, which—"

"Evangelina could have planted. Please, *Special Agent*. Tell me something I cannot tear apart from a distance."

"I made contact with a woman who claims to be her mother. Name of Elizabeth—"

"You saw Liz?! That's—"

"*Michael.*" Mercy's laptop nearly frosted over.

Now that was interesting. She used the arctic silence to continue. "She told me to pass on a message to my superiors. I've already submitted my report to Director Jorstad." Of course, she had left out the details as to how the confrontation had ended. "Mrs. Georges Scales appears to believe that the people she represents are under attack. She'd like us to leave them alone, and 'let them leave.' She didn't specify where they'd be going."

"I see. Michael, stay quiet for all of thirty seconds, will you?" Val rose, took her teacup and saucer into the kitchen, and brought back a full cup. The entire time, Michael kept his affable, silent grin plastered on his face. *Like a marionette whose master has propped it up for a time,* Mercy thought.

His wife sat down again and fixed her eyes on her daughter.

"Please tell me that you and those outstanding new partners of yours, Detectives McMahon and Vue, now have Elizabeth Georges Scales in custody."

"That was impossible. She had backup. It ended in a standoff." Mercy found herself wringing her hands under the desk, and tried to stop. *Hmm. First tell.*

"A standoff. Did you trail her afterward?"

"That was also impossible. Detective Vue was wounded, we believe by a dragon in camouflage. He needed immediate medical assistance."

"Listen carefully, Picklechip. In situations where you have to choose between hauling in the woman identified by Regiment leadership for years as *No Higher Priority*, and getting your new cop friend to a hospital to look after a flesh wound, you leave the backwater boob to bleed out and *bring in the traitorous bitch!*"

Mercy bit her lip. "Abandon a partner in the field. Is that an order, Regiment Proctor?"

"It's a priority, Special Agent. That's why we call her *No Higher Priority*. See how it's not just a clever title."

Unfailing courage, everlasting honor, swift justice.

"I'm sorry I let you down." Mercy turned to look out the hotel room window, which faced east. The sunrise was lovely, and huge V formations of ducks were migrating over the red-tinged oaks and maples. She thought of her early childhood, before they had packed up for England, when her father and she spent autumns in the Appalachians, hunting for fowl with a perky Irish setter she had been allowed to name Wolfman. When she would get upset at a day of bad luck and insist on going home early, her father would always have the same advice . . .

Give yourself ten seconds. Ten seconds is not so long, but it gives your brain time to talk with your heart. Think about what you really want.

She would always count all the way to ten, and then she would choose to stay hunting a little longer.

One . . . two . . . three . . . four . . .

"Picklechip. Are you still there? Is my voice coming through? Michael, I think the connection is . . ."

"The connection is fine, Val," Michael interrupted with an easygoing enough tone. "You're just acting like a complete ass once again, and as a result she doesn't want to talk with us anymore."

It might have made Mercy laugh, had she not been so consumed with finishing her countdown.

. . . five . . . six . . . seven . . .

"Well, if she's going to resort to childish silent treatments, I don't see the point of staying on. I've three more lectures this week, and field research notes to compile in between. Honestly, Picklechip, you know we love you. We'll chat tomorrow. You'll have better news then, I'm sure of it."

. . . three . . . two . . . one . . .

"Picklechip? Did you hear me?"

Am I ready for the hunt to continue?

She closed the laptop. *Yes.*

CHAPTER 37

Mercy had many talents, the ability to run in a pantsuit and government-approved low-heel pumps being merely one of them. So she was able to catch up with Art and Lue in the parking lot as they were on their way back from the coroner's office.

"So that confirms it," Lue was saying as she closed in on them. "That diamond horn on Pamela Pride's brass unicorn is consistent with the slash wounds on the Moorston victims' necks. And I will buy you a whole-grain cookie if you can guess what they found in her backpack at her condo."

"More unicorns," Art guessed.

"*More unicorns!* You *are* good, Detective. She had two—two!—stuffed unicorns in her backpack. Also, printouts of the names and addresses of all the murder victims to date. And a couple more, whom we have visited and found empty houses for. Talk about a Backpack of Murder and Despair!"

"You sound happier than usual," Mercy said, falling into step with them as they entered the station.

"The evidence we found at Pamela's condo suggests strongly we were right about her. It also suggests there are no more targets. I consider that good news, Agent March."

"As do I."

"Diamond horn!" Lue shouted, clearly full of glee. He slapped a patrol officer—she was pretty sure this one's name was Mark, or Jim—on his way to the war room. Mark/Jim gave the detective a look behind the back. "A darned diamond-horned brass unicorn that she scratched marks into exterior siding with, while waiting to kill dragons! What a job!"

They didn't even make it to the war room, when the next dispatch call came.

"No!" Lue cried, and his despair was contagious. "We found them all! How can there be any left?"

"Relax," Mercy said, trying a brave face. "They're calling it a fire. No one's saying anything about a murder."

"So, no one wants to go to the scene with me?" Lue started back for the parking lot.

"Well, I'm happy to drive out there . . ." Mercy started, and then they raced out together.

They all ran to Mercy's car, Art scrambling into the passenger seat and Lue folding himself in the back. Mercy plopped into the driver's seat and gave them quizzical looks. "I meant, I'm happy for *each* of us to drive out there. But sure, I guess this'll work."

"A fearless and royal operative of the majestic Federal Bureau of Investigation summons us with a nod of her head—"

"Never mind, get the hell out." She sighed, slamming her door and starting the engine.

"—and we, mere knights errant in the mysterious world that is joint powers law enforcement, leap to obey her slightest—"

"Shut up shut up shut up," she chanted, pulling out of the police parking lot.

"Doesn't work," Art said. He was settled comfortably beside her and seemed content to follow her lead.

"I do not want to hear from *you*, Art." Lue's bitching from the back was muffled as he wriggled around, stretching his long legs across the backseat yet remaining safely (if not comfortably) belted. "You nearly broke my back in your scramble for the front seat; there was no need to slam me against the adjacent cruiser. Next time simply yell 'shotgun.'"

"Hmph." Art pecked at her, smiling; she grinned back.

The radio cut in: "*. . . units please be advised, building is occupied; witnesses describe a large animal, perhaps a bear, prowling on property, exercise caution . . .*"

She felt her eyes nearly bulge from her head as she smashed her foot down on the accelerator. The car heaved over the curb, barely avoiding a stop sign.

"Whoa, whoa, *whoaaaauggghh!*" She heard a thump and a crack as Lue wailed from behind her, but she didn't look back.

"There," Art said. He was perfectly calm, seated beside her and bracing himself with both feet and an arm, while pointing toward a low brick wall off to their right with his other. "Past the tree line."

She yanked the wheel again, and the car churned up perfectly manicured municipal lawn. At least it was fall, and she wasn't barreling over tender, sweet, newborn spring blossoms. She could see Evangelina racing along the wall Art had pointed out—wow, he was a cool one! She had barely seen the flash of black when they'd pulled onto the block before giving in to her sudden hunch.

Siren blaring, they blasted past the flaming house where fire and rescue were already setting up. The wall Evangelina was racing atop ended; she leaped to the ground and veered away from the street as a wrought iron fence began.

They were in the tonier residential neighborhood of Moorston, which was small but contained some serious money from executives who had made their mark in the Twin Cities and then retired up north in towns like this. Beyond the iron fence, the impressive lakeside estate was not nearly as eye-catching as the sight of this dragon, Evangelina, their *first good look* in unfiltered daylight, streaming shadow-wisps off her black scaled wingtips and coiling tail, flexing her multiple jointed legs more like a galloping horse than anything else, her image interrupted like the frames of a movie reel by a rapid stream of elegantly wrought iron bars.

A groan came from the backseat. "My spine has snapped, you unrepentant harpy!"

"Sorry!" she sang, flushed with the heat and joy of pursuit. *We're all hunters,* her mother had told her once when she was little. *That's why it feels so good always to get the right answer.* "I'll buy you lunch!"

"Yes, thank goodness, that will be more than enough compensation for my spine—aarrggh!"

"Sorry!"

"Turning," Art said.

And so their prey was; she had darted right, farther away from the road, as the property changed hands again. The next estate was smaller but had more trees on it. This is where she would lose them.

Mercy stood on the brakes, bending her neck so the top of her head didn't hit the car roof. "Let's go!" she wheezed. The car smoked to a stop and they flopped back into their seats.

She and Art were out first and jumping past the iron fence to chase into the woods. Lue limped behind them, taking more mincing steps as the woods gave way to a small ravine.

Evangelina was not hard to see: huge and black and winged and terrifying and wonderful and, most noticeably, uninjured. Her movements had an effortless flow devoid of any limping or favoring.

Did Pamela Pride even get a lick in? Mercy wondered.

Had it been spring or summer, they would have lost even this large, black shape quickly in the foliage. As it was, it was a good two or three minutes before they realized they had to give up. The stark tree trunks thickened, the footing loosened too much for anything on two legs, and Evangelina had the advantage of . . .

"Wings." Art looked through the treetops as their quarry, at least two hundred yards distant, took to the air with a startling cry. "Fucking wings."

Mercy pulled up next to him, drew her Beretta, and fired. BAM-BAM-BAM. BAM-BAM-BAM.

Art didn't flinch. "Bullets won't stop her. At least, not the number you have in that clip."

"Then I'll reload." BAM-BAM-BAM. BAM.

"Mercy, it's okay . . ."

"It's *not* okay!" She popped out her empty clip, scrambled for a new clip, and then instead flung her weapon into the woods and buried her head in her hands. *Empty-handed again, Picklechip?!* "You don't understand, it's not okay, I have to get her, I have to bring her in . . ."

"Maybe she won't come back," Art told her in comforting tones. "Maybe it's done now. This house wasn't even on Pride's list."

Lue caught up to them then, piece drawn and looking pale from pain. "Everyone okay?"

"No one's hurt," Art told him. "Agent March is frustrated. So am I."

"Evangelina escaped?"

"Obviously."

"Sounds like another day of dragon hunting." Lue holstered his gun and sat on a felled oak. "I am ready for this to be over. I thought it *was* over."

"Not if Pamela's list was incomplete," Mercy said, trying to regain composure. She set about recovering the Beretta, which was lying in dried thorns several yards away. She winced as she reached through the sharp vegetation to pick it up. "We have to figure out who else is on the list."

"Okay," Lue agreed. "But how can we do that?" Those social networking lists have hundreds of names on them. Even if you narrow it down to Moorston residents who have *not* left or been murdered, you have dozens of residences to consider. How can we possibly be in all places at once?"

"We'll figure it out. There has to be a way." Mercy grimly holstered the Beretta. Her meltdown was over, and the FBI agent was back. "C'mon. Back to the car."

Art began to follow her, and then looked back at Lue as the younger detective got up with a grimace. "You need a doctor?"

"Yes, but not the kind you have in mind. Is it bad if everything hurts?"

Back at the car, which Mercy restarted and put gently into drive, the questions began anew.

"I cannot help but notice," Lue began as he winced, "that I am in the backseat again."

Art ignored him. "Why was this residence not on Pamela's list?"

"We'll have to go there to find out."

Once they were there, they were surprised with the amount of damage the fire had done. Something—a boiler or kerosene tank—had exploded and blown a hole in the side of the three-story, which had lit a nearby oak on fire, which had fallen and set some nearby brush on fire. The structure itself was half-standing.

Walking through the mangled lawn to the smoldering building, they realized there would likely be no helpful evidence inside. Fire and rescue had beaten the flames, but the worst was done: medics were lifting and wheeling out two covered bodies. Art asked and found out the family name: Nuwa.

"I recognize that name," Lue said upon hearing it. "Folks down at the station say that Harry Nuwa started a medical device company down near Minneapolis. It grew like bonkers and he sold it for millions and millions." He looked glumly at the covered gurneys. "He had a wife, and a bunch of kids. They've all grown up."

"Someone should contact them," Art said.

Mercy nodded.

"If they were dragons like all the others," Lue asked, "why would they let themselves burn to death? Why not change shape. Wouldn't dragon skin be flame resistant?"

Art pointed skyward. Even though it was daylight, the gibbous moon was still in the sky. "Many dragons are limited in when they can change shape. They're tied to the moon phase."

"Evangelina's not."

"Evangelina's exceptional."

Lue chewed on the inside of his cheek for a moment. "I hear other dragons can control when they change shape. They use special leaves."

Mercy and Art both turned and faced him. He swallowed hard. "I would prefer not to reveal how I know that, except to say: I am not a dragon."

"It's okay, Lue." Mercy gave a small smile. *We have to trust one another.* "In any case, if those leaves exist, these people didn't have them. Or didn't use them."

"Okay, I guess. So now I wonder: how did the fire start?"

"Evangelina started it. She's a dragon."

"Pretty quick jump, Agent March. Has there ever been a case of Evangelina breathing fire?"

Art shook his head.

"Okay, witness reports from Saint George's suggest she spits something venomous and/or acidic," Mercy allowed.

"No one *knows* if it's flammable or not. But the facility *did* catch fire."

"We'll find out the fire's origin soon enough," Art said. "That's what arson investigators are for."

"I bet they discover it had an entirely human origin."

"What, like an accident?"

"No, Agent March. Like an arsonist."

"Who could be Evangelina Scales."

"Or the Regiment's next Pamela Pride."

"Aw, Lue, c'mon. Aren't you putting the horse ahead of the—"

"Dragon? No, Agent March, I am not."

"Heh." They both looked at Art; for him, that was bursting into laughter. "Horse ahead of . . . heh."

"Great, Art. Glad you liked that. So!" Lue's back must have felt better, because he was waving his hands in the air. "Is it only me, or is it odd that Miss Pamela of the Secret and Terrible Unicorn Panty Brigade is dead and . . . whoops! Evangelina has radically and suddenly altered her behavior, tactics, and activities? Perhaps she has dyed her hair blonde and taken up jogging as well!"

"And started collecting unicorns," Art added loyally.

"Exactly!"

Mercy wrinkled her face good-naturedly at Art and continued. "We're standing outside a smoldering building where we saw Evangelina Scales. Not hanging around, not calling for help, but running away like a guilty demon. That happened, we can agree, right? We've got another big mess and she was on the scene. I can't speak for you guys, but that's good enough for the FBI." *And others.* "I still want her. You still want her?"

"Stay focused," Art said, nodding, and it was the biggest help; she wasn't sure he knew what a big help he had been. Because it was Art, she and Lue knew he meant it in the most neutral way: *Evangelina may, she may not, but either way, let's get her.*

And either way, we are *going to get you, my girl.*

Mercy climbed back into her car, a determined and feisty young sedan that, despite the abuse piled upon it today, gamely started up.

Mercy could relate.

CHAPTER 38

Her mother was impeccably dressed and made up, as usual. Years ago, Mercy had studied how the woman managed it—but even with her front-row seat, helping her mother with hair and makeup in the bathroom, Mercy was still dazzled by the results. She wasn't sure she would be able to carry on that particular legacy herself, as she aged.

"Hi, Mom. Where's Dad?"

"Good morning, Picklechip. I told your dad to go nap. I understand you've been keeping busy."

Mercy snorted. "If you mean have I been following Evangelina but not catching her, yeah. Real busy." She remembered her earlier thought to get a self-reflecting window and practice eliminating her poker tells, then realized that by now, she didn't care. Progress? Or despair? "If you're looking for an update—"

"Can't a mother simply bid her daughter good morning?"

Mercy let the long moment slide by until her mother

broke the silence by admitting, "Yes, well, I *have* gone over the intel you submitted to Bill—what there is of it—and thought you might find a chat helpful."

"I think I will, too, Mom. Because I couldn't help but notice—and neither can any of the state or local authorities on-site—that Pamela Pride is dead, and evidence of past crimes is piling up, and it's almost like—ha, ha—Evangelina might not be guilty."

"She certainly *is*."

"Well, okay, probably guilty for the death of Pamela Pride for sure—"

"I take issue with the word *guilty*." Valera's eyes were slits; her mouth was a line. "It doesn't suit your line of work."

Mercy took a breath, let it out. "What I meant was, I think our investigation has turned up new evidence."

"That's not important. You're close to catching Evangelina Scales. *That's* important. So catch her."

"I don't know that we're going to get very many more chances, Mom. The dragons may have left this area. And in any case, Mom, I'm not sure you get what I'm trying to say."

"Oh?"

"Yeah, I think we're looking in the wrong direction. I need to—"

Mercy heard a hard click and realized her mother had set—almost slammed—down her tea. Four thousand miles away, her dad was in for nasty nap-rousing. "You need to *do your job*, as I have said."

"Mom. I'm trying to do what *you* taught me. What makes me a good agent is attention to detail, and trusting my instincts. And right now my instincts along with some startling new details are telling me we need to consider new possibilities which, naturally, I wish to follow up on."

"Ah, yes, because Evangelina Scales might not be *guilty*. Yes?"

Mercy let herself have a long blink.

"Never mind guilty or not," Val continued. "Let's focus on what we know *will* happen. *When we get her*, all your questions will be answered at the trial, yes?"

"Yes," Mercy admitted. And oh, did she have questions! Hours and hours of them! She was finding herself day-dreaming about the hours and hours of questions. What they could learn! It always sounded so stupid when the science guys said it, but it was really, really true: what they could learn. The thought was dizzying, like a first kiss. "Yes, of course, the trial, that's been the whole—"

"Right, excellent, I'm glad we're agreed. Glad—nay, relieved—as always to have your approval. Of course, if you should see fit, as agent in charge, to kill Evangelina Scales on sight—for example, should you judge her an immediate threat to yourself or your colleagues—I can promise you the full protection of this organization, and a great deal of gratitude from your masters at the FBI for saving everyone a heap of time and trouble."

It took Mercy a few seconds to realize her mom was almost . . . nervous? She had assumed the woman was rushed, but it was more than that.

Val continued. "If you have all the assurances you need, perhaps now you could refocus on the job you've sworn to do?"

"Back to my work," Mercy paraphrased, mocking the accent and watching the immobile, beautiful face on the screen. "The refrain of the authority figure with no other argument upon which to fall back."

"You're pushing your luck, Picklechip."

"Pamela Pride probably never pushed her luck, did she Mom? Whoever she was, wherever she came from . . . I'm sure she was a much better Regiment soldier than I am, Mom. Am I right?"

"You've been in the States for too long."

"Maybe if I had a weird thing for unicorns tracing back

to an odd childhood trauma, or some other ridiculously obsessive neurosis, I'd make a better mindless killing Regiment automaton."

"Mercia Fallon March!" Val's exterior calm crumbled, and Mercy found herself straightening in her seat. "I do not expect mindless obedience from you! I expect you to use your brain and come to sane conclusions! The March family legacy is one of intelligence, courage, and resourcefulness! I expect you to show those qualities and reflect well on your mother, and her parents, and those parents before them!"

Mercy rubbed her palms against her bare thighs in tight circles and swallowed. "Okay. Got it. Give my love to Dad—"

This time her mother was the one to slap the laptop closed.

Mercy sat in her seat for a long time, crying . . . and thinking.

CHAPTER 39

"So," Lue began later that morning in the war room, as the three of them stared listlessly at piles of new information that didn't answer a single real question they had. "Who has the next brilliant brainstorm?"

Mercy scratched her neck under her curls and bit her lip. "I think I might."

"Please regale us!"

She smiled back. "We were asking yesterday: why was the Nuwa family not on Pamela Pride's list?"

"Yes," Art and Lue agreed.

"Well, think of who they were. They were a rich transplant from the Cities—not Winoka—an older and successful couple with grown-up kids and nothing but leisure and volunteer work ahead of them. This world was very good to the Nuwas."

"Until they were burned to death, yes."

"Let me get to my point, Lue. With that kind of wealth,

they could buy a certain amount of secrecy and privacy. They could isolate themselves, cut out a great deal of external observation, and likely confound any conventional attempts to learn who they were."

The two detectives nodded appreciatively. "Okay, that makes sense," Lue allowed. "So they never get on anyone's list. Still, once they saw other dragons—people they knew, who were in their social network— get killed or leave town, why would they stick around?"

"Well, I'm speculating here," Mercy admitted, "but what if they simply weren't afraid? They didn't live in Winoka, so they never saw that town destroyed. What if years, decades of success in this world—starting and selling a company, raising children who survived all the way to adulthood, buying lakefront property, working cleverly around the moon phases, never being discovered by anyone—all that made them feel, I don't know, invincible? Maybe they believed themselves intelligent, courageous, and resourceful enough—a sort of family legacy they felt they needed to live up to." *Thanks for that, Mom,* she thought bitterly.

Lue snapped his fingers. "I like it. Mr. and Ms. Nuwa figure, why go anywhere? We can hold off any threat with what we have. Their children can make their own choices. Speaking of which, our efforts to contact those children have come to zilch."

"They chose more wisely," Art deduced.

"Is it really that wise, though?" Lue stood up and began to pace. "Think about wherever these dragons are going. Elizabeth Georges Scales said, we will not see them again. They want us to let them leave. Leave to where? Is it a dragon paradise of some sort? If so, why would any dragon choose to live here in this world? No, if dragons are forced to go there, it is probably less pleasant than staying here."

"But somehow safer."

"Sure, Art. Safer. Any place that has a lack of law enforcement hunting them twenty-four seven, would probably feel safer to dragons. Dragons are probably at the top of every other food chain in history."

"Yes, Lue." Now Mercy was standing up. "The Nuwas liked what they had. They didn't want to give it up. They decided to take their chances in staying."

"And they lost."

"Yes." Excited now, she sat down at her laptop. "So who else is in Moorston, who's in these networks . . . who is well-off enough to take the same risk?"

Lue hovered behind her. Art wheeled his chair alongside.

Five minutes later, their mouths were all agape.

"How could I not have seen this," Lue muttered.

"She's only one of three," Art said. "What about the other two?"

Mercy got up and checked the Moorston map with red and green pins, and the printed address list alongside it. "The Taylors have been out of town for four months. The Hollenbecks have been missing since early this week."

"That only leaves her," Lue admitted. He looked at Mercy as he began dialing his cell phone. "I have to call her on her day off. You realize, this will do nothing to help local-federal law enforcement relationships."

Chief Linda Smiling Bear did not answer her phone—not even her emergency cell—and no one at the station seemed to know where she was. Mercy drove the three of them; the chief lived less than a mile west of the Nuwa estate.

"Casino money," Lue pondered as he braced himself in the backseat. "We all knew she had it. No one really knew her any better than that."

"I imagine no one tried."

Lue frowned at the back of Art's head. "What do you mean by that—that I was the kind of guy not to try?"

"I didn't mean you. You're new in this town. You didn't have time." Art turned and gave him a reassuring half grin. "You would've figured it out eventually."

Lue slouched back into his seat, and Mercy could see the detective wasn't so sure. Her mother's voice, unbidden, came to her mind: *we're never quite as clever as we think we are, are we, Picklechip?*

By the time they got to Smiling Bear's house, a European châteauesque that featured a football-field-sized front lawn and a brilliant, endless expanse of impossibly tall wildflowers in the back, they feared they might be too late.

"Call it in," Mercy said. Art already was.

The sweeping, steep-pitched roof was already bleeding smoke. Mercy swerved the car into the driveway and then pulled onto the lawn, a safe distance from the structure. Art and Lue drew weapons as they got out, but Mercy went instead to the trunk and opened it up.

"Over there!" Art called.

Slipping out from the back side of the building and racing out through the wildflowers as tall as cornstalks, was a stout but quick figure—more compact than Art, Mercy figured. He had short-cropped red blond hair and wore dark blue jeans and a maroon University of Minnesota sweatshirt. His backpack, Mercy was sure, contained more than unicorns.

As she opened her mouth to suggest one of them chase the suspect while the other two evacuate Smiling Bear—for she was now certain Smiling Bear was in that house—a tenebrous shape pounced out of the middle of the field and wrapped itself around the astounded U of M fan. With a single swift movement of mandibles, the shape let the man go and headed into the house. Behind her, her prey shook violently and collapsed as gouts of blood coursed from his throat.

"Huh," Lue remarked. "She caught up to the second Regiment agent a lot more quickly than the first."

"Pamela Pride was more subtle," Art offered.

"Pamela Pride had the magical, mystical power of unicorns on her side," Lue supplemented.

"Pamela Pride didn't race through fields of wildflowers with no clue as to what lay within," Art continued.

"Pamela Pride was hot," Lue concluded.

"Boys. Shall we?"

Lue shrugged. "You want us to go in after her, after what we saw here? Agent March, you must agree now that Evangelina did not set the fire."

"We can't be sure."

"She came here to save the chief. In less than a minute, the two of them will come through that door."

"We have no more evidence of that than we did yesterday!"

"Mercy." Art approached her and clapped a hand on her shoulder. "We can both get what we want here. Let's take position outside and see what happens."

"If that woman burns to death . . ."

"She won't."

All right. If he can wait, so can I.

They took positions close to the door, Art and Mercy opposite each other, and Lue facing straight into the house. Mercy backed up a few steps after a minute, trying to keep as wide a view of the entire house as possible in case Evangelina chose another escape route. The sound of the fire within was deepening, and they could hear beams fracturing and glass exploding. The smoke thickened, and several upstairs windows suddenly shattered, revealing a surge of bright flame.

The half-dragon monster finally came out tail first, through the same door she had entered, legs scrambling and wings folded protectively in front of her. It was hard to see past those massive triangles, but everyone knew who it was that this thing dragged in her mandibles. After a few seconds, they could make out the bruise on the unconscious woman's face.

Oblivious to any others around her, the dark beast wrapped itself into a new shape . . .

. . . and Mercy got her first direct view of Evangelina Scales. She was hypnotically beautiful, and Mercy recalled childhood stories of spiders who could weave potent sorceries with their very eyes. Dark curls tumbled down her shoulders, framing a sharp face full of worry for the woman who lay before her.

Getting to her knees, Evangelina leaned over the unconscious woman and began CPR.

Mercy looked at Art, who looked at Lue, who looked at Mercy. All three of them had weapons raised. Mercy was the first to put away her Beretta, and the other two followed suit.

They stood there for another ten or twenty seconds, rooted to the short strip of manicured lawn that separated the burning house from the vast, unkempt meadow. Finally, Evangelina's patient sputtered, and Mercy heard Art exhale.

So did Evangelina. She snapped her head around and spotted him. Immediately after, she saw Lue and got to her feet. Mercy, being behind her, remained unseen.

"Easy," Art said, and Mercy could see how nervous he was from the way his outstretched corduroy sleeve trembled. "Take it easy."

Evangelina did not take it easy. She caught Art's eyes, whirled to face Mercy's direction, and then hissed as she broke shape at alarming speed. In less than a second, the full fury of the shadow monster was bearing down on Mercy, fewer than thirty feet away.

Both detectives drew again. "Mercy!" she heard Art cry out. *How sweet.*

And unnecessary. She had used the distraction of Lue and Art to pull out her second weapon—a Paxarms Mark 24B dart gun. Each of the four darts she had preloaded contained a single drop of etorphine hydrochloride, also known as M99. A single drop, she knew, risked death for an average-sized human.

She shot directly into the dark corona, heard a grunt of outrage, and stepped back as Evangelina kept charging.

It's going to take a few seconds you have to wait a few seconds don't fire again unless you absolutely have to because you want her alive okay raise the gun again and aim just in case because she's not slowing down

She fired again. This time, Evangelina shrieked, stumbled, moaned, and crumpled to the ground, inches away from Mercy's feet.

No one moved for some time. Mercy shook, Art lowered his gun as he stared at Mercy, Lue kept his own gun drawn on Evangelina, and the chief stayed frozen on the lawn with a confused look. Behind her, the house continued to burn, and small bits of flaming debris began to spill out the windows above. Approaching sirens suggested the arrival of fire and rescue personnel, among others.

On the grass, Evangelina's shape continued to react to the paralytic agent. The shadows and wings and mandibles melted away, replaced once more by the woman Mercy had seen revive Chief Smiling Bear.

Mercy looked up at Art with tears in her eyes. "I'm a Special Agent of the Federal Bureau of Investigation," she told them. "I'm also a special operative of the Regiment, a global organization dedicated to the eradication of all quasi-human species. I was born into it, really. This is my first assignment as a hunter agent. I think I'm really good at it, but I don't know if I can do it anymore."

She dropped her tranquilizer gun and raised her cell phone. "I texted my chain of command as we took position. They're on the way. I can't stop them from taking her away, but I can arrange for you and Lue to come with us. I know you've been hunting Evangelina for a long time. I want you to be satisfied, too, I swear. I won't shut you out. Please don't shut me out. I know what you are, too, Art. You're a beaststalker. You're not Regiment, but you hunt these things, too. Like me. We all had our secrets but it's all out there now. I'm sorry I lied to you and Lue. Please, Art."

"Son of a bitch," she heard Lue mutter, but she didn't look at him. She could only look at Art McMahon.

Art stepped forward, around the chief and Evangelina. A kerosene tank somewhere on the other end of the enormous house exploded, followed by the sounds of shouting and more sirens, but none of this distracted him.

He was close now, and she bit her lip in worry. He was squinting, wasn't he? He wiped his face with a corduroy sleeve, then his hands on his jeans, and took a step toward her. She set her teeth and didn't take a step back. He raised his hands—oh, no, was he going to hit her in front of Lue and the chief? She deserved it, and she didn't want to cry, but was he really going to do that, allow that loss of control and mark her face with his fists, his hands?

He had her by the shoulders. He was pulling her in, reeling her in, like a fish. Keeping her close. She smelled his tension and sweat. Here it came. *Don't cry don't cry but you can hit him back don't cry and don't let this get back to Mom*

His face, so close it was out of focus. His fingers—no, they were too soft for fingers, they were lips, they were his lips, they were—

Art kissed her on the forehead.

Then let go of her arms and stepped back. Then he crouched down over the body of Evangelina, checked her pulse, and looked back up. "Your prize is still alive."

Thrilled, she touched the spot where his lips had been, that sweet, still warm spot.

A dozen federal agents swarmed around the corner of the house at that moment, demanding everyone freeze.

CHAPTER 40

Mercy didn't realize the magnitude of what she had accomplished until she saw the size of the convoy she was in. She got her own town car in front, with Director Jorstad himself and a driver. Art and Lue got their own town car, directly behind them—Art seemed shell-shocked by the pomp of it all, but Lue seemed game enough. Behind them was the small truck that carried Evangelina.

Mercy had seen at least four agents in lab coats and six in body armor load up the unconscious Scales woman in back. Director Jorstad promised they'd pack enough tranquilizer in her to last the trip, and maybe a couple hours after that. Behind the truck was another truck—this one was full of agents in body armor—and behind that truck were two Humvees with mounted M2s.

All around the convoy, state patrol (some of whom might be Art's buddies, she surmised) kept motorcycles flashing back and forth, screaming to the front to shut off intersections on the state highways until they hit Interstate 94, at which point they kept two fore and two aft.

Also, there were at least three Kiowa gunships floating about a quarter mile behind them the entire way.

Mercy thought briefly of the chief, who was headed for the hospital, and her house, most of which was headed for the woodpile. *She won't stay in Moorston for long now,* she mused. *It won't take long for the Regiment to come after her again. I hope she knows that.*

I hope she gets away okay, she realized.

After some initial warm congratulations, Director Jorstad returned to his formal self, letting Mercy give a quick verbal debrief and only asking one or two questions where her breathlessness left out important detail. At the end, he looked for a moment like he might clap her on the shoulder or even hug her; but then his face grew suddenly tired.

"If you'll excuse me, Agent. I haven't slept for three days. Your reports have kept us all on edge." He looked at her meaningfully. "I could really use the next two hours."

"Of—of course," she stammered as he took off his suit jacket, folded it up, and leaned his head against the window away from her. Within seconds, he was lightly snoring.

Once she was sure it wouldn't be rude, she pulled out her smart phone and sent a message to her mother:

You awake?

Her heart sank upon reading the response a minute later:

Of course I'm awake. What mother doesn't wake up when her daughter texts at 3AM?

Sorry, Mom. I'm fine. We got Evangelina!!!

Terrific. Now make sure the FBI doesn't lose her. I'm tired, honey. Lecture tomorrow. Can I go back to sleep?

Mercy typed furiously:

> Sure, you can go back to sleep, Mom. I mean, it's only the biggest day of my career, and a major threat to international public safety is neutralized because of ME, and the branch director is sleeping comfortably next to ME in a town car at the head of an armed convoy, secure in the knowledge that I have everything under control, and I think I may be falling in love, and the guy's a beaststalker who faced down mortal danger at MY side, and I'm going to take him out to dinner tonight and then maybe to a hotel, but you don't need to hear all this petty crap, just go get your beauty sleep, you ugly hag, because you need it at your age. Tell your superimportant British friends they should be on American time, the overcolonizing jackasses.

Then, after letting her finger linger over "send" for a good twenty seconds, she hit "delete" and sent this instead:

> Sure, Mom. Sorry again to wake you. Bye.

Someday, she promised herself. *Maybe tomorrow.*

She darkened her phone and took in the western Minnesota autumn for a good fifty seconds. The driver looked up into the rearview mirror.

"Hey. Big day, eh?"

"That's what *I* thought."

"You impressed Jorstad big-time. You should have heard him on the way up here. Between calls to the military, he was talking about you. Up-and-comer, credit to the agency . . . stuff like that. You're the next big thing, Agent March."

"Thanks." She tried a warm smile, but she wasn't sure if she pulled it off. Maybe more wan than warm.

"Remember the little people, when you're a big shot." He winked.

"I will. Excuse me."

Her phone buzzed, and she looked down:

Mom mumbled the news before falling asleep. Congratulations, peanut. I told you you'd win!

She smiled and typed:

Thanks, Dad. You can go back to sleep now, too. Love you.

Love you too, sweethearzzzzzz . . .

She couldn't help giggling. As she wiped a tear off her face (what was *that* doing there?!), she chastised herself for thinking of him as the weak one.

It took strength to move your family to a foreign country for the love of your wife, strength to support that woman and let her get all the glory and never complain, strength to put up with the same eternal stream of overjudgmental bull that Mercy had tolerated growing up . . . all for love. Love was strength.

Dad's strong. He's in love. With a bitch, sure: but in love. That's what counts.

She cleared her throat and looked back up at the driver. "You're not going to think I'm forgetting you if I text someone for a while, are you?"

"Not at all, Agent March."

Art. Thank you.

You don't need to thank me, Mercy.

Yes I do. Couldn't have done it without you.

Very kind. Lue wants to know who's texting me.

So tell him.

He has questions. What happens next? Where are we going?

Secure HQ in Minneapolis. We'll debrief her and find out what we can.

How secure?

Don't worry, silly. It's FBI.

You mean Regiment.

Yes. Sorry again. Regiment. Three levels below ground. Armed checkpoints, tear gas, all the other stuff we went into law enforcement for.

Speak for yourself. I'm in law enforcement for love.

You're sweet. Is Lue still reading over your shoulder?

No. He's drifting off.

Good. I have a plan for tonight. You free?

Thought not. Wouldn't we guard Evangelina?

She's not invited. Lue can watch her. We'll finish paperwork and head out.

Out where?

Wouldn't you like to know?

Actually, I would.

Leave it to me. I'll reward your trust.

As you wish. You're the agent in charge.

Exactly the right thing to say. Ciao.

She snickered to herself as she darkened her phone, put it in her pocket, and made her own jacket pillow. *I am in charge. And with me in charge, tonight's going to be spectacular.*

CHAPTER 41

Mercy woke up as the car banked right to follow the interstate as it veered south, so it could skirt downtown along its western and southern edges. Her first action was to turn and make sure the rest of the convoy was there; she half expected it to be in flames, with the gunships gone and a sky full of dragons in pursuit.

The convoy was intact, from the state patrol motorcycles and town cars to the armored trucks and Humvees to the hovering Kiowas. It was difficult to see if Art was asleep in the back of his town car, but Mercy couldn't imagine the man falling asleep at all.

He'll sleep good tonight.

She blushed at the thought, and then remembered to make restaurant and hotel reservations. Even as quiet as she kept her voice, and with her boss still sleeping and the driver presumably focused on the road, she couldn't help feeling a bit embarrassed.

She straightened her spine and decided it was none of their business, anyway. Who could blame her for wanting to celebrate? And who knew if it would really get that far, anyway? They'd known each other for less than a week.

But what a week!

Jorstad woke up a few minutes after she finished making the reservations. They were at the downtown exit now, and soon maneuvering through the streets of Minneapolis.

"Thanks," he told her, rubbing his eyes. "I needed that."

"No problem, sir. I napped myself."

"I assume you and the detectives will want to be present for the suspect's debrief."

"Yes, sir."

"That's fine. We've got some processing of the suspect beforehand—security protocol, medical procedures, and so forth. Leave that to me. Take the time and show the detectives around. Most cops don't get a look inside this building. It's good to give them the chance when we can, for agency relations."

Agency relations, she thought wryly, *are not going to be a problem.* She stifled a chuckle.

"She'll be in Interrogation Room C-3, starting in . . ." He checked his watch. "An hour. You know where that is? You have keycard access?"

"Yes and yes, sir."

"Great. I probably don't have to tell you, Agent March, but I will anyway: this likely isn't going to go down pretty. Evangelina Scales is . . . well, you know what that thing is. There'll be little cooperation, I suspect."

"I understand, sir."

"I'm letting you and the detectives watch because you've earned the right to be part of this. I'm trusting you not to interfere."

"Not at all, sir."

"Good." Jorstad sat back and stretched his legs. "Once

again, Agent March. Outstanding work. You should be proud."

An hour and five minutes later, Mercy didn't know how proud she actually felt. All thoughts of restaurants and hotels had fled her mind, and all she could focus on was Interrogation Room C-3, which lay on the other side of the one-way mirror that separated it from this small observation and control room.

The scene through the one-way was disturbing. Only one person was in the steel room, even though it could easily hold one hundred in classroom seating. Evangelina was awake in the center of the room.

She was sitting on a minimalist plastic stool and cuffed to the small steel table in the center of the room, stripped to the waist, hands spread and fastened to bars on opposite ends.

She had been shaved; her long dark hair was curled uselessly around her ankles. What looked like a steel collar kept her from tucking in her chin. Attached to the collar were two gleaming metal strips—one that traced down her spine, and a shorter one that went partway up the back of her skull. Wires poked out from both ends; some ended in electrodes stuck to her vitals, while others came together in a bundle that someone had duct taped hastily to the floor.

The bundle snaked across the floor until it entered a port in the wall that separated them from her. Similarly colored wires, Mercy noticed, flowed from a port on their side of the wall, into the computer array where a thin, handsome man who had introduced himself as Zarubin sat. He wore a pine green suit and a nervous smile as he checked the equipment.

Mercy forced back the rising bile in her throat. *This was the security and medical processing Jorstad was talking about?* Jorstad himself was nowhere to be seen.

"What is that thing?" Lue asked.

Zarubin took a few moments to respond; he was preoccupied with the readings on the screens. "Experimental device. Some of our research into Winoka's military history suggested some success in manipulating the spine of the creature. Slice the spine just so, and it can't change to its true form ever again. Attributed to the second to last mayor of that town, a certain late Glorianna Seabright. She had a brutal but effective method of neutering these things, and there are many in the Regiment who would be perfectly happy to take a page from her book. There are others who'd just as soon slaughter whatever we find."

"I think we may have met one or two of those," Lue observed dryly. "It seemed to us they had more to do with those murders, than the woman you have in there."

"Detective, please." *This isn't making it any easier,* Mercy decided.

Zarubin sniffed. "My job is the recovery of information, not the plotting of assassinations, which may or may not have happened and/or been authorized by my superiors in the Regiment."

"You sound wonderfully convincing. Did you read that all by yourself?"

"They have their role, Special Agent March has hers, and I have mine."

Jorstad chose that moment to enter the room. He had a single piece of paper in his hand. "Excellent. You're all here. Here's your protocol." He handed the paper to Zarubin.

"Are you kidding me with this interrogation?" Lue asked. He motioned at the half-naked, shorn woman chained to the table. "What you are doing here will never stand up in court."

Jorstad sized up Lue with a raised eyebrow. "You're one of those idealists that Agent March gravitates towards, aren't you, Detective Vue?"

"I like to think of myself as a strict constitutionalist,

more than anything else. And with all due respect, Director, there is no such word as 'towards.' The 's' is unnecessary."

"Hmmm." Jorstad turned to Mercy, who was watching Art, who was staring through the glass. "Do you two have any additional editorial feedback for me, or shall I have Zarubin get started?"

Without looking at him, she asked a question that had been bothering her since before they captured Evangelina. "Director, how many agents did you have assigned to Moorston?"

He shook his head. "I don't follow, Agent March . . ."

Lue snorted.

She looked at him. "Well there was me, of course. And the late Agent Pride. And whoever Evangelina poleaxed at Smiling Bear's house. And of course you would have sent the standard cover pair. And that's not even counting the swarm of agents who were suddenly available on a moment's notice to join us for the military convoy—which by the way was lovely, thank you very much."

"Agent March, why does the number matter? You're the one who took down Evangelina Scales. You're the one who gets the credit. No one's disputing that."

"Agreed. So the number was, what? Three? Six? Twenty?"

Jorstad straightened and adopted an unapologetic expression. "Five, including the two fallen."

"Five." Mercy whistled. "Five's a lot, Director. If I were one of those five, I might read that as a sign that you had no faith in any one of us. Especially since you didn't tell any of us about the others—or at least, you didn't tell me about the other four." She turned to Art and squinted. *Could he be one of the four still alive? Could he be FBI? Could he be* Regiment*? Did Mother send him?!? Aw, crap, that would ruin tonight . . .*

"Agent March, generally speaking, I prefer subordinates to question my direction privately. If at all. That said, I am going to cut you some slack, given your accomplishment today. I will even apologize for the appearance of it all.

"The deceased Agents Pride and Williamson, along with Agents Oshiro and Bahar, were each sent individually, like you, with no knowledge of the others. Each of your missions was slightly different, and I saw no overlap that required coordination. In fact, I would argue that leaving you unaware of the others, allowed you the operational freedom and creativity that made capture of Evangelina Scales possible."

"Capture." She let the word hang. "You mean the arrest for trial."

"I use the words I mean, Agent March. You're running out of slack."

"Very well, sir. What words would you choose to describe this?" She pointed at C-3.

"*I* would use 'bull—' "

"Detective, please." Mercy held up her hand to interrupt Lue. "Director, I believe I can be a successful asset for the Regiment, for a very long time. You've invested a great deal in me, and I'm sure you want that payoff. I need to understand your thinking, to do my best work. Please help me with that."

Jorstad clicked his tongue, scanned the control room, and dropped his head. "My *thinking*, since you asked, is that we have limited time before Evangelina Scales needs to be on a C-130 headed east. We have to get all the information we need before then, because her survival is not guaranteed." He looked pointedly at each of them again. "That is classified information, ladies and gentlemen. You will treat it as such."

"East—you mean DC has already pulled rank on you Minneapolis feds?" Lue couldn't help snickering. "Ah, irony."

"What does DC want with her?" Mercy asked.

Jorstad shook his head.

"I mean, you all see it, right? Art shows up and pulls rank on my local Moorston ass, as a big-shot BCA agent. Then, as I start to get used to *him*, Ms. Special Agent here shows up and shows her Minneapolis, ah, credentials.

"That was heavy stuff—you would not believe how hot my ex-wife is to work in Minneapolis, though I admit I miss the allure—and then when we finally get here, and we have Evangelina . . . BAM! There is always a bigger fish, am I right?" Lue looked at Art, who acknowledged the rant with an eye roll.

"DC won't tell you why they want her out east?" Mercy felt a bitter taste in her mouth. "What, they don't trust us, fed to fed?"

"I didn't say DC, Agent. I said 'east.' And I didn't say federal."

He turned to leave. "Zarubin, you have one hour. It should take you half that long, if that equipment really works. When you're done, call in medical and have them sedate her for the trip. I've got a C-130 to wrangle from Fort Snelling . . . *what now*, Agent March?!"

She had pushed him out of the room and closed the door behind her. "I'm sorry, sir, but you told me to question your direction in private, so I—"

"It's not an *obligation*, Agent March, nor a dare. You could try not questioning me at all."

"It's not DC, and it's not federal authority. Do you mean we're sending her over the Atlantic?"

He looked up and down the empty corridor, and still spoke in a whisper. "Regiment Command wants Evangelina Scales. It's all been arranged, Agent March. Except for the C-130, which I must attend to. Right now."

"But, sir—how can we guarantee a fair trial outside our own borders?" She swallowed, already knowing the answer, but needing to ask anyway. "How can we be sure it was Evangelina who committed these murders, and not . . . someone else? Right now, there's a viable alternative theory as to who committed many of these murders. We need clearer evidence."

"I agree. Now." He pointed back into the room. "Go get it for me."

As Zarubin poked around his computer, Mercy tried to forget the conversation with Jorstad. Her hand went up to the one-way glass. From this distance and angle, she could almost but not quite block out the sight beyond.

The interrogation specialist's fingers flew over the keyboard and track pad, and internal images of Evangelina—infrared, X-ray, magnetic resonance, and several others—opened up on his screen.

"What we hope to do here," he said in a dry educator's tone at anyone who would listen, "is arrive at a more civilized approach than Mayor Seabright's. With the inhibitor—that's that metal strip going down from the collar over the spine—we can duplicate the effect of the spine slice—prevent the change, that is—without doing any permanent damage."

"What good does that do?" Art asked from behind Mercy. She could actually hear his teeth grinding together.

"Nothing, without the initiator. That's the upper strip." Zarubin pointed on his screen to the normal image of the room beyond, at the shorter metal piece that pressed into the back of Evangelina's skull. "This part sends impulses to the part of the brain that clues the rest of the body in that it's time to change shape. Wires on the brain can do amazing things—zap the right part, and you can make any animal twitch a limb, or hiccup, or even smell bacon and eggs."

"So you can get a person to morph into a dragon," Lue observed.

"Well, you can't make a *person* do that," Zarubin corrected. He sharpened the contrast on one of the displays. "It wouldn't work for you or me."

Mercy was surprised to hear no tremor in her voice. "So you get her brain to tell her body to change, and then you prevent the body from doing that."

Zarubin nodded. "Theoretically, the resulting pain should be high enough to incent appropriate behavior, without causing the subject any actual physical damage. Such a subject should be willing to relay information on any topic we wish: the location of a nest, for example."

"I believe most of them live in houses, like you and me," Lue said quietly. He was not looking at any of them, or even Evangelina. If Mercy had to guess, she would have figured he was thinking of someone specific.

"We're about to find out." Zarubin flipped a switch and spoke into the microphone at his side. His voice boomed through speakers on the other side of the one-way. "We have questions for you."

Up until this point, Evangelina had simply stared at the opposite wall. Mercy had assumed the young woman had no choice. Now, at the sound of the interrogator's voice, Evangelina moved. Her arms were still chained, but her shoulders rose, her legs straightened, and she turned to look at the one-way. Instead of sitting passively in the stool, she was now hovering over it, and inviting them with her ironic glare to come join her.

"Have a seat, please."

Evangelina did not move.

Zarubin made a few keystrokes. "Have a seat."

The device did not glow or hum or do anything at all that Mercy could tell. Still, Evangelina shrieked, pounded the table . . . and remained standing where she was.

The keyboard taps turned into smacks. "*Sit.*"

She sat, wailing.

"We have questions for you. When you hear a question, you will answer." Zarubin reached into his shirt pocket, unfolded the paper that he pulled out, and began to read.

"First question: how many like you are left in the United States, including all fifty states and its territories?"

Evangelina seemed to consider nonresponse, but then thought better of it. "None like me. Not anywhere."

Zarubin went back to a gentle keyboard tap. The woman screamed and pounded the table. "None like me! Not anywhere!"

The tapping hardened, and she was back on her feet again, slamming her fists and shaking her head. "None like me none like me not anywhere none like me . . ."

"If I could make an observation . . ." Lue began.

Sighing impatiently, Zarubin flipped off the microphone. "Detective, we need answers. Lies mean punishment."

"Evangelina is telling you the literal truth. There *are* none like her. Not even a dragon is like her. If you simply rephrase the question, I am certain she . . ."

"I follow the protocol on the memorandum. It's not my job to rephrase or improvise in any way. Nor is it yours. Detective, if you cannot control yourself, I will ask you to leave. Now please . . ."

Mercy flinched when Art suddenly stepped forward, grabbed the expensive office chair, yanked it back over its occupant's protests, flipped the switch, and barked into the microphone. "*Tell them how many dragons there are!*"

The woman's reaction was stunned silence for several seconds. Something approaching a smile came to her lips. The readings on the screens showed what was obvious to their eyes: Evangelina had relaxed slightly.

Mercy bit her lip. "You shouldn't do that, Art. Interrogation one oh one. She knows we're divided in here, now."

"Detective McMahon! You will back away from that equipment and leave this room, or I will have you thrown out and fired!"

Before Art could respond, Evangelina did.

"We know of maybe a dozen more, scattered throughout

the states. Most have died or escaped. Another half dozen or so in Canada, mostly Alberta. Maybe a few in Mexico and Guatemala, but none known in lower Central or South America. I know nothing about the other continents."

"Thank you." Art flipped off the microphone, glared at Zarubin, and stepped away from the equipment with a sneer. "Continue your protocol."

Mercy considered her options, to keep herself from vomiting. *Remember,* she told herself, *it's like Director Jorstad said. I earned the right to be part of this.*

One option was to do nothing. Zarubin would continue the interrogation, Evangelina would experience bursts of pain, and then one of two things would happen: first, the interview would continue and conclude, and the Regiment would then dispose of Evangelina; or second, Art or Lue (probably Art) would lose patience and get them all thrown out, the interview would continue and conclude, and the Regiment would then dispose of Evangelina.

"What is your role and position in the dragon hierarchy?"

Another option was to take what Art had done a step further and assume control of the interview. This seemed unlikely, given Zarubin's disposition toward all of them and the low probability that Evangelina would cooperate so fully with every question on that protocol. When she refused . . . which of the three of them would zap her? If they didn't, what would happen next? Worse, what would happen if they *did*? And none of this solved what would happen afterward, and whether they could stop anyone from putting Evangelina on a C-130.

"My mission is to recover as many civilians as possible, before Regiment murders them."

"Please limit your responses to the question asked, or you will be punished again."

The next option was to attempt to pull rank as the special agent in charge of this investigation, and demand an end to the interview until she could sort things out with

Jorstad. But therein lay the question: would Jorstad even tolerate any further discussion? Was he even in charge?

"Are there any like you—or any other dragon—working in law enforcement, for any agency in this country?"

The last option was to do something. Probably something . . . unprofessional.

Something my mother would hate.

"Not anymore. It's too dangerous to apply. Too many law enforcement careers require DNA fingerprinting, and dragon genetic markers are too well-known now."

She couldn't resort to that, could she? It would be the end of her career. Beyond that, the FBI would doubtless fire her—Regiment or no, aiding and abetting a murder suspect's escape was a felony. She would end up in criminal court, and then jail. Jorstad would not protect her. Her mother would disown her. Her father, however strong his love, would be unable to stop any of it.

Her mother . . .

"Do you confess to the murders of Pamela Pride and Frank Williamson?"

And it wouldn't work, would it? They'd never get out of the building. They weren't even in the same room as Evangelina to start; they'd have security on *C*, *B*, *A*, and ground floors; they'd lock down elevators and flood the stairwells with armed guards; it would be over before it began. Career ruination, and Evangelina would still end up dead. Maybe Art or Lue, too. Maybe even herself.

"You have no more real questions for me. You'll kill me now, no matter how I answer."

"Do you confess to the murder of Pamela Pride and Frank Williamson?"

Immediately, she knew she didn't care. What was she worried about here: A bad performance review? A career languishing in the middle management of a criminal network? *Her mother?*

She caught Art's eye, and in an instant she knew she had

him. *Having him gave her hope: he's a beaststalker, too. He can still agree, this is wrong. We can still be on the same side, he and I.*

Art turned to Lue and clapped a meaty hand on the taller man's shoulder. Lue looked at them both and nodded. He looked, Mercy thought, like she felt: pale and ready to puke, but determined as hell.

Eyes flashed to the interrogation station. *I'll take him out.*

Heads nodded to the other room. *You two get her.*

"I killed Pride in self-defense! She was assassinating civilians I was trying to save! Noooooooo . . . please, please make him stop! Please! I want to talk to the other one! I want to talk to him! Please, I was wrong! You were right! I should have told you long ago! NOOOOOOOOOO!"

Art bared his teeth at the back of Zarubin's head. Mercy got his attention back. *Count to ten,* she told herself, hearing her father's voice again. *One, two, three, four . . .*

"One last time. Do you confess to the murder of Pamela Pride and Frank Williamson?"

. . . five, six, seven, eight . . .

Evangelina stood up, hooked the plastic stool with her leg, and flung it at the one-way. It bounced off harmlessly and clattered back toward her. *"Fuck you and that unicorn-loving bitch and that fucking firebug and your entire Regiment! You're all a disgusting collection of homicidal freaks!"*

. . . nine . . . ten!

Sirens blared. Lights dimmed. A calm woman's voice over the public address system: *"Alert. Lockdown. Lockdown. All agents initiate lockdown procedures."*

Mercy, Lue, and Art all stared at each other with identical expressions. *What now?*

There was no time to figure it out. Half a dozen armed guards in body armor entered the room. "We're in lockdown!" one called out.

"Everyone stay where you are! No one in or out of this room! Sir, you need to get away from your station . . ."

Zarubin was too fast and curious. Before the guard could pull him away, he had already called up security monitors for the complex. There, Mercy and everyone else in the room could see the reason for the lockdown.

For the first time since she had entered this building, Mercy wanted to smile. And with one glance she could tell Art and Lue felt the same way.

"What the hell?" Zarubin muttered. "For one woman, we're in lockdown?"

She was in her thirties, a younger replica of the woman who had humiliated and cuffed Mercy in the park. The hair was shorter and the wrinkles fewer, but the face was unmistakable.

Elder daughter.

Her business suit and demeanor, along with what Mercy assumed must have been one or two cleverly falsified documents, had already gotten her past the thickest of the building's security. Whatever had tipped someone off and initiated the alarm, she was now in the soft, chewy center of the building. Her stride was confident and her movements sharp. As guards approached her, she disposed of them: a single smash across the face here, a guard's own Taser there, a roundhouse kick over there. In a suit! A suit with a *skirt*!

"I must find her tailor," Mercy muttered to herself.

"She's two floors above us," Zarubin observed. He turned to the guards in the room. "It's one woman. There's no way she makes it even close, even if she's a trained agent. She can't get past Regiment countermeasures. I should continue the interview."

"Sir, protocol requires a suspension of all ongoing business until we get the all clear. Please shut off those monitors."

"I will do no such thing. And you will not touch this equipment, unless you want to lose your job."

Mercy watched the guard consider his priorities. It appeared enough that Zarubin wasn't actively disobeying the lockdown; as long as he stayed away from the monitors, the guards would, too.

So they kept watching Elder Daughter's progress. The second wave of guards was ready for her and had taken covered positions throughout the corridor, weapons drawn. She turned the corner . . .

. . . and disappeared.

It took Mercy a few moments to realize what had happened. By then, Zarubin was grappling with the guards.

"Camouflage! Shit, she's dragon! Let me turn visual to infrared! Do your guys have infrared? *Check it!*"

Convinced, they let him back at the keyboard. After a few strokes, he had the monitors showing a dark, cool background, against which stood out the bright flare of a distinctly nonhuman shape with wings.

"You've got to warn them!"

The guard was moving to tap his radio, when Art struck.

The first punch went across the chins of the chief guard and the man to his left. The second punch, to the groin of the next opponent, knocked him back against the wall, where he slumped to the floor.

Mercy admired the fighting style. *Krav Maga variant. The Regiment would approve, under different circumstances.*

By the time Art would throw his third punch, the guards were ready. It made no difference. His fists treated their body armor like silk vests, plowing into solar plexuses, kidneys, and ribs alike.

And his speed! My God!

As the last guard went down, Zarubin grabbed his gun, raised it, and got a shot off at point-blank range, blasting a bullet straight into the BCA agent's chest.

"Art!" Mercy caught him as he staggered back into her arms, his mouth open in a howl of pain and disbelief.

Lue flung himself at Zarubin, pinning the weapon and

the hands holding it against the far wall. Mercy thought vaguely of helping him, but she could not let go of the man in her arms.

He was coughing wildly, hands gripping her shoulders so tightly she almost asked him to stop, except she knew the grip would loosen all too soon, and she would lose him . . .

"Art, no!"

Lue and Zarubin continued to wrestle. The detective's knee came up, and the guard doubled over, and again, and he let out a choked moan. A round fired and embedded itself in the one-way. Mercy was too low to see if anyone beyond had even noticed what was happening in this room.

Art's grip tightened, and she winced as she suppressed a cry. "Art, I'm here. It's okay."

He continued to hold her as she lowered him all the way to the floor. His breaths were short, and he was still coughing. She wouldn't look at his chest, wouldn't admit that there was a wound there, wouldn't recognize any blood she would see seeping across his shirt if she looked anywhere but his strong, beautiful face.

Silently, she cursed all three of them for taking off their own body armor once they had secured Evangelina in this building.

You didn't know, she tried to tell herself. *You didn't know what the Regiment really was. Didn't know what they would do. Didn't know what could happen, what they could hide from the rest of the Bureau. From you.*

Lying on the floor with Art gasping in her arms, she wasn't so sure of that.

Didn't know? Or didn't ask?

Lue had Zarubin in a headlock, and the firearm was out of reach. It was only a matter of time before he had the situation under control. In this room, anyway.

Then it would be him and her. What would happen then? What would they do, without Art? She couldn't believe she could feel this way about him after such a short time, but there it was: she loved him, and she was losing him, and she had no idea what she would do without him.

Lost, she looked up at the security screens. The dragon shape was still hot red, working its way down the hall. Even through her grief, Mercy noticed two things: first, there was never a spout of flame, or anything lethal, from the creature.

Second, every guard she left behind still had the warm colors of life pulsing through their unconscious bodies.

Even now, they don't kill. Even now, as they rescue their tortured loved ones from us, they leave us alive.

Then, another thought: *They are handicapping themselves . . . and they're still beating us.*

A sudden certainty cascaded through Mercy, an epiphany that utterly claimed her and embraced all she stood for, even as it showed her a different path.

That is the team I want to work for. That is the team I want to fight for. That is the team I want to die for. And I will. Oh, please, I will.

Art had stopped coughing now. His eyes were closed, his grip on her loosening, his mouth curled in a faint frown.

He never got the chance, but he would have died for them, too. In a way, he's doing that now.

She determined that she could not leave his body here. She would carry it out, no matter how much it slowed them down. Lue could free Evangelina, and they would meet up with this dragon-woman and convince her of their intent, and together they would manage . . .

Wordlessly, the man beneath her opened his eyes, tightened his grip on her, pulled himself up into a sitting position, and blinked.

Wordlessly, she gasped and grabbed him back. *How?!*

Wordlessly, Lue sighed as he dropped Zarubin's unconscious body, got to his feet, and stared at Art with disbelief as well.

They all stayed there as the sirens continued to blare, the woman's voice continued to announce a lockdown, and the screens continued to show the intruder's progress. The pulsing red and yellow shape was a woman's again, and she appeared to be manipulating a keycard panel by the door that would grant her access to this floor.

Mercy opened her mouth to speak before a voice stronger than the loudspeaker emerged in her head. It startled her. It startled them all.

Arthur get me out of here. GET ME OUT OF HERE!

Art jumped to his feet, and something small and metallic clattered to the floor—it was the bullet, flattened as if it had hit a Kevlar vest. He gently but firmly pushed past Mercy and stepped up to the one-way mirror, beyond which Evangelina was staring as if she could see them.

He struck where the stray shot had embedded itself in the glass, and his fist punched through. Mercy began to exclaim in alarm as he dragged his arm back through the jagged, narrow hole, but there was no blood.

Lue approached him cautiously. "Art, we can go through the door over there"—he pointed across the room.

They heard a slamming sound and turned to the monitors. It was the dragon shape, throwing itself against that very door on the opposite side of the room. The Elder Daughter was here for her sister.

"She'll get Evangelina," Mercy said, resting a hand on Art's left shoulder and trying hard not to think of the voice that had called specifically for "Arthur." "You don't have to."

With his right hand, Art brushed off Mercy's touch, and then swung at the glass again—this time right next to the hole, where the web of fractures was thickest. The hole got bigger, and Mercy watched in astonishment as Art's fist and forearm came back through unscathed.

"Art, your arm . . ."

"Looks fine to me," Lue said.

She glanced at him, mouth open but nothing to say.

"Special Agent, you must have figured this out by now." Lue gently pulled her back. "Detective Art McMahon is a newolf."

"What do you—"

"He has anomalous DNA. He fights unarmed. He has obvious evolutionary traits—look at that skin. And . . ." He paused, unsure of how to say it. "He has a life mate."

Art punched the glass a third time, a fourth time, a fifth time. The window began to resemble a rifle target with an overlapping grouping. His entire focus was on destroying the barrier between him and the woman in the room beyond. Mercy kept watching his unscraped arms, his unshot chest, his unpierced neck—*that dart in the park never really broke his skin*—and his unbroken spirit.

"I guess I should have seen it days ago," Lue said, shaking his head. "The whole alpha-wolf vibe fits the profile of how he can get pretty Regiment agents *and* gorgeous spider-women to fall in love with him. Anyway: more guards are coming." He pointed at the screen, which showed the corridors in the floor above crowded with bright shapes. "We have to figure out what to do. I advocate shrieking and passing out."

"Detective . . ."

"No, I know. I have your back, Special Agent. Give me the plan."

She stared at the monitors, and then realized she had no idea what to do. *Perhaps shrieking and passing out is the way to go.*

The monstrous shape took another run at the far door, and the room echoed with the sound of buckling steel. Art growled and punched faster and harder. Four or five more strokes, and the opening was large enough. He pulled himself through with a grunt and spilled onto the cold cement floor.

At the same time, the opposite door slammed open, and a brilliant blue dragon tumbled through. She somersaulted and rose to her feet as the stunning thirtysomething woman in the business suit once more.

Art did not even look at this new woman. He stepped up to Evangelina, grabbed hold of the lower end of the spinal restraint, and ripped it, and all of the attached electrodes, from her body.

In an instant, he and Evangelina were lost in a billowing cloud of shadow. As it consumed them, Mercy heard the sound of snapping steel. Small metal fragments flew about the room, and the table creaked under a sudden added weight.

The Elder Daughter gave a dry grin. "Are we ready to leave?"

"We don't need you," Mercy heard Art growling from the depths of Evangelina's shadow. "I can get her out of here myself."

"No doubt, Arthur. I should have realized you had everything under control when you sent your message from the car. Your devotion is unquestioned, and you've proven that Evangelina needs your help after all. But why not leave together, now that I'm here? After all, I did all this hard work getting in."

Arthur's stout frame emerged from the gloom. "I said *we don't need you*. I sent that message as information, not a request for help. She's mine!"

The woman chewed her tongue and turned to the massive shadow. "As charmingly protective as ever. Isn't this why you dumped him?"

Please. Let's just leave. Together.

Art growled but relented. "Guards have cut off your escape route."

"Then I guess we'll have to plow through them. We

can't stand here arguing, Arthur. Susan is waiting at the rendezvous point with our vehicle. She's worried sick for Vange, ever since the Saint George's incident resulted in that Regiment sketch." The woman nodded at Mercy and Lue, who were still staring at them through the hole in the one-way. "Speaking of which, I need to take care of the immediate problem."

"Whoa . . ." Lue whispered as he backed away from the window. "We had better go. Flee. Vamoose. Pick a verb."

Mercy could not move her feet. It was not fear, it was determination. *It can't end like this. Not after what we went through. Not when I want to fight alongside them.*

"Leave them be, Eldest," Art growled.

"Yes, Eldest." Lue pointed. "What he said."

Eldest? Mercy looked at the woman again. She had thought thirties, not "eldest." *Wow—could she be in her forties?*

"You suddenly care about Regiment soldiers?" the woman asked, even as she stopped. She looked Mercy and Lue up and down with silver eyes. "Why?"

"They're not Regiment. They're my partners."

Niffer, please. I want to go.

Still chewing her tongue, "Niffer" assessed Art's partners. "Are either of you going to make me regret *not* beating you unconscious?"

"I was hoping to follow you out," Lue replied. "Cringing with gratitude the entire way."

Mercy swallowed. "Let us help you."

Niffer snorted. "We need neither your help nor the distractions you'll cause by following us. If you really want to assist us, stay here until my sister and I are gone."

With that, she turned. "Vange, ready?"

The shadow's rapid movement toward the door, a murky

current that seemed to sweep Art along, was all the answer Niffer needed.

"Remember, sweetie. We're trying *not* to kill anyone."

We'll see.

"Hey!" Mercy reached up and pulled herself through the glass, wincing as her fingers, shoulders, and hips scraped jagged edges. She fell into the room on her back and grunted. Niffer turned as the others left the room.

"I told you to stay. *Stay.*"

Mercy was quick enough to track the woman's movement into a swirl of vapor, but not quick enough to protect herself. Something pricked her neck, and she felt the numbness spread. *Son of a . . . my mother is never going to . . . frezzleblennhh . . .*

Her vision faded, and her mind spiraled into timelessness.

Six Months Ago

"I don't care what you say, I'M GOING AFTER HER!"

"Vange, please, you don't have to yell. In fact, I'd hope you'd be smart enough by now to know that yelling only attracts attention. The walls are thin here. Please, sit down and listen."

She kept pacing across the room, brunette locks swaying about her tense face. "To what, Mom? What else is there to hear? They have Aunt Susan. They've got her in that fucking mental hospital, and they're going to drill holes in her head until she spills everything she knows. Or doesn't. Either way, she dies."

"They're not going to kill her, Vange."

"How do you know that?"

Elizabeth sighed and sat on the hotel bed as her daughter continued to pace. "How to explain? I know these people. I know how they see people like Susan. Killing her, even hurting her . . . they'd see it as impolite, even anti-

thetical to what they do. They want to protect Susan, in their own distorted, horrific way. They'll lock her up. But they won't harm her."

"It doesn't matter. She doesn't deserve to be locked up!"

"I agree. Give me three or four months, and I'll put together a team—"

"Give me three or four hours, and I'll have her back here tonight."

"You already have a mission. Focus there."

"Niffer would understand. In fact, I'd be surprised if Niffer isn't breaking her out this very moment."

"Your sister is at a critical stage. We are taking the first few steps into a completely refashioned world, Vange. Only she can—"

"What, again with the Great Creator speech? I've heard it, Mom. I've been hearing it for years. It's why she was never there for me when I was younger, why Aunt Susan had to be my big sister instead. That's fine, but now Aunt Susan is in Regiment hands. If Niffer's doing something she thinks is more important, I'm doing this myself."

"You're putting a lot of people in danger if you do."

"Who, besides me? No one else has to go."

Elizabeth stood again, and her regal posture made Evangelina pause in her pacing. "How about those people in Moorston your sister expects you to save? What about them?"

"I can still get to them. I told you, this won't take more than a few hours . . ."

"The Regiment only needs to stay a few hours ahead of you to kill every one of them. Vange, we don't have a full list for each town, anymore. The remaining dragons are harder and harder for us to find. Some of them don't want to be found, or they think they're perfectly safe. The Regiment has all the resources we have, and more. I can guarantee you they have deployed at least one assassin, probably more, to the area already. They'll track down dragons and start killing them."

"I know the stakes, Mom. I wish you would trust me."

"I wish you would trust me. *That's the problem, Vange. You don't trust anyone. Not for months. Not since you discarded Art—"*

"Oh, I cannot believe you're going to bring him up again."

"I'm not saying you have to date him again, Vange. But he could be helping you. You found so many people when you worked together."

"That's because he has excellent stalking skills. I expect him to show up in this hotel room any second. You probably told him I was here!"

"Don't be ridiculous. You made your wishes clear. And you're right; he is obsessive. What do you expect? Newolves mate for life, Vange. You seduced him, brought him along on your mission, performed miracles together . . . and then dumped him. He's been inconsolable ever since. He won't stop looking for you, whether we help him or not."

"Maybe I should leave Minnesota."

"Moorston, Minnesota, is the only place for thousands of miles where we know there are dragons to save, Vange. He probably knows that."

"Yes, well, it's also the location of the so-called hospital where Aunt Susan is. So I guess I'm headed for that town anyway."

"Forget the hospital for now. Let me draw up—"

"I'll be back later tonight, Mom. With Susan. Have the Mustang ready."

"Vange, please." Evangelina turned at the pleading sound. Her mother's tired face was streaked with tears. "If they capture you, there's no one to come get you. Your sister can't come. Art won't be enough. And I'm too old."

"Nobody will need to save me, Mom. Saving is my *job. Let me do it."*

Elizabeth exhaled. "They'll get you on video."

"Not if I tear the place apart."

"Please don't kill anyone."

"I can't guarantee that anymore, Mom. Not with the Regiment getting bolder. Heaven knows they've already killed plenty of us. They deserve what they get."

Her mother sat down on the bed again. "The world has not truly improved during my lifetime. It makes me sad."

Evangelina turned and gave her last words as she opened the hotel room door to leave. "I thought that's why Niffer was building a new one."

CHAPTER 42

When Mercy woke up, the sirens were still blaring, and she was still in the interrogation room. The worried face of Detective Lue Vue hovered over her.

"Agent March, can you move?"

She tried to open her mouth but could not. Instead, she blinked.

"Blinking is good." He rubbed her cheeks with his hands. Flecks of frost sprayed up, and she realized she was breathing vapor. "Once you have warmed up, we can get out of here. I imagine you want to leave as much as I do."

Art, she tried to say.

"They have quite a head start. About twelve minutes. The monitors"—he motioned to the system in the room behind the one-way—"suggest the Regiment, even with the resources of the full Bureau at its disposal, is running out of ideas. Also technology. Art with the two of us was pretty good. Art with the two of *them* . . ." He whistled.

His words twisted her gut, and she squeezed a cold tear out onto her cheek. *How could I be so stupid? How could I think I was good enough?*

"Try to sit up," he suggested.

With his help, she raised herself. The lockdown warnings echoed through empty halls, and she knew the fight was far away. She tried to tell herself she wanted no part of it, that they were gone, and her best bet was to stay here and rebuild her career, her life.

Sit. Stay.

She got up to her feet without Lue's help. Her limbs were blue, but she could feel the tingling sensation of renewed blood flow.

"Let's go."

It was not hard to trace the escape route. In places the guards were so thick, the unconscious bodies were heaped on top of each other. Mercy did random pulse checks as they went; every one of them was faint but steady.

Three floors up, they were back at ground level. Here, they saw the first evidence of unrestrained violence: the corridors were filled with smoke, and the acrid smell of burnt flesh was in the air. Bullet holes peppered the walls, and in places, Mercy was sure she spotted bloody claw prints.

"The Regiment did not want to give up their prize," Lue noted.

Mercy rushed over to the closest body she found. It was a special agent she didn't know—unlikely to be Regiment, but ordered all the same to defend the Bureau. The woman's charcoal hair was smeared with blood, and her young face had the pallor of death. She had no pulse.

There were at least half a dozen others like her, whom Mercy and Lue could not save. A few others were crawling, screaming, their body armor smoldering. Tear gas canisters sputtered across the foyer. Sidearms, assault rifles, flamethrowers (?!)—an entire armory was spilled across the proud marble floor, twisted among the remains of metal detectors and other trappings of security.

Lue settled down next to one older agent who had suffered obvious blunt trauma to the throat. It took Mercy some time to realize who it was. The bruises on Jorstad's face were fist-sized.

"Art . . ." He trailed off, and looked to Mercy. "I wish I could say for sure that he had no choice."

Mercy wiped her face on her sleeve. "Who cares about his choices anymore? It doesn't matter. We keep chasing them. We'll find them."

Lue looked around. "Maybe we should help some of these . . ."

"No." Mercy pointed through the shattered plate glass walls, to the streets of Minneapolis. Sirens from beyond joined the internal whine, gathering and nearing. "Let them do their job. We have ours." *That's what Mom would say, right?*

"Are you seriously still trying to stop them? Agent March, they *made it out*. They could be anywhere in the city! At least two of them can fly!"

Mercy pointed at the floor. "Blood trail. Check it out."

"That could be anyone's . . ."

"Heading outside?" Mercy stormed out of the foyer, through the empty panes that faced the courtyard outside, and down the cement path that led alongside the building. Lue followed her reluctantly. The trail led around the corner, away from the sounds of sirens.

"It's an odd path for a wounded FBI agent to take."

"If Evangelina, or her sister, is bleeding this badly, maybe flight's not an option after all. Where could they be headed?"

"My guess is the river. It's only three blocks away, gets them off the roads, and leads out of town."

"Very logical. We could investigate, certainly. Or we could do the sane thing, which would be to lie down quietly and wait to be ministered to by angels disguised as EMTs and waving sphygmomanometers."

She lurched ahead of him, in the general direction of the river, and he sighed and caught up with her. "EMTs? Who needs medical attention? Surely not we." He slung an arm around her waist. "That sound you hear? Aside from my vertebrae smashing together, that was my career imploding."

"Left up here," was her grunted answer, and he obligingly helped her lurch in the right direction.

This part of Minneapolis was the old mill district, with multiple four-to-seven-story buildings renovated for commercial and residential use. The structures were tall, the corners tight, and the alleys narrow. Staggering as much as tracking, Lue and Mercy followed the drops and spatters as they kept to those alleys and narrow spaces, crossing streets at low traffic points, and inexorably heading toward the river.

It was in an alley a mere block from the river, just north of Washington Street, where they finally caught up.

There they are! The blonde was limping dramatically, holding her shoulder. The other two were moving only slightly faster.

Mercy drew her Beretta and aimed it at the back of the shadow monster's head.

"FREEZE!"

CHAPTER 43

Niffer calmly turned. Her left hand pressed into a bullet wound in her right shoulder, her face was covered in ash, and blood trickled down her left thigh.

Beyond her, Art seemed winded as he pressed his palms against his knees. His corduroy jacket had been incinerated, his shirt was blackened and torn, and he bore a nasty burn across his right side. Multiple quarter-sized bruises marked his forehead and chin—*bullets,* Mercy guessed—and his eyes were bloodshot.

Evangelina remained in monster form, and her shroud hid any damage she may have sustained.

Niffer was the first to speak. "Agent March. What is your intention?"

Mercy opened her mouth, but could not find the words. Even Lue was looking at her hopefully, as though she was saving an inspiring, Churchill-esque speech for this moment.

Well. What *did* she want, now that she had them? Evangelina she had already captured once, to no end but disaster. Surely her sister would be an even more potent curse. And Art . . .

Niffer watched her gaze. "Ah. I see. You're not here to arrest us. You're here for *him*."

Beyond her, Art straightened, and Evangelina stirred. Mercy tried to still the gun in her hand, tried to show she was in control, even though she knew she would not fire. She took a tentative step forward. Lue, who had drawn alongside her, kept pace with his own piece steady, and the gesture meant everything to her.

I'm not crazy to be here. I'm not alone. Surely he must see that I'm right.

Evangelina's voice echoed in their minds, tinged with irony and bitterness.

Here to win him, or to kill him?

"Either way, Vange, it looks like you're in for one more fight," Niffer observed. "Unless, of course, you wish to keep Arthur well and truly dumped. That would seem churlish, at least on the day he rescued you."

"Eldest. Evangelina." Art was finally catching his breath. "Let me handle this."

Neither sister moved. Art came back toward Mercy and Lue, a small hitch in his stride. When he was ten yards away, he stopped. He looked at Lue first, and gave him a grim nod.

"You've been a good partner."

"Thanks. You, too."

"It ends here."

Lue bit his lip. His gun came down slightly, and he glanced at Mercy for advice. She had none to give.

"You lied to us," Lue said after another long pause.

"Only to lead you to the truth."

Lue's gun lowered further. "How Zen. Where are you going?"

Art closed his eyes. "To finish a chapter."

"That makes no sense."

"It doesn't matter. You can't follow."

Mercy watched the struggle on Lue's face. He wanted to go, she could tell. *Someone could be waiting for him there,* she suddenly realized.

She knew how he felt.

"Why not?" she asked.

Art faced her, and she caught her breath. She had thought he would be hard and simple, like he had been with Lue. Now, his face said so much more. There was tenderness there again, and possibly even desire.

The words spilled out before she could stop them. "I know this is crazy, Art. I know this has only been a few days. I know you have every reason to despise me. I don't think you do. I see you standing next to her, and I understand now you loved her once. I don't think you love her anymore, Art. I think you've evolved past her. That's what you do, right? You evolve? You're next to her, but I can see it. Even now, after all this, I can see it. I can see you care for me, that you see the part of me that can live up to my word, that you want to give us a chance . . ."

He reached into his holster, drew his sidearm, and shot her twice.

"FUCK!" She collapsed, holding her leg. One shot had blasted her patella, and the other had hit somewhere even worse.

"Art!" Lue raised his gun again. "This may cause me to think you are an asshole!"

Art dropped his weapon, held out his hands, and motioned to Mercy. "She needs medical attention, Lue."

Cursing, Lue dropped to his knee next to Mercy, holstered his gun, and checked her leg. "Aw, cripes, Art. You hit the femoral artery . . ." He whipped off his jacket and wrapped the sleeves around her thigh, fastening as tight a knot as he could manage. "You monosyllabic jerk! What were you thinking?"

"Good-bye."

Detective Art McMahon turned and followed the sisters down the alley, ripping off his tattered and scorched shirt as he went.

"I *never* liked you!" Lue yowled, but even Mercy could see he didn't mean it.

CHAPTER 44

Mercy gritted her teeth as Lue searched himself frantically for a radio. He finally came up with a cell phone, but she batted it out of his hands and it clattered onto the alley pavement.

"Ow! And what are you doing? Keep your hands on the wound, and let me call for help!"

"I don't need help."

"What a joke. He *shot* your *femoral* . . ."

"I know what that bastard shot." Something inside Mercy broke, and she began to sob. The choking groans filled the alley, and she knew how pathetic she sounded. She also knew Art and his dragon-bitches were still close enough to hear her. She didn't care.

It's not fair. I've tried so hard. For so long. I was supposed to win. Dad promised I would win. He promised!

Lue kept one hand on hers and used the other to pull off his tie. "I am sorry, Agent March."

It was impossible to stop, as humiliating as this was. "He wasn't chasing her because he wanted to stop her . . . He was chasing her because he was obsessed with her!"

"Apparently." Lue wrapped the tie around her leg above the wound and began to knot it. "I admit I only figured it all out when I saw he was bulletproof, down in C-3. Until then I thought the same that you did: that he hated Evangelina."

"He didn't hate her . . . He hated *me*. Because I lied to him."

She sensed his careful gaze. "We all lied to each other, Agent March. Art was quite taken with you . . ."

"Yeah, I could tell how taken he was with me from the way he *shot me in front of his girlfriend!*"

"Twice."

"Shut up!"

"That was a mixed signal," Lue allowed dryly, tightening the tourniquet.

"I can't believe he did that." *Why would he want to leave with her? His sister said she dumped him. Ugh, this is so high school. It has all the hideous, petty elements: jealousy, dumping, gunplay.*

Lue's hands went back to her wound, checking to see if the blood was coming more slowly now. "So this is about more than being fooled by Art, right? You were hoping for . . . what? A date? A boyfriend? A fairy tale?"

She gained control of her sobs. "I know how this sounds. I know we only knew each other for a few days. I felt . . . I don't know if I was even expecting a relationship, just . . . anything but *this*."

The three refugees were still within sight, about thirty yards down the alley. Evangelina had finally turned back out of her monster form; her slender hand squeezed Art's muscled arm. The three of them were seeking a pace and style that would blend in, no doubt.

Mercy hissed bitterly after them, "Why would he do this?"

Lue didn't look at her face, instead focusing on the

bleeding wound. "He may not even know what he wants right now. The guy has spent, what? Years among us, alone? Part of that time with a girlfriend, helping her on a secret mission, falling in love. They save a lot of people together, face danger together. It would have all been very romantic, until she ended it.

"If Evangelina dumped Art like the elder Scales said, it would have been so trying for him—abandoned by his life mate, his mission in doubt, trying to follow the cases to protect her as law enforcement closed in . . ."

"You're not convincing me that he was right to shoot me, you ass."

"Oh! Well. Yeah, that was wrong. Very absolutely wrong. Again, I am sorry. I only want you to see what I see: just because he did what he thought he had to do here, does *not* mean he was right. Give him time to see that."

Lue's reasonable tone made her feel worse. Anger resurged within her. "I'll give him more than *time* . . ." She pulled one hand off her femoral wound and picked her Beretta up off the pavement. She tried to focus the muzzle on one of their heads . . . any of their heads would do . . .

Lue pressed her arm down. "Could we fix one bullet wound before opening up another?"

"I don't need fixing!" She shook off his hand, raised the Beretta, and then lowered and holstered it, cursing as Art and the others rounded the corner and vanished.

She tried bending the knee, but quickly stopped. It wasn't time yet. This wasn't like slipping on a pickle slice at a formal dinner party as a child, before the withering laughter of her parents and their gathered peers—an event that had wrenched her leg, bruised bone, and unintentionally revealed a unique feature about her body.

Lue picked up his cell phone from the ground, where she had knocked it out of his hands, and hesitated. "I will try again. The hospital is nearly a mile away. Do you have a better idea than calling for an ambulance? Please do not say: ride Lue like a pony."

Sniffling, she pushed his hand holding the cell down again. "I'll be okay. Give me a second."

"Mercy." It was the first time he had used her first name. "Look. At. Your. Leg. You must go to a hospital, or you will bleed out and die. Think of the paperwork!"

"That's not going to happen. *You* look at it." She took her other hand off the femoral wound, and took some satisfaction from Lue's expression. "We all have our secrets, Detective."

"Impossible," was all he could say.

"Not at all. Some beaststalkers have interesting mutations of their own, you know."

"Whuh—"

"Perhaps nothing as impressive as being bulletproof, or standing on their hind legs and acting like a BCA agent for several years without barking, but still."

He wiped his hand over her inner thigh in disbelief, his nose inches from her bloodied flesh.

"Detective. You're getting a little fresh."

He blushed and almost snickered. His eyes went down her leg. "What about the knee?"

"Bones don't heal as fast."

He looked up. The alley was empty. "They *are* getting away."

"I can see that."

"If we called for backup, we could at least get a vehicle . . ."

She stood up and pushed him back a step. "Screw that. I am Regiment. I am the *best* in the Regiment. Even if they don't live up to their own principles, *I* will. *Unfailing courage, everlasting honor, swift justice.* The suspect is here, right now. We wait for a car, we lose him—lose *them*. No one else can do this."

After two tentative steps, she felt the flesh in her thigh start to pull together. The knee was reknitting bone, which felt like army ants moving sand under her skin. Uncomfortable, to be sure: but in a moment, she would be able to run.

She pricked her ears—yes, she could still hear them. Their footsteps on the asphalt were fading.

"You need help?"

"Does it look like I need help?"

"I mean you, Agent March. Not your leg. I would like to go with you."

She began to nod grimly, until she thought of her mother and managed a smile as well. "I'd love the company, Lue. You up for a race?"

"I could always use the practice for next month's 5K."

"You know who we're pursuing."

"*Whom.* Yes. We are pursuing Evangelina Scales and her associates, all persons wanted for questioning regarding the murders of Pamela Pride, David Webber, Amanda Coolidge, and several other civilians and federal employees."

"Real questioning, Lue. Not what we saw in there." She pointed vaguely to the building with Room C-3. "Questioning that sees daylight. That reveals what's happening out there. No more secrets, Lue."

"Right. Okay, my ex-wife is a dragon."

"Good for you, Lue. I hope she makes it through."

"I do, too." He straightened. "I thought I was done seeing the incredible today, Agent March. But you look ready to run. Maybe even run faster than I can."

"Almost."

"Almost faster?"

"Almost ready." She crouched and closed her eyes. Her leg felt fine. Wiping the sweat from her brow, she reached down with her other hand and felt the comfort of her Beretta in its holster.

She wondered whether she would use it or not, when

she caught up with them. Then she wondered if it was right to try to catch them at all.

She exhaled. *Count to ten. One, two . . .*

"They are getting away. Did you want that?"

. . . three, four . . .

"Agent March?"

. . . five, six, seven . . .

"Mercy?"

Her eyes popped open, and she sprang forward. "Let's get 'em."

HUNKY WEREWOLVES, DELICIOUS DEMONS, AND DROP-DEAD SEXY WITCHES ALL HAVE THE SAME ADDRESS...

MYSTERIA

By

MaryJanice Davidson

Susan Grant

P. C. Cast

Gena Showalter

Hundreds of years ago, in the mountains of Colorado (just close enough to Denver for great shoe shopping), the small town of Mysteria was "accidentally" founded by a random act of demonic kindness. Over time, it has become a veritable magnet for the supernatural—a place where magic has quietly coexisted with the mundane world.

But now the ladies of Mysteria are about to unleash a tempest of seduction that will have tongues wagging for centuries to come.

M299T0708